6

SIGN'S ON

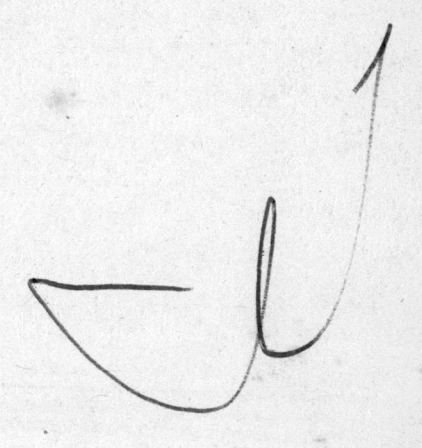

SIGN'S ON

Jacinta McDevitt

POOLBEG

This novel is entirely a work of fiction. The names,
characters and incidents portrayed in it are the work of the
author's imagination. Any resemblance to actual persons,
living or dead, events or localities is entirely coincidental.

Published 2002
Poolbeg Press Ltd.
123 Grange Hill, Baldoyle,
Dublin 13, Ireland
Email: poolbeg@poolbeg.com

1 3 5 7 9 10 8 6 4 2

A catalogue record for this book is available from the British Library.

ISBN 1 84223 002 6

Cover designed by Slatter-Anderson
Typeset by Patricia Hope in Sabon 11/15
Printed by Cox & Wyman

www.poolbeg.com

About the Author

Jacinta McDevitt has had many short stories and articles published and broadcast. This is her first novel. She lives in Malahide and has two grown-up children. She works in an architectural practice.

Acknowledgements

I'll try to keep the thankyou's as short as possible because I'm just dying for you to get stuck into reading my book. So, first off thanks to you, for buying it and reading it, hope you enjoy it. To Poolbeg for publishing it, especially Gaye and Paula – it's been fun. To Jane Conway-Gordon, my lovely agent. A collective thankyou to all the wonderful people who encouraged me to write – there are lots but in particular Eileen Casey, Celine Naughton and also Spilling Ink. Thanks too to Michael and all the gang in work who don't mind being used as a sounding board for my stories – or if they do are kind enough not to say so.

Thanks to my friends, old and new, who shorten the road and lighten the load – you know who you are.

Warmest thanks to Bethia, Carmel and Mildred – how very lucky I am to have friends like these. A big hug to Helen, Sara, Katie, Frank, Hannah and Sam who never complain about their mad aunt or at least not within earshot! Michael, Tony and

Maeve – in-laws to die for. Margaret, Lucy, Frank and Mary, the best siblings ever – we love each other, warts and all. Endless love and happiness always to my parents, Frank and Helen – thanks for the safety net. All my love and thanks always to my two children, my lovely young adults, Alan and Lucy – they make being a mother a joy and have a wonderful knack of always making me happy.

Love the bones of you all.

Now get reading . . .   Once upon a time . . .

For Alan and Lucy
and
Dad and Mam

CHAPTER ONE

"Jesus, wait till I tell you! You'll never believe it!"

I dumped the bulky shopping bags on the floor. I could hear the noise from the television. Dick was home. The telly was always on when Dick was home. At least there was someone in to hear my bit of news. Well, if I'm to be honest, it wasn't news. More like gossip really. I don't normally spread it but this was such a rare bit. I couldn't resist. Anyway, passing it on to family doesn't count. Dick, God help me, was definitely family.

I really wished it were Suzie, my long-suffering friend, that I was sharing it with. I was dying to tell her. She appreciated scandal of any type. But when I'd phoned her earlier, Bill, her husband, said she was still at work. She'd be back around six. I guessed I would just have to save her, like the best wine, till last.

I pushed through the door of the telly room. The catch was broken. It had been broken for years. It was one of the things on my list. I had started a list a few months back and now the notebook was full. I was way into the second one. One day I would tackle all the jobs. Soon.

Dick was slouched in his armchair. Assuming his usual position. Dressed to kill in his worn-out grey track suit and threadbare socks. His thinning hair trying to make up its mind which way to lie. Not being able to decide, it was standing upright on his head. The stubble on his chin was anything but designer. He was where he was happiest: on his bum, glued to the television.

"Hey, you know Doreen? From five doors up?" I shouted at him over the racket from the TV.

"No, Doreen who?" Dick barely looked up.

"You know Doreen, Larry's wife, Doreen?" I shouted even louder.

"No!" he shouted back.

"Ah, Dick, you do know her! Doreen, Larry's wife from five doors up?"

"Jesus, Linda, will you keep it down!" he shouted back, not bothering to lower the volume, his own or the telly's. "Can't you see I'm watching the telly?

I'm telling you I don't know any Doreen. How many times do I have to say it?"

"Ah, you do know her, Dick – she's always tarted up, never wears anything out of Dunnes or Penneys. Always designer, even her knickers are designer. Her clothes have the labels on the outside."

"Doreen who? For the last time, Linda, I don't know any Doreen."

Tuned in to the telly, not me.

"Well, she's Larry's wife. Larry who drives the BMW you're always ranting and raving about. Sure you know them well – five doors up." Jesus, was he thick?

"Ah! Larry and Doreen! Navy-blue Beemer – of course I know them."

At last!

"Well, you'll never believe it but Doreen's only having an affair. Honest to God! Jean told me, Audrey told her and her sister-in-law who works with someone who's a brother-in-law of someone else whose wife is best friends with Doreen told her, so it must be true. Imagine it! I wonder does Larry know? He's so taken up with the new car he probably wouldn't even notice if they were doing it under his nose. Not unless they were doing it in the back seat of his car, of course. God, imagine it,

3

his wife's having an affair and all he's worried about is the sparkle off his car. Pity he wouldn't put a bit of sparkle into his marriage."

"He's only looking after his new car, nothing wrong with that. It's terrific. In fact, I was thinking of getting one myself."

"Think again. We couldn't afford it – that car was an arm-an'-a-leg job. Anyway, it's bad enough Larry waxing poetic about his car, without you starting. He has the good polished out of it. He'll cause an accident. The bloody car is so shiny you'd need sunglasses when he's on the road."

"Where's the harm in him spending a bit of time looking after his car?"

Of course Dick would say this, with his love of cars. Our 95D red Fiesta hardly came up to scratch – an embarrassment to Dick but I loved it. Dick wouldn't have been seen dead washing our car – he left that to me. The willing horse. The car had opened up a whole new life for me – life beyond public transport and Shank's mare. Unlocked a world for me outside our four feckin' walls. The car was all ours. The bank manager owned none of it. It was the only thing that the bank didn't have a share in. They owned half our house and furniture. I only hoped theirs was the tatty half. I liked to think the newly decorated half was mine.

"Pity he didn't spend a little time on his wife," I suggested.

"I'm sure he's very attentive to Doreen," Dick said. "You just expect too much. I like Larry. I think he's very personable."

"Well, personable or not, there he is now, the poor bastard, hail-fellow-well-met to all and sundry and they all talking behind his back about his frisky wife. I never knew anyone who was having an affair. Imagine, in this estate! God, who'd have thought it? Wonder who the fella is? Who'd have her, come to think of it?"

"For God's sake, the poor woman probably isn't having an affair at all. I was talking to Larry on Saturday when he was washing his car and he never said."

"Well, he's hardly going to tell you about his affairs or should I say his wife's affair, is he, Dick? I can just hear him, 'Oh, by the way, was I telling you my wife is having it away with someone?' Cop on, he'll be the last one to talk about it. All the same, it's odd for him to be out in public if he does know. Most fellas would run for cover. Stay indoors and engage in a bit of weeping and gnashing of teeth."

"God but you're cruel," Dick said. The pot calling the kettle black.

"I didn't do anything. I'm only telling you what I heard." And I was.

I just couldn't get over the news. I know I was going on a bit but this was major excitement around our estate. And coming from the least likely quarter. I mean, Doreen of all people! Not that she didn't look well – on the contrary, she kept herself very well. Too well for my liking. Rumour had it she spent a fortune in the new beauty clinic in the village, getting exfoliated and toned on a regular basis. Jesus, if they exfoliated me there'd be none of me left! I'd be one big pile of dead skin.

All the same, I'd have thought Doreen'd be a bit beyond having an affair. I mean, she must have been fifty if she was a day. She had four grown-up sons, all living in very exotic places around the world. All doing very well for themselves in computers or something. Running different international companies, calling the shots and earning telephone numbers – according to Doreen. Sending her a few bob every now and again. Doreen had a perfect life. For someone that had reared four boys she was very genteel, prim and proper. Butter wouldn't melt. You know the sort, always eager to tell you that she saw your little Johnny or Mary hanging around the corner smoking with some ne'er-do-well or other. Trouble had never knocked on

Doreen's door. It had found its place with me, overstayed its welcome, never felt the need to move on.

"Isn't she the dark horse all the same? God, can you imagine it?" I picked up the shopping I had abandoned when I came in and hoped that nothing had melted.

"Well . . . no, not really . . . I can't imagine it and I don't think I want to, either."

Dick went back to watching television. I headed for the kitchen sink. I tried to wash the ice cream off the lettuce without much success. If I chopped it and mixed it with mayonnaise no one would ever notice. I was trying to imagine Doreen in a state of gay abandon with some handsome hunk, but I just couldn't. I couldn't even imagine her having sex with her husband never mind a stranger. I would have thought she wouldn't want to upset her hairstyle or risk breaking a nail in a moment of mad passion. Actually, it's a terrible job to try and imagine two people you know having it away with each other. Like when you tell your kids about sex for the first time and you know they're imagining you doing it and you try to imagine what they're imagining. No, not a road I normally like to go down.

"I wonder who the fella is?" I persisted, going

back into the TV room. "He must be blind or desperate or something."

This wasn't going well at all. I needed someone to talk to, to be as shocked as me at the carryings-on. Dick was useless. Where was Suzie when I needed her? "Dick? Are you listening to me?" I shouted again.

"Of course I'm listening to you! Amn't I a captive audience? I can't help listening to you – you keep repeating the same thing over and over again. Doreen, five doors up with labels on the outside of her clothes, is having an affair with a desperate blind man."

I knew by his tone of voice that he was fed up and wanted to end this particular conversation. Or any conversation.

"Oh you can laugh! What would you do if I was having an affair? You wouldn't be such a funny man then, would you? Oh no! Your resident washer and cleaner would be missing half the day. Up to all sorts, with all sorts. See what a funny man you'd be then! Me off out day and night with all an' sundry. Now there's a thing. I wonder do they meet up in the day or at night? I can't say I've ever seen anyone strange hanging around but then again I suppose I haven't been watching. I must keep an eye out now though. There could be hot love-making, earthmoving stuff going on our doorstep, Dick, and we wouldn't even know it."

"Hardly on the doorstep, Linda. Move out of the way. You're blocking the telly."

It never ceased to amaze me. No matter what the catastrophe or disaster we were in the middle of, Dick was capable of watching telly. I swear to God, if the roof had fallen in on top of us, Dick would still have been sitting upright on the couch, covered in rubble and moaning that he couldn't find the zapper and the reception from the bloody cable was getting worse and worse.

"Linda, shift yourself. You're still blocking the telly!" he shouted, louder this time.

He was back in TV-land and all I would get out of him now would be the odd grunt in between flicking the remote. He could flick for Ireland. He was having a run-down now over and over until I didn't know whether Jack Duckworth had joined the staff of the Queen Vic or Marian Finucane had run wild and held up a bank on *Crimewatch UK*. Anyway, it was obvious he wasn't a bit interested in the affairs of state or estate. I suppose he felt secure in the knowledge that I would never have an affair. I agreed. I could never imagine myself having any sort of a fling. Not that I had had a whole lot of offers. Oh, the mind was perfectly willing. I imagined Clooney types, and Sean whispering "The name is Bond, James Bond" into my shell-like but then I looked in the mirror.

My mirror must have been the one used by the wicked queen in *Sleeping Beauty* it was so honest. Every line and wrinkle showed up. Every bulge. Even when I sucked in. It was not a pretty sight. The years had not been kind to my poor bod. Neither had the fact that twice in its thirty-nine years it had swelled to beached-whale-like proportions for nine months and then within twelve hours been deflated, leaving an excess of soft, wrinkly flesh hanging where my once-flat belly had been. It felt weird, kind of soft and warm, yet ripply. As for the boob department! To go from a 32B to a 42DD and then back to a 36C is more than one pair can take. My perky bosom was a thing of the past, a thing I remembered with great fondness. I was the first to admit that my Rubenesque bod was definitely not up to having an affair. If I was going to have an affair, if I was going to embark on the thrill of a lifetime, I would spend at least six days a week in a gym – swimming, working out. But I'd never been to a gym. Even on a social visit. Didn't know where to find one. The nearest thing to exercise I got was walking around town on a Saturday seeking out ensembles and making a mad dash back to the çar park just before it closed. So my exercise regime was nil. I didn't even own a pair of runners. I was more your heels-and-stockings type person.

My eating regime on the other hand was fine. Nothing wrong with that. Every Monday I started a diet. I'd done the Hay, banana, ice cream, Scarsdale, Uni-slim, Weightwatchers and C-food diet (see food and eat it). Nothing wrong with any of them. I was sure they all worked perfectly well. Oh yes, you'd lose stones on any one of them if you stuck to eating what you were told. But I couldn't. I had great intentions but no willpower. I started off great – Day One was always easy. It's Night One I had the problems with. Someone always produced a bar of chocolate on Night One. I loved all types of chocolate, hadn't met a piece yet I didn't like. My name is Linda; I am a Chocoholic. As a result I was one of those women who can pinch much, much more than an inch. More like a little ruler. So with this combination of diet and exercise I was not, as you can imagine, getting ready to audition for *Baywatch*.

Don't get me wrong. I'm not saying I was like the back of a bus or anything but I knew my limitations. Leotards and affairs were out. I was just normal. A bit overweight and floppy around the edges but I cleaned up nice. My children told me I was still in there in the Looks Department and who was I to contradict them, even if I had spent nearly half my life brainwashing them into thinking that their mother was one terrific human being, the nearest thing to perfection they were likely to meet this side of the Pearly Gates. So what if they were biased? I liked it that way. When I asked Dick if I looked well, he always told me that I looked fine. 'Fine' from Dick was a terrific compliment. 'This is a fine meal, Linda.' 'That was a fine holiday.' 'That was fine.' The last when I was lying star-positioned on the bed, sweat pouring from every orifice after a night of the best passion I could give.

My God, wouldn't I love to have an affair, I thought. Love to have sex that was more than just 'fine'. Doreen must be so confident in the nude. No cellulite, no stretch-marks, no soft floppy bits.

"Dick?" I risked tellyus interruptus.

"What?" He'd started flicking again.

"Dick? Do you think I'm still attractive?" I asked.

"What?"

"What do you think of my body, Dick?" Sometimes you have to be blunt, ask straight out.

"Ah, for God's sake, can't you leave a man alone

to watch a bit of telly? You're fine. Your body is fine. Everything about you is fine," he grunted.

Fine. I had been listening to fine for years now. Fine didn't quite do it for me any more. I wanted wonderful, terrific, fabulous. Every once in a while I wanted beautiful and sexy. I knew Suzie's husband, Bill, told her she was sexy and beautiful.

"But am I fine enough for you to have an affair with?" I asked, reasonably enough I thought. Now this was a very good question. A fine question even. I dared him to give the wrong answer with an eyeball-to-spectacle-look. (He had only been wearing glasses for the past six months and I still couldn't decide whether they made him look distinguished or shifty. At that actual moment I was thinking obnoxious.)

"I would have an affair any time." He tried. I'll give him that much.

"But would you have an affair with me?" Dickhead.

"Who else?"

"Is that who else would have you or who else would you love enough, think sexy enough to have an affair with?"

I know, I know I was being childish but how in the name of God was a girl to get a compliment unless she set one up for herself? It was hard work,

13

this compliment-getting. As I got older it was getting harder. I was pissed off having to set them up myself. Sort of took the good out of it.

"You are the sexiest woman in this house."

Our teenage daughter, Chloe, made an entrance at the wrong time.

"Oi, what about me? By the way, I'm going out." She always made an entrance, never just came into the room. She flung the door open and five seconds later her long legs appeared and then the rest of her. She ended every sentence with 'by the way, I'm going out'.

"Well, you're both sexy," said Dick the diplomat.

Our son and heir, Carl, barged in just behind Chloe. Afraid he was missing some meal or other.

"Well now, what have we here?" his loud voice boomed in competition with the telly. "A man, with a pot-belly – a very large pot-belly I feel obliged to point out, Dad," he prodded Dick in the stomach, "a man in his early forties – granted with some hair still on his head – mousy but real – telling a middle-aged wrinkly and a young voluptuary how sexy they are – and all this before tea. I worry about you, Dad. By the way, what is for tea?"

Carl ended every sentence with 'by the way, what is for tea?'

14

"For Christ's sake. Clear off the lot of yous and let me watch the bloody telly!" Dick finally lost it. Started thrashing his arms and legs all over the place. Pointing the zapper at the three of us. I think he was actually trying to push the 'mute' button.

"Now, now, Dad, no need to get stroppy." Chloe risked laughing at him. "You can watch *The Simpsons* – no one is stopping you."

Chloe, me and Carl left Dick to it. Chloe continued talking as the three of us filed into the kitchen. "Hey, Ma, did you hear your pal Doreen is having it off with someone? Proper little knocking-shop we have on our doorstep!"

"Now, Chloe, that's enough of that! I did hear something as a matter of fact but I'm sure there's no truth to it." Well, I had to defend my generation. "Who told you anyway?" I had to play this cool. After all, I was dealing with a teenager and if experience had taught me anything it was that the more interest I showed the less I would be told.

"Jean. Her mother knows someone who knows someone else who knows Doreen."

"What did she say?"

Oh! Oh! Had I given the game away? Asked one question too many? One was usually too many.

"Well, she just told me, you know."

"No, I don't know. If I knew I wouldn't be

asking. What exactly did she tell you?" In my anxiety to hear more I had played it all wrong. I had lost the moment. I should have feigned a lack of interest, then Chloe would have spilled her guts. Talked ad infinitum.

"For God's sake, if I had known I was going to be on *Mastermind* with 'Doreen' as my chosen subject I would have taken notes. All she said was that Doreen was having a bit on the side and she wasn't talking about salad. I think it's disgusting. She should know better – at her age."

Red rag to a bull.

"What's wrong with her age? She's only about eight years older than me." I couldn't contain myself. Anyone over the age of twenty-one was past it. Past everything.

"That's what I mean, she's old. Not a good example to be setting for us young ones! When I think of the time she gave me daggers just because she thought my skirt was up around me bum. The cheek! What's that you're always saying about people in glasshouses, Ma? Well, your woman and her posh conservatory mustn't have ever heard of that one!"

"What's her conservatory got to do with her playing away?" Carl interrupted. "Don't tell me they're doing it in the conservatory? That's disgusting.

16

In fact the whole thing is enough to make me puke. She's ancient." Carl was talking with his mouth full. Full of the chicken-leg I had earmarked for the dinner. He was gnawing his way around it. It looked delicious. So much for the chicken and mushroom pie.

"Oh, God, Carl, you're so slow sometimes," said Chloe. "If you'd only stop sitting on your brain – you're stifling it. Move around, get it to work now and again and you'd know what people were talking about."

Chloe can be quite cutting. Carl has a knack of setting himself up as the perfect target.

"I don't think Doreen's too old to have an affair," I protested. "In fact, I'm sorry I'm not having one myself. Might keep the lot of you on your toes."

"And I'm sure you've had lots of offers?" Chloe laughed.

"God, Ma, you're disgusting!" Carl hated any hint of his mother's sexual activities.

Two teenagers in the one house was one teenager too much. I was worn out with the pair of them. Always sniping at each other. They couldn't agree on the time of day nor would they give it to each other. I opened the door of the fridge and stood staring. Nothing happened. I was looking for inspiration for the dinner. Now that the second leg of the chicken was in Carl's hand I was going to have to come up with an alternative menu. Loaves and fishes.

That's another thing about teenagers – they're either eating everything in sight or on a starvation diet. I never got it right. Then again I never got anything right so why should that be any different? Anyway, they never let me know which eating regime they were observing at any given time. It was all a guessing game. When I filled the fridge they were dieting. When it was Old Mother Hubbard time they hovered like locusts, chanting the same old war cry about there never being 'anything to eat in this house'. Mary Ellen, John boy, Jim Bob and every other goddammed teenager on the block always had lots to eat in their houses. Home-made bread and soup, perfectly baked everything. We were always on war rations. Out of guilt, every now and again I half-killed myself and bunged a batch of buns into the oven. Iced and decorated them. Hundreds and thousands all over the bloody place. 'Nobody eats that rubbish nowadays,' I was told. Apparently it wasn't healthy. Again, out of guilt, bearing in mind all the poor starving children in the world, I ate the dozen buns and before I knew it, it was Blimp Time – again. Could I win?

Why did I keep trying? Who was I trying to kid? Jesus, this mothering thing was hard.

Now that the chicken was gone I wondered if I could give them mushroom pie? Well, I suppose not, as I only had a handful of mushrooms. Funny, but whenever Carl stood and looked in the open fridge he was rewarded. He always found something. A plate of cold sausages or some leftover cold meat. I had been too slow today, preoccupied. He got to the fridge before me. I should have hidden the chicken carcass. Mushroom and sweetcorn pie? Oh, great, a couple of rashers, lurking in the corner. He must have missed those. Mushroom, sweetcorn and rasher pie?

I chopped the rashers, onion and mushrooms and fried them up with the sweetcorn. Threw it all into a white sauce. A bit of pasta and hey presto Carbonara à la Linda. Mouth-watering. A fine meal.

After dinner I made myself a cup of tea and went out into the hall. I sat on the bottom stair and rang my friend Suzie again. Thank God, she was in this time. I was bursting with the Doreen news. (I know I said I didn't spread gossip but Suzie was like family.) Glad to say she hadn't heard yet and was agog, a terrific audience. I had known Suzie for yonks. She was my best friend in all the world. We shared the same 'Shit Here' sign. Yes, a huge sign that hung over both our heads. No one else seemed to have one. Or maybe they did. They were hard to spot. I had always been a member of the 'Shit Here' club. Suzie was a relatively new joiner. Membership is easy. Everyone and everything dumps on you, even God.

I can remember the exact date Suzie joined the ranks. It was January 1st. It's a date you remember easily. It was also Suzie's birthday. She rushed home from work. Pulled on a pair of soft white evening trousers and ripped off her skirt. She threw on her white crochet top and we were off. We went to a few usual haunts, having a bit of *craic*. I thought I saw a light shining over Suzie's head. I ignored it. Then I noticed. Suzie was still wearing her slip – over her trousers. Sheer black, inches of lace at the bottom. Everyone was looking at it. I distinctly saw a 'Shit Here' sign hovering over her head as she made a dash, at breakneck speed, for the toilet. Now we were partners in the club. When the sign was not illuminated over my head it was flashing bright lights over Suzie's. We checked in with each other regularly to see who had custody of the sign, who had had the most disasters befall them on any given day.

"Do you think everyone knows about the affair?" Suzie was still aghast.

"Well, Suzie, if Audrey knows, everyone knows.

I'm not telling anyone. I don't want to be quoted. I suppose poor Larry will be the last to know."

"The poor bollocks." Suzie was a kind soul.

"I think we have a new member in the club, Suzie."

She agreed.

"Listen, Suzie, remember that suit I was telling you about, the grey short –"

"Skirt. Yeah, we said it would be nice with the pink thing," Suzie finished.

"Ma, quick, quick there's water all over the floor!" Chloe shouted from the kitchen.

"Feck. Have to go, Suzie, the washing machine again. Don't worry about the sign. It seems to be well and truly shining directly over my head. I'll talk to you later."

"If you need me you know where I am." That was the thing about Suzie – she was always there when I needed her. Every crisis. Big and small. Suzie was there. I hoped I was always there for her.

I hung up the phone and waded into the kitchen. The feckin' washing-machine had indeed decided to spew its guts all over the place. There was a slope on my kitchen floor which formed a waterfall-like feature if water should happen to spill. The water runs like rapids down into the dining-room. The dining-room floor boasts the only nice plush carpet in the house. I ran in there in true cowboy fashion to head the water off at the pass. I was the Lone Ranger. Everyone else was doing something else, watching the telly, painting their nails, stuffing their faces again. All confident that I would fix everything. No matter what else they thought of me, one thing was sure. They all thought I was able to do everything. On my own.

"Oh, it's all right – I can manage," I shouted in between brushing the cascade of milky water out the back door. "No, no, you just all carry on relaxing, watching the telly! Don't let me disturb you! No, I insist stay where you are! The Suez washing machine has erupted in the kitchen but don't worry about me. I'll just don my wetsuit and flippers and have the place back to normal in jig time. You all sit there and wait. It will be no time at all before I surface again. Not to worry if I'm a little longer than expected as I might just hang around down there and catch a fish for tomorrow's dinner. *So don't stir yourselves – I'll have everything under control in a jiffy, tickity boo!*" My voice rose higher and higher. Hysteria setting in. *"For God's sake, get up off your arses and give me a hand!"*

I totally lost it. Sarcasm does not work on my family. You have to be direct. Direct works.

CHAPTER TWO

I knocked back a Bacardi and blackcurrant. Well, I had had a very traumatic evening. I rang Suzie in desperation after my deep-sea diving episode. Mouth-to-mouth was lacking from my nearest and sometimes dearest. If I hadn't escaped the flicking of the telly, the swinging of the legs and the picking of the nails, not to mention the foibles of the other two, I would have killed one of them. Or all of them.

So in true Hannibal-over-the-Alps style me and Suzie made a forced march to the pub. We only had five pounds thirty between us but it was enough. Well, enough for us to forget the messes we'd left behind and have a good laugh anyway. We were both dolled up. Suzie always bordered on the bohemian. She wore flowing, soft dresses, tight crochet tops and loose, baggy trousers. Velvet bags and lace-up boots. Not all at the one time. Different combinations for different moods. She would have loved to be a free spirit only for the fact that she had a husband and three children who had broken her spirit long, long ago and after forty-one years she was too sensible to think anything is free.

We must have looked like a right odd pair. I am about six inches taller than her, dark and brown-eyed. Due to the fact that I'm always trying to look inches thinner, I wear very tailored clothes. Short skirts and jackets. Trouser suits. Boring. Tonight I was poured into my little beige dress with matching jacket. Suzie was wearing one of her long, flowing dresses – a pastel blue that reflected the colour of her eyes. Her blonde hair was piled up on her head loosely – mine in stark contract was cut short and wispy. It is black, black as the ace of spades. My tights had a ladder in the foot but a blob of scarlet nail varnish had cured that. Suzie never wore nail varnish on her nails or on her tights. She had no nails and never wore tights. Her legs were a 'Sun Haze' colour naturally. Mine are a white, plucked-chicken colour naturally. My long nails were always chipping and my tights laddering. I always carried nail varnish.

We always dolled ourselves up going to the pub.

You never knew who we'd meet. After all, Doreen must have met her new sex-partner, her Clooney, somewhere. Maybe in this very pub. A Clooney, if you don't know, is a perfect man. As in George Clooney, him of the brilliant good looks, boyish charm and to-die-for grin. Suzie and me were always on the look-out for a Clooney. We knew one would walk up to us some time, when we least expected it. There could be one lurking somewhere right now, I thought, as I sat in the pub. Eyeing me up. Taking stock of my stockings, ladder an' all.

"Excuse me."

Jesus! I nearly jumped out of my wrinkly old skin. A Clooney appeared from nowhere. He was the business. Dark, dark brown hair, matching eyes. Both his eyes were indeed the same colour but they matched his hair colour as well. Although there was the odd strand of grey. Not in his eyes, in his hair. Tanned skin. All over tanned, I'd guess. Blue denim jeans, brown cowboy boots and a fabulous soft brown leather jacket. A genuine Clooney. Maybe even a rich Clooney. He had a terrific smile and a brilliant set of teeth. It was the smile that did it for me though. He was saying something to me, staring down into my eyes, which were half-closed and bloodshot from the Bacardi.

I'm not great with drink. It has a peculiar effect

on me. One glass of anything alcoholic and I'm anybody's. It starts off with a distant feeling, like I'm sitting beside myself. My brain takes a little holiday from my body. Both of them work independently of each other. Messages leave the brain. They are never received by the body. The brain instructs 'pick up your handbag'. The body parts start flying all over, aiming two feet away from the bag. Then my lips go numb. Very numb. I lose all feeling in the mouth area. Asking for assistance with the bag is impossible. Taking a sip from my drink is not on. Just as well, I suppose. I misjudge the position of the glass in relation to the position of my mouth. If by some fantastic feat of concentration I get the glass to my mouth I have to manoeuvre my mouth, numb lips and all, around the glass. This is a particularly hard trick. I usually dribble. It is very embarrassing. A middle-aged woman with bad co-ordination, dribbling at the mouth, is written off as a lush even if she has only had one drink. I have tried several other drinks to see if the effect is the same. Vodka, whiskey, gin. I have even tried cocktails and liqueurs, Drambuie and Sex on the Beach. Obviously I take these one by one and usually on different nights of the week although I will admit to taking more than a couple of Harvey Wallbangers one night or so

I'm told. That night is one I would prefer to forget. Thank God I have never been able to remember it anyway. So you see I am not great with drink. Neither am I great with Clooneys.

"Excuse me," Clooney crooned again.

"Yeeeessss?" I tried to cross my legs but only succeeded in kicking Clooney where it must have been very, very painful.

"Jesus Christ!" His eyes watered and he seemed to be gasping for air.

Maybe he's going to ask me where I have been all his life, I thought. Or would I like to make mad passionate? Or how was my belly for a love-bite?

He finally got his breath back. "Is this stool taken?" He spoke rapidly.

"No, you can sit there if you like," I whispered. I rubbed the multi-coloured velvety top of the stool and patted it encouragingly. "We are quite alone," I continued. "We aren't waiting for anyone else, are we Suzie?"

"No, no." Suzie looked eager. Too eager.

I went to cross my legs again. Clooney jumped back.

He grabbed the stool up into the air. "Great, I'll take it over there then." He pointed over in the direction of a group of the most gorgeous women I had ever seen. All implants and face-lifts.

"Oh. Sorry. No, yes, no I mean I thought you were asking something else. No, we are not using the stool. Go on, take it. Take it. You're welcome. Us two old hags, with all our natural bits still natural and untouched by scalpel are on our own and will no doubt remain that way for the rest of the evening. Yes. Yes. Go on. You can have the stool."

I nearly cursed at him. He looked over at Suzie who was making Bambi eyes at him, which would have been all right if only one row of her false eyelashes wasn't hanging off her eye, giving the impression that she had a permanent wink. She looked like one of the pictures you flick back and forth and the image winks at you.

If it hadn't been for Suzie's eyelashes I'm sure he would have joined us.

Suzie and me watched him as he beat a hasty retreat, balancing the stool on his hip. If truth be told Suzie and me watched his tight little bum move across the pub and wished we were the stool. So there we sat, Suzie and me, holding our drinks, nibbling our dry roasted peanuts, watching the beautiful people holding hands and nibbling each other's ears.

"Jesus, I envy Doreen."

Me and Suzie often escaped, far from the madding crowd that was our families. We headed for other

far madder crowds that had nothing to do with us.
That we were not responsible for. We went on Day
Release. A shopping centre, cinema, coffee shop or
fish market. Anywhere. We had this need to recharge
the batteries every now and again.

Suzie worked in the local bookshop, Hardbacks.
She said you'd need a hard back what with all the
lifting and stacking the shelves, with the books
getting bigger and thicker every day. More and
more pages. Less and less plot. There was a notice-
board in the shop. It was a great source of information
on what's on and where to go. We would never
have gone to the series of talks on antiques only for
Suzie. It was good *craic*, everyone thought we were
experts and Suzie and I didn't let on that the only
antiques we had were my washing machine and her
hoover. Both examples of excellent workmanship.
Both around a quarter of a century old now and
both given to bouts of nervous exhaustion when they
were most needed. Suzie could often be spotted
running from my house with my vacuum cleaner
under her oxter five minutes before her mother-in-
law arrived and likewise I carried large black sacks
of washing to and from her house in my times of
greatest need. Like that night.

We did things for each other. She forgot the
things I didn't want to be reminded of, like the fact

that I was nearly forty or that I had just started a diet and it wasn't the Bacardi and blackcurrant diet. She told me things I love to hear. Like what a great friend and confidante I was and how terrific we both looked. This last she kept repeating over and over just before we opened the door to enter the pubs where the beautiful people hung out. Neither of us suffering from an over-abundance of confidence, we had to psyche ourselves up before we went anywhere. Sad, wasn't it, at our age? But that was the thing about Suzie and me – we were born into the wrong generation. A few years earlier and we'd have had all the confidence of the Flower People and few years later and we'd have popped out of our mothers' wombs with the confidence and arrogance that our own children have.

Suzie and me were a perfect match. We complemented each other, knew when we were getting on each other's nerves and backed off. In fact, if Suzie was a man she'd be perfect. But she wasn't and as neither of us had tendencies in the gay department we had to settle for a terrific friendship. Use each other's shoulders on a regular basis. We had saved a fortune on counsellors. We dug one another out of impossible situations and traumatic events. Sure, wasn't I there for her the day she got her hair permed? Now I must tell you she had very fine, silky blonde hair. The type you see in the ads on telly. Anyway she was fed up with it but no matter how much I tried to put her off she just had to have a perm.

"Look at me!" she cried when I met her after the event. "Look at what they've done to me! And I paid them for it! I bloody parted with a week's wages to look like this! I even felt obliged to give the fecker a tip!" She pointed both index fingers in the direction of the mop on top of her head. "I'm l-l-like a-a-a-a c-c-cartoon," she started stuttering. She never stutters unless she is in a grave state of chassis. "Now d-do-n't t-t-tell me its l-l-lovely cause I'll know you're l-l-lying." She took a deep breath and continued without the stutter. "Say nothing, Linda. I don't think I can bear it. I would prefer no opinion at all rather than an honest one. Oh God! Linda, what do you think of it? Now be honest! What do you really think?" she cried again – in fact, she cried for days. I swear her normally dark blue eyes turned into the watery blue colour they are today because of all the crying she did over that perm.

"In fact it's quite nice," I lied. Well, what was a friend for only to lie when it was necessary?

"I look like bloody Shirley Temple!" She just wouldn't stop crying.

31

Granted, she did look like Shirley Temple and if she had any sort of a decent voice I might have joked with her and asked for a bar of 'The Good Ship Lollipop'. But I was her friend and wanted to remain her friend. This was serious stuff, definitely not the time for jokes, no matter how good. Unfortunately, Suzie is very small, five foot one, and has a small cherub-like face or 'full moon in a fog' as she calls it. So the resemblance to Shirley was uncanny. It took weeks of washing and crying before Suzie and her hair returned to normal.

Doreen's hair was always perfect. Like Doreen herself. The real reason Suzie and me were so gobsmacked with Doreen having an affair was that Suzie and me had only ever slept with one man. Well, one man each. Not the same man. Honest to God. We had only ever slept with our husbands. Each to her own. Imagine in this day and age having to admit that! Even twelve-year-olds have had more than one partner. So lately I had been wondering . . . well . . . well, I would have loved to know if it was true – you know, about size not mattering. I had only ever seen one. I mean I'd only ever seen Dick's dick. Nobody else's. I couldn't have told you if it was M, L or XL if you know what I mean. I had no yardstick. Well, it certainly wasn't a yardstick, that I did know. Can you see my problem? There was nowhere I could ask, nowhere to make enquiries.

Suzie was as ignorant as me. Her Bill's dick and my Dick's dick seemed to be about the same. So we wondered if there was a standard size, if all the fuss was just something that men had hatched among themselves. Another 'Let's fool women, ha, ha,' scheme. Like when we were fooled into thinking that men, by virtue of the fact that they have a penis at all, should be the only ones to vote or be paid more than women for the same work. You know what I mean. The penis factor. It's everywhere. Stand at a bar for a drink and unless you have a penis you won't get served. Complain about anything from a rotten meal to the service on the boiler and unless you are sporting a penis you won't be taken seriously. How many times have you had to enlist the services of your husband or father or brother or son just to overcome the penis factor and get attended to? I am sick of being a woman in a man's world. I often thought of hanging a little silver penis around my neck and waving it around when appropriate. I could make a fortune, if I went into business, selling them. Overnight I could eliminate the P-factor.

Anyway, getting back to Suzie's and my problem, there is no Consumer Affairs Department of Body Parts. I could have been hard done by. I could have been missing out on something great in my life. I could have been settling for second best in the lovemaking stakes and not know it. Doreen must have moved up a grade or two, so why not me? I suppose you're thinking 'Oh, she was obsessed, having a mid-life crisis, it being her fortieth birthday and all that year'. But it was a serious issue. It had been taking up a lot of my time lately. That and thinking what it would be like with someone else. And there was Doreen all the time having it off with God knows who.

I loved Dick. I thought. I had grown up with him. He had been in my life longer than he had been out of it. One year courtship and nearly twenty years married. It would be our twentieth anniversary at the end of the year. Fifteen of them were wonderful. I just went along with everything he said. The last few had had a bit of the same ol' same ol' feel to them. But I was used to him. After all those years there were no surprises with Dick. Well, no pleasant ones anyway. He thought he was the best husband and father ever. And when he tried really hard he could be – when he wasn't glued to the shaggin' telly. I wasn't complaining or maybe I was but we were inexperienced when we got married. I was young and foolish. Foolish enough to fall for all the 'death us do part' and the 'happy ever after' lines. We were carried away on the moment. I thought Dick was all I would ever want in a husband. Then again what did I know? Before I met him I had only been out with a couple of other blokes. Holding hands, a quick grope and a goodnight kiss was the order of the day.

Dick and I met by accident really. I was living at home with my parents and the three of us were having dinner one evening. A very civilised affair compared to my own household where dinners were eaten off laps and if I had asked anyone to set the table they would think I was talking about setting up an arrangement for a still-life class. We watched the telly while we were having our dinner. No one spoke. Dick didn't like it. Tomato sauce and bottles of milk rested at people's feet begging to be spilt, asking to be knocked all over my dreadfully impractical cream carpet. I bought the carpet in a moment of madness when I thought that, as my youngest child was eighteen, we could handle a cream carpet. I now realise that eighteen is only a numerical age – it has nothing to do with the development of the adult *per se*. So the cream carpet is now a mottled cream, grey and spotted red colour. Who are cream carpets made for anyway?

Most parents fall into a black hole, a bottomless

pit, when their children reach the magic age of eighteen. They think, and this is due mainly to the fact that they are conditioned, brainwashed even, by their children to believe it, that as soon as a person, male or female, hits their eighteenth birthday they become adults. Can drink, smoke and have sex without the parents' permission. Not that they had the parents' permission when they were fourteen or fifteen years old and started drinking in the first place.

Children seriously believe that on the eve of their eighteenth birthday they are given special powers. Think they know it all. Parents hope that on the morning of their children's eighteenth birthday the scatterbrained zombie that was their seventeen-year-old son or daughter will wake up and caterpillar-like will have turned into a mature, rational, sensible adult. Don't be fooled. Believe none of the propaganda that the teenage section of society is spreading. Oh, there is a change all right. They emerge on their eighteenth birthday thinking they are invincible. They can legally drink so they drink as much as they can swallow. At eighteen they get great swallowing powers.

Anyway, getting back to how I met Dick. There I was, as I said, having my dinner when the phone rang.

"Halloo, can I speak to Linda, please?"

"This is Linda. Who's that?" I asked.

"Hi, Linda. It's Richard from work."

"Hi, Richard." I didn't know any Richard.

"I was wondering . . . well actually . . . I was thinking."

God, I hadn't a clue who he was. I hadn't been working that long and there might have been some fellas I didn't know but I seriously doubted it. I always made a point of sussing out the talent. There was a quiet fella called Tom. Oh horror of horrors, suppose the fella called Tom wasn't really a Tom but a Richard and I'd been calling him the wrong name?

"Well, I was wondering really would you like to go out with me some time? Just if you wanted to, like, nothing special. Maybe for a drink or to the pictures or something?"

"What?" He didn't sound like Tom.

"Well, only if you want to. I won't be offended or anything if you don't want to. It's just that I like you and I think we get on really well in work and I'd love to see you, sort of to go out with you if you thought you'd like to? Linda, are you still there?"

I couldn't remember anyone I got on well with in work. Oh, I didn't go around insulting people, telling them about their BO problems, casting aspersions or even asparagus. I just kept myself to myself, being new and all that.

"What? Oh yes, yes, I'm still here." I still hadn't a clue who he was.

"Linda, what do you think?"

"That would be lovely."

There it goes, my mouth acting before my brain told it what to say. Running off opening itself and getting me into deep shit. There must be exercises I can do to get my mouth to wait for sensible instructions from my brain. All right, so my mouth would have to wait a while, sift through all the foolish suggestions put to it too. Select the most suitable words for every occasion. Stall before I speak. I'll have to work on that.

"When?" he asked.

"What?"

"When do you think you would be free?"

"Free?"

"To come out with me! What we have been talking about? You and me going for a drink or something. When do you think we might be able to go?"

"Oh, right, tomorrow night." There it goes again, my mouth, letting the side down. Eager feckin' beaver.

"Great. Where do you want to go?"

"The pictures would be nice." Jesus, Mary and Joseph. I would have to get my mouth stitched up if this continued. The pictures for a necking session, I may as well have said. What would have been so wrong with meeting for a drink to suss the guy out. He could be one of the Kray twins and I was going to sit with him for at least an hour and a half in a pitch-dark room. A noisy crowded pub would have made it too hard for the guy. Better, if you are going to sacrifice yourself to a total stranger, to go the whole hog and offer yourself up on a platter.

"Terrific. Will I pick you up or meet you there?"

"I'll meet you there." Great. Now, not even my parents would get to interrogate him. They were terrific at the third degree. Sweat poured profusely from the last friend I brought home, after my parents had done their usual grilling. And that was only Suzie. They would have been Gestapo-like with a member of the opposite sex. Now, they wouldn't even be able to identify this Richard person in a line-up after he had had his evil way with me and then thrown me on a scrap heap to rot. Defrocked. I offered myself up to Richard on a platter with glazing.

I spent most of Saturday applying the glazing. Preparing for what could have been my last social event. I washed my hair and put extra conditioner in. It was a mop of unruly curls. I tried ironing it. It singed. I forgot to put the brown paper between the iron and the hair. My hair never grew down like most humans. It grew with frightening rapidity. Not down but out. Like a clown's wig. In fact, I should have been a professional clown – I had all the requirements. Anyway for the famous date I put on a strip of pale powder-blue powder eyeshadow, as young eejits of girls did way back then. I lashed on the navy-blue mascara. I tried on all my skirts – not all together. I wasn't happy with the messages they were sending out. 'Easy pickings'. I settled on the safety of my favourite denim dungarees. Lots of buttons and buckles. A blue check shirt I had been given for my birthday completed the Bozo look. I, of course, saw no resemblance to that particular entertainer. I was thinking more Debbie Harry. I marvelled at myself in the mirror. I was the business. This Richard guy didn't know how lucky he was. I hopped on the bus and arrived at the cinema half an hour too early.

I stood by the main door waiting, with half the female population of Dublin. All praying to St. Jude not to be a hopeless case. Not to be the one who would be stood up. By the law of averages one of us had to be. We snuck a look at our watches when no one else was looking. We never made eye contact. We needed anonymity. It ensured a less embarrassing time when no one arrived and we had to slink off with our tails and pride between our legs. Only when our dishy fella arrived and gave us a peck on the cheek would we smugly make eye contact with all our peers, pitying those who were left still waiting and wondering. We stood like lemmings waiting to take that leap from the cliff edge. I peeped at my watch. Five minutes to go to the start of the film. Where was the bastard?

I saw a man hovering. He had been loitering in the foyer since I arrived. He was a bit older than me, two or three years at a guess. He had straight light-brown hair, blue eyes and looked normal. In fact, he looked very above normal. Really very good-looking in a rugged sort of way. Not too fat, not too thin. He had navy corduroy trousers and beige desert boots, obviously new, no brown marks on the toes. He had a tee-shirt on with some sort of writing across the chest and was carrying a grey sweatshirt with a hood. The athletic type. I kept looking at him. It couldn't be him. I didn't work with this guy. I'd have remembered if I did. Finally he made eye contact.

"Richard?" I asked. He looked around, over his shoulder, to see if someone was standing behind him.

"Are you Richard?" I couldn't believe my mouth. It was being so brave.

"Yeees. And you are?"

"Linda. I'm Linda. You know, who you're supposed to be meeting?"

"No, no, you're not Linda."

"Oh, yes, I think I am."

"But you're not."

"Well, I think I might be the best judge of who I am and I am most definitely Linda." Was I that ugly?

"But, no, you can't be, I'm meeting Linda from work here. You don't work in Kavanagh Solicitors now, do you?"

"No, no, you've got me there but then again you were the one who rang me, remember? So you must work in U R Insured. Right?" I said.

"Wrong. So you're not Linda. I rang Linda from work and asked her to the pictures. She's not a bit like you."

"Hold it. I'm Linda and you rang me. How many other Lindas did you ring? Is that how you get your kicks? Pick a name you like, arrange to meet a whole bunch of women with that name. Choose one of the poor bunch of suckers for a snogging session in the cinema?"

"Excuse me, I most certainly don't go around ringing Lindas nor do I snog in the cinema, thank you very much. There has been a mix-up. You're the wrong Linda."

"Well, all I know is you rang and arranged to meet me. I foolishly enough said yes so here I am. Now are we going to a picture or not ?"

"You mean to tell me that a total stranger rang you and asked you out and you said yes?"

"It wasn't a total stranger. I work with the guy."

"Well, then, where is he?"

"Jesus, are you brain-dead? It was you that rang me!"

"I keep telling you I rang Linda from work – thin, blonde girl. Nothing at all like you."

"Well, you rang the wrong number. Look, one out of three ain't bad. I am Linda and I can dye my hair if you want but the thin? Well, you'll just have to pretend. Now am I to go home or do you want to see a film?"

"Oh, God, this is terrible. We may as well stay now we're here. What do you want to see?"

"James Bond."

My mouth again. I should have gone for a safe film. One without Pussy Galore.

Richard bought me sweets and popcorn and paid for my ticket. Just as well as I had forgotten to take the ten pounds off my dressingtable and had just about enough change for my bus fare.

I needn't have worried about the snogging. There was none. Not that I would have minded – he was kinda cute. But I think he was in a state of shock. The blonde bombshell he had been expecting had turned into Coco the Clown. After the film he kept apologising. He was a decent guy and he knew he had insulted me. I allowed him make it up to me by bringing me for a cup of coffee. I didn't drink in those days. No one had driven me to it. We went into a small hotel up the street. A total kip. Auld fellas falling down drunk, women shouting at them to 'bleedin' well fuck off' and snotty-nosed kids whingeing from lack of sleep and lack of interest. Richard said he had his car with him and he'd take me home. This was a major point in his favour: wheels. We chatted easily. He told me he was studying to be a solicitor. I was duly impressed. Then I spoiled it all by asking what his Linda was like. He said he couldn't remember and asked me if I would go for a drink with him the next night. I agreed.

At this stage we were outside my house. I didn't want to appear too eager and ask him in, neither did I want him to go. So we just sat there. I inched my way closer to him and I could see him adjust himself in the seat trying to do the same. I recognised the Old Spice – my father wore it. Everyone wore it in those days. His face looked smooth. You'd think no hair grew on it but you'd know it did. You know that sort of tempting shaven face. Makes you want to touch it. Well, honest to God, I don't know what came over me but I did. I watched as my very own hand left my side and touched his cheek. If I had slapped him full on the face, he or I couldn't have been more surprised. Really my body parts were becoming a definite disadvantage. First my mouth, now my arm. Jesus, Mary and Joseph, my mouth was at it again. It was only leaning over to kiss him. Holy God, he was a great kisser. Soft at first then a little firmer, full suction of our lips and then the tips of our tongues touched . . . Jesus, it was great. I won't go into too much detail and bore you but suffice it to say the breathing exercises taught to me by Sister Mary Frances at choir practice came into their own.

So Richard and me became an item. He met my parents. I met his mother. That was a strain, I can tell you. He's an only child, only boy, need I say more?

"Richard is very committed to his studies, you know. He hopes to be a fine solicitor one day like his late father."

By late she didn't mean that the man was stuck at the nineteenth hole in Royal Dublin. No, the man was actually dead. She always referred to him as late. As though it was a total inconvenience.

"My late husband never over-indulged."

"My late husband always knew the right thing to say."

"My late husband was never late."

I felt sorry for the poor late bastard. He seemed to have had a miserable life and then popped his clogs before he got a chance to have any sort of a fling. He was a great ad for never doing the right thing. Lived a proper boring life and just when he found something he liked doing he dropped dead doing it. Honest to God, he'd only joined a golf club. Wasn't in it a wet day. He'd maybe used the facilities six times in all. Out he goes to have a bit of R&R, picks up a five-iron to hit the ball. Then out of the blue, literally, he was struck by lightning. I'm not telling a word of a lie, the man was literally struck down in his prime by a bolt of lightning. Dropped down dead. They say he was cooked from the inside – he was still holding the golf club. Like a microwave apparently. I don't know all the medical details, nor, can I tell you, do I want to but I must admit it's a great talking point if you're ever stuck for something to say at a dinner party. "Did I mention that Richard's father was struck by lightning?" It's marvellous. A crowd of fifty has been known to gather on occasions when Dick and I gave the golf-club and lightning story at a function.

Particularly a golf outing. His father would have been proud.

But that left me with the mother. Now, she isn't all that bad really but, you know, she's one of those people that looks like a skunk has just passed her by and she's looking to see what direction he's travelling in. Her head is permanently on a swivel, for fear she'll miss something, like me making an eejit of myself , as I am prone to do. From the start I found myself not being myself when she was around. I put on a voice that I only put on for her. My impress-the-mother-in-law voice. I couldn't help myself. I wanted her to think I was Superwife, Supermother and Superdaughter-in-law all rolled into one. In those early days when she came to visit, I nearly somersaulted into the room balancing a cup of tea on my nose and jumping up – "Ta-Da!" – with my arms spread out, star-position, holding a plate of ham sandwiches in one hand and home-made black forest gateaux in the other. It had gotten no easier over the years. Time had made me realise that as I got older it was getting more and more difficult to somersault around the room. Try as I might I had given her no evidence at all of my superpowers but she was Richard's mother after all so there was no doubt in my mind that he had filled her in on each and every one of my little foibles. She firmly believed I wasn't good enough for her darling son.

I can't fault the woman on that. As a mother I can understand it. Feel the same way myself in fact. No one is good enough for my own two children. But as long as we start from there and come up with the very next best thing I'll be happy. As long as they pick someone that will make them happy and keep them in the style they have been accustomed to, then I will be delighted. So what I'm looking for is two single people, one male for my daughter and one female for my son obviously, although nowadays you might be forgiven for wondering. But I can assure you both of them have proven themselves in that department. I am sorry to say that both have, in their time, been seen from the back-bedroom window in compromising positions with members of the opposite sex. They are both unaware of the vantage-point this window offers. Anyway the applicants for the position of partner to the two best kids in the world would need to be able to cook, iron, sew, write endless large cheques, hammer, drill, paint, hoover, wash . . . a more detailed list is available on request.

If my mother-in-law would only lighten up she'd have a great life. I tried my best but my best was never good enough. Fell short of perfect. Richard always said I imagined it but then that's 'don't rock the boat' Dick for you. My friend Suzie agreed with me. She was in the same boat. The one that Richard or her husband Bill didn't want to rock.

Suzie is lucky. She never sees her mother-in-law. She moved away to Majorca seven years ago. The mother-in-law, that is. Just upped stakes and high-tailed it off to the island. Suzie's husband Bill thought his mother was having some sort of a brain seizure. It was dreadful. He tried to have the poor woman committed but the mother kept telling him she wanted a bit of heat. Poor Bill got the natural gas central heating installed for her but it didn't help matters. Bill said that the trouble was that she had been allowed to go away on holidays to Majorca with the Sociable Elderly Club in her village and had lost the run of herself. Turned out he was right. It was body heat she was looking for. Hadn't she only gone and met an old Spanish guy, Carlos, and had been going out to get a bit of heat off him every chance she got. Bill and Suzie had been thinking that the Sociable Elderly Club went on holidays far too often: Christmas, Easter, summer and at the drop of a hat. Bill went down to the Sociable Elderly Club to complain that his mother was spending more and more time in foreign parts. He didn't know that his mother was only interested in Carlos's private parts. The club told him that they had only arranged one trip to Majorca and that his mother had been very disruptive on the trip. Drinking and hanging around with the locals. Bill was mortified. It wasn't bad enough that his three children were fond of a drop – now, in his early fifties, he discovers that his mother of seventy-two is not all he had built her up to be. Bill was raging. You'd know by the way the veins were bulging in his neck.

"If she thinks for one minute that she can high-tail it off to some godforsaken, flea-ridden hole of a place to live with some flea-ridden Carlos or other she has another think coming. No mother of mine is going anywhere foreign. Do you hear me, Suzie? She's not setting foot outside this country. If I have to go around there myself and lock her up she's going nowhere."

"But, Bill, she's a grown woman. You can't stop her," Suzie said, reasonably enough I thought.

"Oh, I knew you'd be the one to egg her on! I suppose you'll be around helping her to pack. You never liked her anyway. You can't wait till she's off your back. If it was your mother it would be a different story! Oh yes! Then the whole country would be put on alert!"

This was a particularly cruel thing to say as Suzie's mother had died when Suzie was seventeen.

Eventually anyway Bill and Suzie and the three kids gave his mother a great send-off. Bill went out to Majorca to suss out this Carlos person and was pleasantly surprised. Word from Bill's mother in Majorca was that life with Carlos was sensational – all sun, sea and whatever you're having yourself if you get my drift. Every time it rained here I thought of Bill's mother and Carlos. So I thought of them daily. I secretly envied them. So that was Bill's mother and Doreen. I'd better watch out. The envy list was getting longer.

CHAPTER THREE

Believe it or not but the next day Suzie and me were still full of the affair. This would keep us going for a long time. But, to be honest, we were a bit peeved and rightly so. We had hoped to be providing the gossip around here. Doreen had beaten us to it. Stolen our thunder. We had wanted to be the ones to shake our families up a bit. Now, with this Doreen business nothing would shock them, short of a bit of inappropriate behaviour with the president. Even that was out of the question now that two women had overcome the 'P' factor and managed to keep a candle burning in the Aras. But Suzie and me were making daring plans, daring for us that is, very mild for Doreen.

We always made daring plans over coffee.

When I say coffee I really mean tea as neither of us drinks coffee. Holding court over a cup of tea doesn't have the same ring to it, does it? We always went out. We never discussed anything private in the privacy of our own homes. There were always little rabbits and big ears in our houses. Big rabbits with even bigger ears. So we headed for Amelio's. Amelio's was the only place to go when we had something important to discuss. It was in Amelio's, a couple of years back, that I first told Suzie Dick was mean to me. I was sorry after. I should have kept it to myself. Like everything else.

"Jesus, Linda, you'll have to do something. Tell someone about it." Suzie was near to tears.

"Don't be silly, Suzie. It's nothing. He just gave me a shove out of his way. He promised he'll never do it again."

"And you believe him?"

"Yes. Of course. He promised. He honestly didn't mean to hurt me. I banged my arm when he shoved me. It was an accident. He was so sorry after. The only thing I'm worried about is Carl and Chloe. They saw the bruise on my arm and I don't think they really believed me when I said I had walked into a door. I hope to Jesus they don't suspect anything, Suzie. They kept asking me how in the name of God I didn't see the door. If they find out it was Dick they'll tear him apart limb by limb. They'll kill him, Suzie. You have to promise me not to say anything to anyone."

"Linda. You can't let the bastard away with it. You're too good for him."

"You're making a mountain out of a molehill!" I wanted her to shut up. "I love him. It was my own fault. He doesn't mean it, Suzie. He's sorry. Look, you can't even see it. No one will notice it. It wasn't a hard wallop and I had annoyed him." My arm did hurt but I was damned if I was going to let Suzie prattle on and on, making more out of it than there was. I could cover up. I was good at it. I had my own unique way of handling it. Kept going as best as I could until the next time. In between times, I loved Dick. Now and again he forgot his promises and blew his top. So what? He always promised he wouldn't do it again. He didn't break his promise that much. But more and more lately. I wondered what triggered it. If I knew I could avoid annoying him. Best to be always on his good side. Dick was a man you didn't argue with. It was hard not to argue with him. Suffer the consequences. I always kept quiet about the consequences. That was easy. I didn't want Carl or Chloe to find out. My secret was safe with Suzie.

Amelio's was the place for sharing secrets. We

couldn't figure out why it was called Amelio's. There was no Amelio in the place. There was a Lotty and a Deco but no Amelio. Lotty and Deco might have been married, even to each other. There was no body language between them. In fact, there was no language of any kind between them. A bit like me and Dick. Lotty and Deco worked independently of each other. Unlike me and Dick, she was much bigger than him. She was definitely lacking in the finesse department, born with less of the silver spoon in her mouth and more of the wooden one. She was one of those people that you would automatically be afraid of. Your instincts would tell you to take care. Suzie and me always followed our instincts. We had healthy yellow streaks down our backs.

Lotty was a big red person. Big red face, bee-stung red lips, bright red neck. Her hair was a halo of fire. Always at right angles to the rest of her. She liked wearing red. More a rough ruby than a well-cut diamond. Deco on the other hand was a small, thin man. He had a lisp and always wore an artist's cap hiding what me and Suzie suspected was a shiny, pink head. He had no facial hair and very scrawny eyebrows. He was as white as Lotty was red.

Deco fancied himself as a bit of an artist and Amelio's was littered with 'art deco' paintings for sale. You know, the usual 'paint by numbers' type. He once asked me to pose for him but I declined on the basis that if I was ever going to pose for anyone he would be called Leonardo – da Vinci, di Caprio. I wasn't fussy. Take your pick.

Amelio's was a bit of a kip. A mixum gatherum of all styles. Plastic and crystal side by side with delph and a very odd scattering of china. Nothing matched. The big plum carpet was worn in places and bright green rugs were scattered everywhere except on the threadbare patches.

Every time Suzie and me went to Amelio's we swore we'd never go again. Swore that we'd head for the high spots. Plush hotels with afternoon tea. Clean crisp tablecloths and sparkling cutlery. Not that Amelio's was dirty, it was just not clean. It was the sort of place you love to go home from. Makes you feel good about the torn wallpaper in your own hall and the yellowing paint on the skirting boards. A bit of a kip all right. Handy though. If we went further afield then Dick would know I'd been out enjoying myself and that would never do. The danger would be I might enjoy myself too much. Amelio's was safe. We sneaked in after being at the shops. Then moaned when we got home that we were dead from all the shopping and queuing at the checkout. My kids couldn't get over how unfortunate

I was. Whenever I went to the supermarket there was an enormous queue. When they went it only took them ten minutes.

The trouble with Lotty and Deco was that they needed customers to keep the place going. People dropping in for coffee or tea like Suzie and me. Deco and Lotty didn't seem to like people popping in. Didn't seem to like people at all. Today was no exception. I ordered my usual toasted turkey-salad sandwich and tea. The tea arrived in a teapot with no knob on the lid and a crack down the spout.

"Excuse me, but could I have one with a knob on?" I was polite.

"A knob, what do you want a knob for?"

"Well . . ." I was afraid. "I don't know what I want a knob for. Perhaps to keep the tea warm or to prevent dirt getting into the tea. Or maybe, just maybe, because I like the look of a knob on a teapot. As for the crack down the spout, well, let's say that one cracked thing around here is more than enough." I looked conspiratorially at Suzie. She was chuffed. I could sense how proud of me she was. I had at last stood up to Lotty.

Lotty grabbed the teapot and disappeared into the kitchen.

"God, Suzie, I'm so brave!"

"I hope you didn't overdo it. She could be doing

anything to our tea. Spitting into it or whatever it is they do when you complain."

"Ah, Suzie, that's base! Lotty wouldn't have the smarts to spit in the tea. Would she?"

We both glared at the door to the kitchen. Neither of us having the benefit of x-ray vision we couldn't see what Lotty was doing. Only imagine. A million times worse than what you're imagining. After all, we were there. We were on the spot and going to be doing the drinking.

I examined my cup. It still had the dregs of a previous drinker's tea in it. There was a print of very unfashionable bright orange lipstick on the rim. Lotty came back. I was a bit afraid to point out the fault with the cup. At the same time I didn't want to drink out of it. God knows what I would have caught. I mean anyone wearing that colour lipstick could have had anything, if you know what I mean.

"Now there's your teapot. I hope that knob meets with all your requirements." She plonked the knob-bearing teapot so hard on the table that the milk spilt all over the yellowed plastic lace tablecloth.

"Would you mind giving the table a wipe?" Suzie whispered.

"Gimme me a chance, would you?" Lotty stormed off in the direction of the kitchen again. This time she was muttering to herself and I could have sworn I heard the word 'fucking' and 'who do they think they are – Lady Mucks – with knobs on'. Then a very frightening thing happened. Lotty threw her head back – it was still attached to her neck but it was very far back indeed. Nearly right back against her back. She started laughing. Loud, raucous, her whole body vibrated like a big strawberry jelly. Suzie and me were terrified. I decided to nip it in the bud.

"Could you bring me a clean cup?" I shouted. It fell on deaf ears.

When Lotty returned with a well-used cloth she was not laughing. Not even smiling. Suzie and me wondered if we had imagined it.

"Now," she said through the side of her mouth. An aside to herself while rubbing ferociously at the plastic tablecloth. She turned to us. Glared. "Is that better now? Are yous two happy now?"

"Well, actually, I need a clean cup, if it wouldn't be too much trouble." I was grovelling.

"A clean cup, is it? And what's wrong with that one?" She pointed a chubby index finger at my cup.

"It's dirty," I apologised.

"All right then."

Credit where it's due she snatched the cup from me and trundled off towards the kitchen to get me a fresh one. Halfway there she had second thoughts. She took the cloth she had just used to wipe the table and started to scoop out the inside of the cup. She kneaded the cup into her wobbly belly. Gave it a rub of the relic of an apron she was wearing.

"Now how's that?" She stood over me smiling. Her four front teeth missing. Lost. Like a child about to make its First Holy Communion. No doubt some previous customers had irritated her and she had bitten their heads off, losing the teeth in the process. No need to guess what would be top of her Christmas list next year.

"Well, well." I was dumbfounded. If I asked for a fresh cup I knew she'd just go into the kitchen and bring out the same cup again. "Well, yes," I said, "that's fine but I really would like a second cup."

"What for?" Lotty asked.

"To have one cup of tea cooling while I drink the first." I can think quickly when cornered.

"Oh, I see, all right then."

She waddled off meek as a lamb. Never suspecting my ulterior motive. Not big in the IQ department is Lotty.

The sandwich was all right. All lettuce and very little turkey. Suzie and I settled down to business. Suzie produced the brochures.

We were going on holiday!

Just the two of us. On our own, with nobody else.

We had to plan it like military manoeuvres. It had to be produced as a fait accompli or else it would be a non-starter. We thought it would stir our loved ones, our nearest and sometimes dearest, into action. Action at the front. The home front. We wanted to go somewhere hot. Nowhere near Suzie's mother-in-law. But if we needed to we would use her as a decoy.

"Excuse me." Deco said over my shoulder. He was wearing a grubby white overall and his cap was perched on his head. A blue flowery cravat was tied loosely at his neck. There was a blob of something stuck to the cravat. Mayonnaise or paint.

"Yes?"

"I want to thow thome pictureth to that gentleman over there and we can't thee them properly. Would you mind if I balanced them on the back of your chair. I could lean them againth your thoulderth."

Deco's lisp was very pronounced. He always spoke like a baby. He moved his head from side to side and the hand movements were all over the place.

"Am I hearing right?" I looked at Suzie. "Is the 'Shit Here' sign over my head, Suzie?"

But Suzie couldn't speak. She was open-mouthed and staring from me to him.

"Do you seriously expect me to eat my tea and sandwich under one of your paintings?"

"Well, if you're going to be like that! I only wanted to thhow my painting but it doethn't matter. You continue on chatting. Don't mind me. I can rig thomething elthe up."

I couldn't believe it. He headed off with the picture to another poor unsuspecting soul. A gobshite. She was so stunned she agreed. I declare to God the woman disappeared behind a landscape of Howth Head. A very bad landscape of Howth Head. Looked like a chocolate Swiss Roll on a pale blue plate to my artistic mind. There the poor woman stayed for at least fifteen minutes while they all discussed the colour, tone and price of the dreadful object balanced on her shoulders. Flattening the back of her hair. I nearly choked on the lump of turkey I found in my sandwich. We swore we would never come into Amelio's again. But of course we didn't mean it. Anyway, Amelio's was the only place that didn't pass any remarks on Suzie's habit.

Now as you know I love my friend Suzie dearly, let me say that again up front. She is my best friend but she has this habit. In fact, she has a lot of habits. Most good. Some bad. One, the pits. I can't handle it. She is oblivious to it. She engages in it every time we go out anywhere. I cringe every time. I am nearly too embarrassed to mention it at all. There we were, sitting, having a laugh at the woman who had turned into an easel. Then Suzie went quiet. I knew she was going to do it. I looked around and thanked God that the majority of the coffee shop was distracted, enjoying the easel entertainment.

Suzie plonked her big black bag onto her lap. I felt my nervous rash erupt on my chest. It knew what was coming. It always appears in times of stress. Suzie started to root in her bag while furtively looking around. Bright red weals were popping out all over me. Throbbing. She pulled bits and pieces out of the bag. Tissues, notebook, two biros, purse, set of keys that looked as if they opened every lock in Dublin, bottle of make-up, three lipsticks and a million receipts and bus tickets. She plonked them all onto the table. She was only short of upending the bag. The bag is not leather. Not even imitation leather. The bag looks and is black plastic. She has had the same bag for as long as I have known her. Nearly twenty years. She also has a velvet bag that must be the same age but it is only ever brought out on state occasions. It looks alive.

She made a final rummage in the bag. With a large

toothy grin, in a flourish akin to a magician, she pulled a Fry's Peppermint Cream bar out and pressed it towards my face. I nearly hit it out of her hand. She whipped it back before I had the chance. She shoved all the rubbish off the table back into her bag along with four salt sachets, two sugars, two peppers and four portions of butter wrapped in gold foil. She laid the bar on the table before her. My rash was starting to itch. She opened the wrapper, exposing all the sections of the bar. Then with the skill of a surgeon she started to cut each section. They oozed cream. She bundled them up inside their wrapper again and stuck them back in her bag. She left the bag resting on her lap. Open. The bag not her lap. My chest was itching and stinging. Then she took a section of chocolate from the bag with a rustle of paper. She examined it in great detail, turning it over and over. Then she popped it into her mouth and sucked. Savouring the taste. Letting the chocolate melt on her tongue.

"Orgasmic," she announced. "Would you not try some?" She then proceeded to do the same with the other sections, one by one.

You have no idea what this little ritual did to me. Every time she did it, every single time. I was mortified. She never cared where she did it. At lectures. In places where the 'no consumption of food is allowed on this premises' signs are in three different languages, even in graphics. My nervous rash was now of the all-over variety. I was getting more like Lotty by the second.

"Now, Suz –" I decided to get it out into the open once and for all. Confront the issue. We were both adults. I would state my case and Suzie would be sensitive to my needs. "Please don't get me wrong, Suzie, but if we are to sit here plotting how to escape for a fortnight I have to have a clear head. If you sit there in the middle of this kip eating that bar of chocolate out of your handbag then I will have to leave. My rash is breaking out on my chest. Look." I pulled down the neck of my bright pink Dunnes Stores jumper and revealed a bright pink matching chest. "I'm sorry, Suzie, but I can't stand your habit of bringing bars of chocolate with you everywhere we go. It's unnatural. I've tried to put up with it but I can't. I just can't."

I had stated my case.

"Where's the harm in it?" Suzie was obviously offended and stuffed the last two squares of chocolate into her mouth at once. Just to annoy me.

This was not the reply I wanted. What happened to 'Well, if it's upsetting you that much I'll stop'?

"If you're going to get snotty about it then I'll stop," Suzie continued. "Never mind if it's the one pleasure I have in life at the moment."

On she went.

"You didn't even think about that. Did you? No. No. You did not."

And on.

"You didn't even stop to consider what is going on in my life – that maybe I'm at the end of my tether. Maybe something dreadful has happened to me that I don't want to talk about."

And on and on.

"Just because we usually talk about everything doesn't mean that when something absolutely awful happens I will be able to talk, does it? No, it doesn't and maybe eating a chocolate bar out of my handbag is the only thing that makes me feel better. Did you ever think of that? No, of course not. So I'll just sit here like a stuffed image and drink my tea."

Oh God, now I'd really upset her. She was rabbiting on like a demented idiot. She only acted demented when she was really, really upset. If I wasn't careful she would start crying and stammering and drag up another hair story. Most of Suzie's disasters revolved around her hair. She could remember every boring detail, in detail. And she could – and did – tell the same story to me countless times and think she was telling it for the first time.

"This reminds me of the time my mother cut my hair."

67

Oh Jesus, what had I done? What had I brought upon myself? The eating of the shaggin' chocolate paled into insignificance when compared to a hair story. Particularly one with Suzie and her mother as the female leads. Particularly the one about her mother cutting her hair when she was only eight years old.

"I was only eight years old."

Oh, Jesus.

"Eight. I didn't want it cut." Suzie was on her soapbox. I could hear the violins in the background. "I loved my hair. It was my crowning glory. I loved plaits. When I was eight my mother plaited my hair one day. Then took up a pair of scissors and cut my two plaits off. Just cut them off in their prime. I still have them."

I looked pointedly at her head, trying to lighten the mood.

"Not on my head. In a shoebox – Clarks. It's at the bottom of my wardrobe. The plaits are lying side by side in the box. Pink ribbons on the ends – of the plaits." Suzie's eyes started to mist over. Waterworks coming. Jesus, I was so bored with hearing this story. I felt faint.

"I nearly fainted," Suzie said.

"You what?"

"I nearly fainted," she repeated.

I knew the feeling. "When?"

"It was terrible looking at all my hair lying on the floor."

"I thought you said it was in a shoebox?" I said meanly.

"It is now. When I was eight it was lying around on the floor, like dead things, so I started hyperventilating."

That sounded like a good idea. I could hyperventilate and end the story now.

"My poor mother had heard that you must breathe into a bag when confronted with a hyperventilating crisis. She gave me a Magic Cooking Bag. I breathed in. The bag stuck around my face. I was like an oven-ready turkey."

I didn't laugh, not even a grin. I am a good friend. I was pinching my leg.

"I seriously nearly died. Only for the fact that my mother had long, long nails – well, God knows what would have happened."

This incident had had a lasting effect on Suzie. She had an aversion to having anything done to her hair. Lately I'd been helping her to get over it. That's why the perm venture was a great step forward. The fact that it didn't work was two steps backwards. Too much too soon. I was a support group for Suzie. But now was not the time to remind her of that. She wouldn't thank me for it. Now she would only remember my criticism of her. Unfortunately she'd never let me away with it. It's not that she bears a grudge, it's just that she never forgets – her and the elephants both. She would be able to quote the date, place and time of this conversation in ten or fifteen years' time. I have a very short, selective memory. Particularly for things that I don't want to remember. It's a great ability, I think. Suzie thinks it's better to remember every little thing about a person. Particularly things they've said about you. And more particularly things I have said about her.

"Look, you're right, Suzie, about the chocolate. I'm sorry. I shouldn't have said anything. I probably do lots of things to annoy you."

I didn't like the way she was nodding or the fact that she had opened another bar of chocolate.

"I don't know what's going on in your life at the moment, Suzie. Come on, eat up your chocolate. I'll even take a square myself."

"Feck off. This is my chocolate – get your own if you want some. There is nothing wrong with me at the moment, Linda. Everything is all right – I think. Bill seems a little bit worried lately about work. He has to stay late a lot but other than that everything is normal. Normal for me, that is. Come on, let's talk about this holiday. I can't wait!"

"Me neither. Wow, Suz, look at that," I said, pointing at the best example of manhood I had seen in ages. He was in the brochure. "Pity it's not a male order catalogue!"

"There'll be lots of them on the beaches. We can take our pick – wait till you see."

Poor Suzie was an optimist.

I never knew what to make of Suzie's husband Bill. He was pleasant enough but he was never there. Suzie and he had an arrangement. He earned the big bucks and was never around; she earned smaller ones and did all the household bits and pieces. I felt Bill got the best deal. Suzie always felt sorry for him working so hard. He always bought Suzie gifts. Impractical, frivolous things like garden gnomes. Bill used to be a butcher. In fact, that's how they first met. Suzie was buying a lump of rump for her mother and Bill asked her how tender she wanted it and would she go out with him. To a dance. She married him six months later. Darren, their oldest child, was born three months after that. Very premature. I was the only one who was told the full story. Everyone else just guessed. For a while Bill and Suzie were on the pig's back. Or, to be more accurate, the pigs were on Bill's back as he carted them into the butcher's shop and sawed and chopped them to bits. Then all of a sudden he started vomiting every time he saw raw meat. A definite disadvantage in his line of work. The blood and guts got too much for him so he got himself a little office and went into another world of blood and guts: the dog-eat-dog world of self-employment. He had a couple of agencies selling bits and pieces. In the beginning it was tough but Suzie helped him and in no time they had built the business up. It was at the stage now where it could almost run itself, Suzie said. Suzie thought the sun shone out of every orifice Bill had. I didn't like him. I don't know why. Maybe I was jealous of their lovey-dovey relationship. He got on my nerves. He was the sort that when you asked him how he was he'd tell you.

"I have a bit of phlegm on my chest but the doctor gave me a bottle of stuff to shift it. It should loosen and be grand in three weeks."

Oh and I wanted to know that.

"Bit of trouble with the old waterworks. Terrible, terrible stinging. The doctor had a good look and a bit of a root. It'll be clear enough if I keep putting on the cream."

And I'm interested in your plumbing problems. I'd sooner go on one of those Japanese challenge shows, you know the ones where the contestants wear snakes and have creepy crawlies do what they do best all over your body while you're hung upside down from some pole or other, than listen to Bill wax poetic at a dinner party about his ailments. The vasectomy being his favourite. The graphic details of where the needles went and didn't go left every man in the room in a cold sweat, all holding themselves between the legs with tears at the corners of their eyes. All the women sat gaping, staring at Bill's jewellery and imagining a little prick into his little prick. Bill never noticed. Suzie always looked on doe-eyed. Nearly applauding at every little medical story he related.

Dick on the other hand never talked about personal things. When he talked it was in metaphors.

"I call a spade a spade. Never mince my words. I shoot from the hip and call it like it is. No bullshitting with me. I'm straight with everyone," was his proud boast.

I never had the nerve to tell him that I wished he'd call a spade a shovel, leave his gun in its holster and bullshit me sometime. There is a very thin line between telling it as it is and being hurtful. The line was so thin that Dick wasn't able to see it. He was always crossing it. It hurt every time. Dick liked his women in their place. The bonfire with the bras was lost on Dick. He was not a new man. More a prehistoric one. He had left the cave so recently that there were still cuts on his knuckles. I craved someone to talk to and Suzie was it. She had Bill. She talked to Bill and me. I listened. I suspect Bill didn't. As Carl and Chloe got older I talked to them too. They listened. I would never groan about Dick to the kids though. That would be a betrayal. I could, on the other hand, moan to Suzie about Dick. I didn't moan all the time, just every now and again when things got me down. Basically I felt I wouldn't swap the guy for the world. OK , so we didn't always agree but when we did, when I did my best to please him, it was terrific.

Suzie thought Bill and Dick were worlds apart in personality. I knew they were nearer than she thought. All right, so I always had to bow and scrape to Dick because Dick liked it that way. But Suzie bowed and scraped to Bill because she liked it that way. But they were both masters in their own homes. They were both members of the Begrudgers' Club, their glasses always being half-empty. You know the sort. You finally manage to scrimp and save to get a brand-new car and they tell you that you wasted your money. You should never buy brand-new.

"Always get one that's broken in. Had its few teething problems. You'll be stuck with that, mark my words."

Bill was good to Suzie. I sometimes envied that. Dick was good too, sometimes, in his own little way. Bill treated Suzie like a lady. Poor Dick had a medieval view on woman without a hint of the Sir Galahads.

Suzie did all the courses that were advertised at 'Hardbacks': assertiveness, self-esteem and positive mental attitude. She went to them all. You could see the difference. Bill could see the difference. He didn't like what he saw. He preferred the old barefoot and pregnant Suzie. Chained to the kitchen sink. I never did the courses. I was afraid I would discover something about myself.

Like the fact that my self-esteem compartment was bashed and broken with very little chance of recovery.

CHAPTER FOUR

The holiday plans were going well. The most difficult part was keeping it hidden from everyone. This was harder for Suzie than for me. I am, after all, a master of the cloak-and-dagger. In fact, I sometimes think I was born not with the lucky caul around me but with a cloak and dagger. I am very secretive. Hate people prying into my business and give very little away. Suzie is the exception to this rule. I am in deep water, up to my neck, and over, if Suzie ever decides to spill the beans on me. She could make a fortune blackmailing me. Of course it would be her word against mine and I'd just have to deny everything she said. Pretend she had made it all up. Everyone would believe me. They'd never think the master of the cloak-and-dagger would confide in anyone. So I'm safe. For the time being anyway.

We had got as far as picking one brochure and three locations. Crete. Tunisia and Majorca. We were each going to pick the place we most wanted to go to. If we picked the same venue we would go there; if we both picked different places we would go to the third place. It was easy. I really wanted to go to Crete. I was sort of afraid of Tunisia. I don't know how it had made it to the final three. But anyway I vaguely thought it was one of those countries where they cut your arm off for doing things and the way my body parts acted I was sure to come home missing more than a few. If I was going to go to some godforsaken country where they cut your bits and bobs off, I'd like to make sure that they would be able to stitch them back on again. I didn't think they had quite as good a name for their handicraft and deftness at stitching people back together as they had for mutilation. You'd like to think, if they cut your arm off, that someone would make the effort to store it in a bowl of milk to keep it fresh and sew it back on later. But I didn't think they were into that sort of thing in Tunisia. I hoped to God we didn't end up there. I'd have to be on my P's and Q's.

Majorca would be all right from the missing

limb point of view but the danger was we might run into Suzie's mother-in-law and that would be just too much for Suzie. What's the point of escaping from your husband for two weeks only to end up spending it with his mother? From the frying-pan to the fire, bad to worse, the divil you don't know always being better than the divil of a mother-in-law.

So my vote was for Crete. Island of sun, sea and sex. I had heard lots about it from the girls in work. The only drawback they said was that you couldn't flush the toilets. I presumed they were only joking – after all, the Greeks invented the drainage system. They invented it thousands of years ago so surely they had kept improving on the system. If you're going to be known for something, surely you'd make some sort of an effort to have it in proper working order? Being able to flush a loo was fairly basic stuff, I would have thought. No, I'd say they were messing, like telling me that I'd have to pay for the sunbeds. Who'd believe that? But they did say that Crete catered for my two hobbies: sun-worshipping and shopping. Not wanting to boast about my prowess in my chosen hobbies but I have turned both into an art form. According to the girls, the shops on Crete stay open well into the middle of the night. I would be in heaven. Sun all day. Shops all night. Paradise. Shopping would be treated with the same respect as military manoeuvres:

1) Plan well – earmark suitable shops with reduced items or sales

2) Carry the right ammo – plastic card being the best

3) Execute without hesitation – if you do not make a purchase when it is available the moment is lost.

In Crete I could lie back while the sun belted down on my chicken-like flesh. Plunge into the clear blue sea and lie back in the sun reading some terrific romance or other. Bliss. Then by night, Dracula-like, I would suck the lifeblood from the shop-owners. I could spot a bargain from fifty yards. I was so excited. I had never been away on my own before. For years people had brought me back things like lighters and ashtrays from foreign places. Nice enough gifts for a person who smoked but I don't. I eventually figured out that they had forgotten, only remembered me when I enquired how their holiday had gone.

"What are we going to give Linda? We've given everyone else a classy bottle of wine or beautiful pottery. How did we forget Linda?"

"Well, she's such an insignificant person I suppose. Oh look, here's that ashtray we robbed from the hotel. We can give that to Linda."

"Great. She'll be delighted we thought about her."

I had promised myself that I would never again grovel and thank anyone for a gift I knew took no thought at all.

The gifts I would bring back from my holidays would have great thought put into them. Maybe. Then again I might just buy a few dozen ashtrays. It was my first time abroad so they'd all be expecting great things I supposed. I had missed out on holidays with the girls years ago because I married and had children when I was very young. Everyone else had been off living life to the full. Sowing their wild oats. I never got to sow mine. Still have lots of them lying about the place. So I reckon now that the kids are grown up it's my turn. My turn to do something for myself. I had to grab the chance or else it would be gone again for good.

For years I had done everything for Dick and my two children. They never thought of me as a person in my own right. All my life I had been someone's daughter, wife, mother – now I wanted to see what it was like being Linda. OK, so it might be scary but Suzie would be there. Oh, oh. Did that mean I'd just be someone's friend?

I wanted everything to be fine, as Dick would say. I wanted him to say it was fine for me to go away. After all, it was only for two miserable weeks. Well, hopefully not miserable but anyway two weeks wasn't a lot to ask, was it? If Dick wanted to go away on a foreign holiday for two weeks I'd be, well I'd be, well . . . OK, I admitted, I wouldn't be exactly over the moon but that was different. He was a man, and the nature of the beast is to be ruled by what he has hanging between his legs. I, on the other hand, was a woman and ruled by my heart which had no interest in sex – well, not all the time anyway. I was more interested in romance. No one would go to the trouble of romancing a middle-aged wrinkly on a hot beach on some little island, would they? Or would they? God, I might get my bikini-line done before I went. Just in case.

We were so looking forward to it, Suzie and me, that after the temporary interest in Doreen's affair, we spoke about nothing else only our secret holiday. We became obsessed. It was the main, indeed only topic of conversation. Which was stupid. After all, we were two grown women. Acting like teenagers.

"Guess what I bought today." Suzie held a parcel above her head.

"Give me a clue."

"You wear it, or nearly wear it."

"Bathing suit?"

"Close, but smaller. "

"Bikini?"

"Very hot, but smaller."

"I give up. What is it?"

She opened the bag, plucked a skimpy black bit of material out and started swinging it around her head, singing: *"Da Da Da Da Da Da Da Da Da Da Da Da Da Da Da Da Da Da . . ."*

Now this might have been grand if Suzie could sing and we were sitting in the safety of one of our own homes but we weren't. We were in Amelio's. It was full of the stuffed-shirt brigade. All braving the elements and having scones and tea. I was waiting for the big boys in blue to come and bodily lift us off to a private room in the Bridewell or the smaller ones in white coats to take us off on a special little holiday with no sun or sea.

"For God's sake, Suzie, people are staring."

"I don't care. For the first time in years I'm doing something for me – well, for us really. Go on, Linda, guess what I bought us."

"I can't."

She swung the string from her index finger down onto the table. There it sat resting on the plastic bottle of tomato sauce, in between the salt and pepper. I grabbed it and put it on my knee. I couldn't make head nor tail of it. I didn't know what way to put it on.

"Suzie, what am I supposed to do with this thing?" I was pulling it in all directions. It wasn't getting any bigger.

"You wear it. It's a thong."

"I know what it is. It's what you're going to do with it that I want to know."

"I'm going to do nothing with it. You, on the other hand, are going to be wearing it on a sun-soaked beach. I will be wearing a red one. Unless of course you'd prefer the red, I just thought you'd like the black. You sex kitten, you!" She was chuckling loudly and it was infectious.

"You can't possibly be going to wear that thing?"

"Not thing, Linda. Thong."

"Well, Wild Thong, you can't wear it and you certainly can't expect me to wear it. I assume that it's not a suit. There is no top, is there?"

"Oh Linda, you're such a prude. No one wears tops abroad."

"Well, I, for one, do. My boobs have not seen the light of day since they were five years old. I hid them when they were in their prime and now that they're well past their sell-by date I am most certainly not dragging them out. Sure, if I lie down on a sun-lounger they'll just flop to either side and I'll spend the day hauling them back from the cliff edge. There is also the little fact that I most certainly do not want my nipples to burn, fry even."

"Did you never hear of sunblock? We have to go topless. And we have to wear the wild thongs otherwise it'll be a case of 'spot the two Irish birds'. We have to blend in. Well, blend in as best we can considering we'll look like two stuffed chickens for the first couple of days. At least we can dress right. When in Rome and all that."

"Well, Rome isn't even on our list and anyway even if I lost three stone overnight this thong wouldn't fit me. If I put on that thong it will disappear into all the creases and folds around my nether regions."

"Well, I'm wearing mine!"

"Oh, what the hell! It'll cut down on the packing, I suppose." She was infectious.

"So where are we going?" Suzie couldn't sit still on her seat.

"Right, Suzie, get out a piece of paper and write down where in the world – only out of the three we've picked – you'd love to go with all your heart."

I wrote 'Crete' on my page.

We swapped pages.

Suzie had written 'Crete' on hers.

We jumped up and down, hugging each other, holding onto our thongs singing, *"We're all going on a summer holiday!"*

When we heard the old fogies clapping, thinking we were the in-house entertainment, we sat down. Jesus, it was dead exciting.

"Right, now let's make lists of what we're bringing. Condoms and drachmas, condoms and drachmas and more condoms!" We were bordering on hysteria.

Lotty was glaring at us.

"God, I can't believe we're really going ahead with this," said Suzie. "We have to pay the deposit on Tuesday so I think I'll tell Bill over the weekend."

I didn't know when to tell the family, before or after we paid the deposit. I knew my kids wouldn't mind fending for themselves for a couple of weeks. If truth be told they'd be delighted to get rid of me for two whole weeks. Nobody snooping in their rooms looking for evidence of drink, drugs and sex. Nobody following them every time they looked a bit shifty. Nobody getting in their faces about the amount of money they spend. The fact that it was my money never seemed to register with them. No, they'd be quite happy to fend for themselves. Not that they'd do anything other than ring the takeaway and let the washing and ironing mount up to Everest-like proportions. I would come home to a mess. They would have had great intentions of having the place nice for me coming home but then the path to our house is paved with good intentions, mostly my children's.

I decided to tell the kids before I told Dick. That way I would have time to bribe them and they would be on my side, supportive, when I broke the news to him.

"For God's sake, Ma! It's like something out of *Shirley Valentine*."

Things weren't going according to plan. I hadn't anticipated Carl having an opinion really. I was surprised he had even seen *Shirley Valentine*. He had remembered the plot. I hoped he couldn't remember the ending. Where she doesn't come back.

"What are you going away by yourself for? Why don't you go with Dad? Are you getting a divorce? Is this a nice way to let us know? Well, it's not nice at all!" Chloe was distraught.

"At your age, Ma. It's well – it's sick. You watched *Ibiza Uncovered* – that's what Crete is like. Is that what you want?" Carl was trying to reason with me.

I was gone well beyond reason. "No, no, I'm not going to Ibiza, I'm going to Crete. It's very historic and civilised. In fact, it was one of the earliest civilisations."

"It's probably a kip then," Chloe said. In a puss.

"No, it's a beautiful place and me and Suzie just want to chill out and relax in the sun with a few good books."

"Then why don't we all go? I could do with chilling out on some hot spot. Why don't we go together as a family?" Carl was delighted with himself for coming up with this little suggestion, solving all our problems.

This was proving more difficult than I had first thought. How could I explain to them that I wanted to get away from the responsibility and drudgery of being their mother just for two weeks, without hurting them? I was walking on eggshells. In my bare feet.

"Well, maybe we can go somewhere later on in the year but now I'm telling you both that I am going away on holiday with Suzie. When you want to go away with your friends I won't be inviting myself along, you'll be glad to hear. Now are you with me or agin me?"

"Oh, go on then, Ma." Carl gave me a hug.

"Only if you bring us back plenty of duty-free and a nice pressie. And you have to promise you won't do a Shirley on us." Chloe joined the hug.

"Ah thanks, kids!" We all squeezed.

"As for Shirley Valentine I am nothing like her and the F-plan is one diet I won't be trying. Don't worry, you won't be getting away that easily. I'm definitely coming back so keep the place clean." Under my breath and out of earshot I added "But if I meet a Costas he can kiss my stretch marks any day."

Two down, one to go. I was drained with the effort of it all. I couldn't face telling Dick immediately. I would tell him on Monday, then pay the deposit on Tuesday. Monday was a good day to tell Dick. Everything happened for me on Mondays. Diets, leaf-turning-over and savings, always on a Monday. Monday was a terrific day for me.

CHAPTER FIVE

On Monday I woke up with a fright. I hadn't heard
Dick leave for the office. He was usually noisy in
the mornings. In the mornings he did his 'martyr
for the cause' routine.

"Any chance of a pair of socks? Linda, for
Christ's sake, you have to stop the kids robbing my
socks. I never have a matching pair and one white
sock and one scarlet sock will not impress the
clients. Linda, wake up! Get up and help me find a
clean shirt. This place is gone to hell. Nothing is
ironed! I can never find anything."

I always wanted to tell him to fuck off, that I
had ten more minutes of a lie-on and he was
invading every one of them. But Dick was not the
sort that would take kindly to being told to eff off

in the mornings. So I normally kept quiet while he ranted. Banging doors and opening drawers.

"Never a damn hairbrush in this house."

When Dick was awake we all had to be awake. All had to suffer. If ever, after all his barging about the place, I was not fully awake then it would have been a good idea for someone to test my breathing. Make sure I was alive. Hold a mirror to my mouth or my face. With the first, the glass would fog over and I'd know I was alive. With the second, the fright of my face first thing in the morning was sure to make me scream. Proving I wasn't dead.

When Dick had a day off work I crept out of the house. No one knew I was gone. I slid from the bed with the stealth of a python. Showered without singing and only flushed the toilet once. I never, ever, felt the need to look for an old pair of shoes that had been made redundant, with no golden handshake, years earlier. I respected the fact that everyone was asleep and enjoyed having the place to myself. But not Dick. Gather round, gather round, all hail to me getting up for work before everyone else. All hail to the breadwinner! Not that he ever won anything or that we would have been impressed if he had won a loaf of bread but you know what I mean.

This morning it was different. I knew I was the

only one in the bed because I was lying on the flat of my back, star-positioned, and no one had thought to lie on top of me and prod me to life. So I was definitely alone. I prised open my eyes and squinted around the room. Dick was nowhere to be seen. I could hear nothing except the famous sound of silence. I looked at the alarm clock and it said half past six so in fact it was really twenty past. Dick had this annoying habit of never setting the alarm clock to the right time. It was always ten minutes fast. We all knew it was ten minutes fast so I didn't see the point in it really. He said it's great to wake up knowing you have ten minutes to kill before you get out of bed. So why not set the alarm to go off ten minutes earlier? I ask. Fair play to Dick, he had in his time come up with some pretty good ideas for the ten minutes. Most of them involving me.

Maybe he had to be in work early but I didn't remember him saying he was going to be leaving early that day. That was unusual. If he was going before seven he would have started his 'martyr for the cause' soliloquy the night before. He was very quiet the night before. In fact, he seemed very quiet all over the weekend. So much so I wondered had he found one of my holiday brochures. I had been tempted to tell him about the holiday a few times on Sunday but he was so gentle and reflective I thought it a pity to spoil his fun. My peace.

Something was bothering me. I couldn't put my finger on it exactly but I had this awful sense of foreboding. I often get it. It is usually followed by some monumental disaster. A death, chronic illness, plague of locusts, that sort of thing. I'd have been great in biblical times. I knew something was about to explode in my face, hit the fan and all that, so I wished Dick was still in the bed to hold me and tell me everything was going to be all right.

Where was he at this hour of the morning? I got up and went to the toilet. No sign of him having had a shower, no wet, soggy, cream-coated soap lying in the bath. The top was on the shower gel. The towel was hanging where it should have been. No, Dick hadn't had a shower. This was unusual. He was a person of habit, was Dick, and it was his habit to have a shower every morning when he got up, every evening when he came home from work and last thing at night. Yes, Dick is a three showers a day man. He had had twenty-one thousand, six hundred and twenty-seven showers since we got married. Please don't insult me by checking this. So why hadn't he showered today? What was different about today? Maybe he was down having breakfast first. I crept down the stairs, frightened of what I might see but no, no sign of anything. There were no dishes in the dishwasher. No spilt sugar on the worktop. No little puddle of milk drying into a big blob for me to clean. No evidence of Dick having been around that morning at all. The post was still lying in the hall. I picked up the letters, mostly bills, and left them in a pile to look at later.

My stomach was sick. Something was wrong. I pulled back the net curtain and looked out into the front garden. The grass needed to be cut. Daisies and dandelions were vying with each other for space. As with humans, the biggest weed was winning. Our car was still there in the driveway. Where could he possibly be gone without the car? To the office, of course. Sometimes, if he was going to be drinking at a business meeting at lunchtime he took a taxi to and from work. Lately there had been a lot of meetings at lunchtime and teatime. He must be gone into work early. Just because he forgot to tell me about it didn't mean that something was wrong, did it? I mean this awful, awful feeling in my stomach could be anything from the bar of Fruit and Nut, the Creem Egg, the tortilla chips to the ice cream I had eaten last night. All the sugar and spice was probably fermenting. Getting ready to explode in my stomach. I was just being silly. Dick had an early appointment and was sitting at his desk now, I hoped. I went back out to the kitchen and put on the kettle. Now that I was up I'd stay up. Have a nice leisurely breakfast and read a bit of my book. I was at the exciting part where whatshisface was going to ask your woman to marry him. I was hoping she'd refuse.

I took down my cup. We each had a designated cup in our house and there was war if someone used someone else's. It was not a cleanliness fetish. None of my family suffer from that. It was just cups we like we use all the time. We share towels and socks and things like that but not toothbrushes or cups. All mouth things – maybe there was some significance in that. I wondered. I got out the tea bags. Thinking about the cups tempted me to break with tradition and drink from one of the children's mugs. But which one? It would be unfair to use one without using the other. Favouritism is not something I can be accused of. I stuck with my own cup which was just as well because there, tucked inside my cup, an obscure place by anyone's standards, was a little note. How romantic, I thought! Married nearly twenty years and Dick was leaving me little notes, granted hidden in weird places, but none the less the thought was there. God, I was such a bitch sometimes complaining about him. Checking up to see where he was. Of course he was in work. I promised myself I'd make a terrific meal for him tonight, get out my most sexy nightdress, if I could find it. I hadn't seen it in nearly five years. The last time I had worn it was on our fifteenth anniversary.

It had been a great success. Sex, sex and more sex. I wondered if Dick ever thought about that night. The yoghurt and the chocolate sauce. The kids banging on our door in the middle of the night telling us how disgusting we were and what a bad example we were setting. Dick merely shouted at them that it was all legal and if they had a problem to get married and get out. We giggled like school kids and finally fell asleep in each other's arms. I had spent the whole night lying on Dick's left arm. He woke up the next day and thought he was having a heart attack. He had lost all power in his left arm. He was so worried he asked me to drive him to the doctor, him not being able to change gear or go around corners with a dead arm. He was distraught, so distraught that when he showed the doctor the dead arm he also described our night of passion in gory detail. He asked the doctor if it had all been too much for his heart. The doctor just said that if any other bits of him went dead to go straight to hospital. Dick was mortified. He felt the doctor was laughing at him.

"No wonder," said I when he got back into the car. "He thought you were bragging about your bonking session. He probably felt sorry for you only having the one shag in fifteen years. I can't believe that you said you may have had a stroke while making love for Christ's sake. He'll think I'm a nymphomaniac. You could have let on you were wallpapering or painting or something. The detail you went into! I'll never be able to look him straight in the face again!"

"For God's sake, I thought I was going to drop dead. I had no feeling in my left arm. A classic case. I couldn't lift it from my side. I swung it onto the table for him to look at. I thought you had killed me. A slow death like you're always threatening. I thought it had started in my arm and would spread with the speed of money from my wallet over my entire body. I didn't know where it would strike next. I might have tried to walk and fallen down in front of him, crawling on my belly to regain my dignity. It might have affected my head next. I would have to go around with my eyes and mouth open, a permanent surprised expression on my face. That after-dentist feeling forever with me. Jesus, I'd never be able to eat again without dribbling and spitting. So your mortification was the last thing on my mind. I thought if I left anything out, like the two tubs of yoghurt I ate and all the chocolate, that when I'd croak he'd only say 'It's a pity he didn't tell me about the mixture of yoghurt and chocolate – I could have given him an antidote.'"

"It's not an antidote you need, it's the Antichrist. I can't believe you told him about the two pots of yoghurt. It's a wonder you didn't tell him the flavour!" I glared at him. He turned puce. I nearly crashed the car on purpose. "You did, you did! You told him the flavour!"

"Well, he asked. He asked was it natural. I said no the kids had used the last natural for their lunch so we had to make do with Fruits of the Forest."

"I am changing doctor." I was looking for something hard to ram the car into. Like Dick's head. I needed to see Dick suffer, something that would involve him suffering a terror worse than a numb arm for the last few seconds. I didn't want to hurt anyone else. Just inflict sheer turn-a-person-green terror into Dick. A cliff edge would be ideal. At a push a large sturdy tree would do. That's the trouble with living in a neo-Georgian semi in suburbia: you can never find a good cliff when you need one.

"Thanks to you, Dick, I can never be ill again in my life. Never have that little luxury. No, in future

I'll have to suffer in silence. If I ever do get a cold or fall down and spout blood from each and every one of my veins you will have to patch me up yourself. Bandage what you can as tightly as you can. Not if every limb I own is hanging by a silk thread will I be able to go to the doctor with so much as an ingrown toenail. Whenever I go to him, with whatever complaint I have, he'll ask about the yoghurt. Well, I'll tell you this much for nothing, Dick. It's not only your arm that's dead. It's your brain and if I ever get out of this car the rest of you won't be far behind."

He sat in silence holding his feckin' arm all the way home.

It was well into the afternoon before he regained the feeling in the arm. It was a long time before I regained any feelings I had for him.

Tonight I would make sure not to fall asleep on his arm. But he still might need to go to the doctor tomorrow! Once it wasn't me going to confirm my worst nightmare it would be all right. My worst nightmare is, of course, having another baby. At my age it is definitely a non-runner. I was very, very careful after I had Chloe. We tried one of the natural methods and were just getting into the rhythm of it all when we discovered it really wasn't working at all. Carl was born nine months later.

Not that I'd swap him for anything. Well, sometimes. But only for a conservatory and only when he's really pissed me off. But we thought it better not to take any chances after he was born so we decided not to rely on anything natural or supernatural.

We needed a foolproof system. A belt-and-braces job. Not total abstinence. We were both allergic to that. It made us ratty and irritable. Intolerant of other people. We used to hallucinate. Imagine everyone else was engaged in marital and extra-marital shagging all over the place and that we were the only ones left out. We tried it for three days. Well, when I say three days we had a lapse for a quickie on day two but that was short and on the living-room floor so we didn't count it. No, a vow of chastity was not for us. We knew it wouldn't work. The three days off only made us more active for the following seven. What's the point in being married to someone, able to sleep in the same bed, feel the heat from their bodies, be legally and morally allowed to carry on and yet not be able to? Something not quite right about that. So I investigated medical contraception in great detail after Carl was born and it has worked well for eighteen years. In fact, you could call me a bit of an expert on the old preventatives.

I tackled the subject like someone whose life depended on it. I examined all the choices available. You know, the coil and all the other stuff. In fact, speaking of the coil, that was the one that actually frightened me the most. They wanted me to let them put a piece of plastic into my innards. A piece of plastic that looked like it belonged inside an immersion heater or a kettle. I was supposed to think it was a good idea. I ask you. Suppose the doctor put it in wrong, or suppose it moved and fell out and I didn't notice? You know, in the middle of a bit of passion or something it could suddenly decide 'Oi! I've had enough of this kip! I'm not hanging around here any longer, places to go people to see and all that.' It would probably recoil at the lack of room in my womb. 'Feck this for a packet of crisps' it would say and make the great escape without the assistance of Steve McQueen. They assured me that once installed it can't move. Then again they said cloning would never happen and Dolly the lamb bleats for herself. I don't trust anything I'm not in control of.

I could control the cap but have you ever seen it? It looks like a rubber Jewish hat. I don't care what the experts say, anything that is called after and looks like an item of headgear is not conducive to being shoved where the sun don't shine.

Anyway it looks enormous and very unsavoury. All that fiddling and saying, 'Hold on, hold on while I put on my cap'. Here's your hat and what's your hurry?

Then there's the female condom, now there's a thing. Very, very long. If one of those went astray you'd be in right trouble. Lose one of those and you'd be requesting a doctor with a very, very thin, very, very, long arm to retrieve it. That or let it land where it will and leave it there. Nine months later when the child was born it would be gift-wrapped. So that too was out.

The male condom: toffee with the wrapper on. And it's the age-old after-party problem: what to do with the leftovers.

So after all that I opted for the pill. 'No mess, no pack drill.' What does that mean? No pack drill? Do not pack your electric drill? Maybe it's something to do with the army drill? I use it all the time but I haven't a clue what it means. No one I know knows. Even Suzie doesn't know and if she doesn't know I doubt if anyone does. So I pretend to know and go on using it. No pack drill.

Well, anyway, out of the blue a couple of months ago I realised I didn't need to take it any more. The pill, that is, not the drill. Just as well because I kept forgetting to take it anyway. I'd miss two days and have to take three together. Or forget to buy it and have to take Mon., Tues., Wed., Thurs., Fri., all at once. Then all of a sudden a couple of months ago there I was when my body-clock stopped ticking. Suddenly ran out of batteries so to speak and started screaming: 'Men, oh, pause! Pause and do not come near. For I am now the infertile one. The Barren One.' The Barren One of biblical fame. No more begetting or begotting for me, thank you very much.

Dick and I went out for a slap-up meal to celebrate. It was very sudden all the same – not the meal, the menopause. Everything stopped. A total shut-down of the womb department. Like factories all over Ireland it was idle. My shut-down was easier than theirs though. No one was hurt. No one lost a wage packet. In fact it was easy, nothing like I expected. No hot flushes.

Well, there was the one time I did get a wicked hot flush. I had rung my boss to say I was sick. He rang back an hour later to ask me something or other about a client. I wasn't home. My kids told him that I had fecked off into town to buy an outfit for the office party. They thought he had given me the day off for purchasing an ensemble. That's how gormless they are. 'Tell her I want to discuss something with her – like the terms and conditions of her employment,' he shouted at Chloe. When I arrived home with the little black number I had bought she was in tears. It took the good out of the purchase. Well, nearly. I went into a major hot flush then. The full flush, neck and all. The following morning when I went into work I was still flushed. I lied and told my boss that the kids had got it wrong and that I was really down at the doctor, not in town. Had it not been for the hot flush I think he would have believed me.

Later that evening when he saw my stunningly successful ensemble at the party he made some reference to the doctor being damn good at sewing. I had another hot flush and up and told him about the time the same doctor had stitched my finger back on after I caught it in the lawnmower. The doctor had done a terrific job. Nothing fancy mind you but the finger was in perfect working order. I wiggled it about under my boss's nose to prove the point. It's something I share with Richard Madeley – you know, him off *This Morning with Richard and Judy*. He got his finger sewn back on after a lawnmower chopped it off. Good job it wasn't at the same time as me or we might have ended up with each other's finger. I would have a famous digit. He would be stuck with mine. I would be able to point, Richard-fashion, to all and sundry. I would in fact have labelled mine, got a tattoo *'Richard Madeley's Finger'*. Mine would be useless to him, although it was damn good at typing, a talent I'm sure he never bothered with. Imagine it all the same: I could caress places of my body and sell my story to the newspaper: *Richard Madeley Fingered Me*. He couldn't sue. I'd be rich.

Anyway, as that was the only time I suffered from any hot flushes, I didn't believe all that stuff about the change. Embrace it, I thought. Say "Come on, Menopause! Come and get me!" Lie back and enjoy it. Look upon it as the great freedom. The one and only true liberation of women. For once in your life you can have endless sex with no consequence. All the pleasure and none of the pain. Terrif. I was certainly making the most of it.

The kettle clicked off. I popped the teabag into my cup and opened the note Dick had left in it.

My darling, darling, Linda,

Wow! What an opener! Dick was always good at openings. Even at forty-plus he was still good at them.

I am sorry.

This was not good. The words I am sorry are never followed by good news. No one ever says I am sorry but I love you loads or I am sorry but you are the most precious person in my life or I am sorry that I want to spend the other half of my three-score years and ten loving you and being with you. No, the 'I am sorry' beginning was a bummer. I knew it and my stomach knew it.

I cannot tell you this to your face . . .

Another hit to the stomach. Get her when she's down. Anything Dick could not tell me to my face after all these years of telling me to my face how shite I was at everything was something I didn't want to hear. Could do without.

. . . so I am writing this note.

The feckin' coward. I didn't want to read on. I knew pain was on the way. I held onto the worktop to brace myself for it.

I cannot stay in the house with you and the kids any longer. I feel I am being stifled. I have no thoughts of my own or no place to be alone. I have been taken over by all of you and there is none of me left. I have to leave.

What was he saying? What did he think we were? Martians? Jesus, he'd left us. I felt alien, sick. The room went black. The pain started very slowly, deep inside my chest at first. Then it gathered momentum and moved with frightening speed into my head, my eyes. Tears flowed uncontrollably and a large lump took up residence in my throat. It felt as though someone was sitting on my chest. I couldn't breathe. I cried out. Then put my hands over my mouth so Carl and Chloe wouldn't hear. I didn't want them coming down to find me like this. Crumbled and broken.

"Sweet Heart of Jesus, what am I going to do?" I was talking to myself or God or whoever was listening and could help. "Please, Jesus, don't let this happen!" I felt a panic rise inside me. I ran upstairs to the safety of my own bedroom. I was in turmoil. In the last five minutes my life had been shattered by the one person in the world who was meant to love and support me, Dick. I was helpless. I lay on our bed and sobbed. I wanted Dick to hold me, comfort me. Tell me everything would be all right. But he was gone. I was crying uncontrollably. Sobbing deeply. I went into the shower en-suite and ran the water. I didn't want the children coming in. I scrubbed and sobbed and wailed and washed. I rinsed and reasoned. The note rang loud in my head. The betrayal.

I am going away on my own for a couple of weeks to find myself. Somewhere warm. Where I can relax and think.

The selfish bastard. The dirty rotten abscess on a crocodile's snout.

We had seen a documentary on crocodiles one

time. One animal had an abscess on its snout. Dick and I agreed it was the most disgusting thing we had ever seen. The water and muck had an adverse effect on the growth and it was like . . . well, I don't think I'll go into exactly what it was like. Suffice to say that in all the forty shades you have never seen a green like this one. It was the pits. Dick was the pits.

Please be patient with me and I will be in touch with you as soon as I can.

Don't bother your arse.

I love you all.

So I'm going to show it by clearing off on a little holiday for a couple of weeks on my own to find myself. Jesus, I thought, if I ever found myself I'd frighten myself to death. I'm happy with thinking that I am the very nice person I've convinced myself I am. What a shit to discover yourself only to discover you were one truly obnoxious person! I hoped Dick found his obnoxious self.

Love always, Dick.

Love always but from hundreds of miles away. Easy. I could do that love from a distance. No responsibility for anyone, just love. Love is more than a word, Dickhead.

"We're off, Ma! See you later!" Carl shouted.

"Bye, Ma! See you!" Chloe joined in.

"Bye, loves, see you later." I hid my sobs and annoyance.

I sat dripping water and tears on the bed and read the note again and again. I must have been misreading it. I was still asleep, that was it. I would wake up now any minute to find Dick looking at me through his new glasses. OK, so they're not rose-coloured. He would see me warts and all.

I have a couple of warts on my hand and I have tried every known cure but I can't shift them. Most cures involve some sort of pain or other and call me silly but I try to avoid pain of any type. I just don't do pain. Usually. I was overdoing it now.

Maybe it really was a nightmare. Maybe I would wake up like Bobby Ewing and discover I had been in one huge realistic dream. Yeah, that's it, I thought. I'm dreaming. What a relief! I'd die if Dick had really left. I'd really and truly die. I read the note again. It was true. I felt sick. I wished Dick were here so I could talk to him about how I was feeling. Funny that I wanted Dick here so I could ask him what he would do if he were me and his husband had taken off into the sunset without warning. My God, Dick was gone to find himself! God knows where he was gone. Certainly not to the Lost Property office. "Have you seen me anywhere? Did anyone hand me in?" No, wherever he was gone it was far away. I felt sick, headed for the bathroom again and retched into the toilet bowl, still holding the note. I sat on the toilet, and read it again. I felt weak. So I read the note again. I was a glutton for punishment, a real masochist. I kept reading. The words were the same every time. I was in deep, deep shit.

CHAPTER SIX

I needed someone. Anyone. I managed to dial Suzie's number.

I was crying desperately. Sobbing my guts out. Deep loud sobs, to be more specific.

"Halloo," Bill answered the phone. I was doing my 'I am a blabbering idiot' routine. Trying to ask for Suzie. Sniffing and snorting into Bill's ear.

"Oh, uh, uh, Bill, it's Linda. Uh, is Suzie there, Bill? Uh!" Big loud sniff.

"Hold on a sec, Linda. I'll get her for you now." He put his hand over the mouthpiece but I could still hear his muffled voice. "Suzie, it's Linda for you. She sounds awful. I think she's crying again. Wonder what the hell's wrong with her now?"

"Oh, shut up, Bill, and give me the phone!" I heard Suzie shout at him.

"Linda? What's up? Are you all right?"

"Oh, Suzie!" Major sob. "I'm in deep shit again."

"Linda, what's wrong? What the hell's happened? Linda, are you still there? Speak to me, Linda! What's wrong? Is someone hurt, Linda?"

"Yes, Suz, I'm very, very hurt." I started sobbing again. From there on she couldn't understand what I was saying. I tried my best to speak but I couldn't. I was one big loud sob. The floodgates opened and I poured forth deep down deep into the valley of tears.

"Hang on, Linda. I'm on my way over. Stay exactly where you are. I'll be right there."

I put the phone down. I wasn't going anywhere. I was a mess. I stared at the mess in the hall. The mountain of multi-coloured coats on the pole at the end of the stairs. The unlucky one on the bottom getting ruined. It was all creased. Being moulded for a hunchback. I rooted to see whose coat it was. Mine. Feck it.

The plain, deep-blue carpet now had a pattern. The footwear pattern. Runners, sandals, boots, platform and plain. All scattered, all over. When I was a child I had two pairs of shoes. One pair more than most of my peers. A sensible brown pair for the weekdays and a pair for Sundays and special occasions, shiny black patent, with bows, brilliant.

My young adults, unemployed students, had more than one pair of foot apparel for every day of the week, all colours, all competing with each other for the glamour factor. A variety for special occasions. Not a sensible shoe among them. We were suffering from a plethora of shoes and a dearth of feet. All the poor students' shoes were in the hall. All lined up and standing to attention. The hall was small.

In fact, the whole house was small. Remember that song 'Little boxes made of ticky-tacky and they all look just the same'? They wrote that song about my house. Matchbox. The neo-Georgian frontage fooled us. We thought we were getting a work of art. Art Magee, the builder, assured us of this. I believed him. I was not alone. All two hundred and fifty of us in the estate believed him. But he forgot to mention the ticky-tacky. Ticky-tacky is not a great material for building houses. My ticky was very tacky and my house, in sympathy with my life, was falling apart. I had replaced bits of it over the years. It was easier to replace the bits of the house than bits of my life. It had taken me years to get to the stage I was at now, rock bottom. I had fixed the house bit by slow bit. Windows, doors, skirtings, wardrobes, walls. The first well worn out before I had saved enough to do the last. I would have loved to revamp the whole house at the one time. Once and for all be done with it. Gut it. Then rebuild. I would have loved to do the same with my life. The hall was depressing. I was depressed. I decided to be depressed in a nice room.

The kitchen was a nice room. I kept it clean, white and bright. It was rarely used by the rest of the family. Unless to remove food, food to be consumed anywhere else but in the room that was designed for the ritual of baking and eating. No one used the kitchen except me. I loved it. The rest of the family hated it. Machines they didn't understand were housed in the kitchen: iron, washing-machine, dishwasher, cooker, hoover. Objects of servility. Frightening. I felt safe with these symbols of my drudgery. They confirmed the rut I was in. Now I was in more than a rut. More your deep crevasse. Grand Canyon style.

Suzie's finger was planted on the bell. I let her in. She put her arms around me and hugged me. I took up the sobbing again. She didn't know why I was crying but when I eventually let go of her I could see she was crying too. *Mi casa es su casa.*

"Oh God, Suzie. What am I going to do? You have to help me."

"I will, I promise." She was pulling at the end of her mohair cardigan. Poor Mo must have sacrificed a lot of hair for this particular cardigan. It was down to Suzie's thighs. This particular Mo must have had blue hair. Suzie kept plucking bits of Mo's blue hair from her cardigan.

"Has something happened to the children?" she asked, hoping it hadn't.

I am passionate about my children. Love the bones of them. Oh, I complain about them, see their faults, each and every one of the vast assortment of them. But that is my right. Only mine. I know my geese are swans. I carried them for nine months. Vomiting and waddling. I spent hours giving birth. Screaming and crying. Then it was their turn. Endless vomiting and waddling. Screaming and crying. Only I have earned the right to criticise my children.

"No. It's not the children." I could see Suzie was relieved. She stopped plucking her cardigan.

"Then what is it? What's happened?"

"Dick's gone, Suzie."

"Dick? Gone? Gone where?"

"Left. He's up and left me, Suzie."

"No, Linda, he can't have!"

"Well, he just did."

"You had a row?"

"No, he was gone when I got up. He left a note."

117

"Jesus! Where are the children?"

"At college. I didn't want to upset them. I got them out before I rang you. Bought myself some time. It took all I could muster not to break down in front of them. Jesus, Suzie, what am I going to do?" I was sobbing again. Detached. Looking on at myself, crying. I didn't know what was happening to me.

"I'll put on the kettle and we'll have a nice cup of tea first. Then you can tell me all about it." Suzie linked me into the kitchen. Tea was the cure-all for everything, according to Suzie. I swear to God, if you told her you were having a brain haemorrhage and had lost all your swallowing power she'd still insist on force-feeding you with tea. I could see her pale pink satin nightdress underneath her mohair cardigan. The flowing red and blue cheesecloth skirt nearly hid the torn lacy hemline. If I had been normal I would have laughed at her little tartan slippers. I didn't even giggle. I would never be normal again.

"Sit down, Linda." She pulled out a chair and took the folded newspaper off it. I noticed words were left on the white painted seat. Backwards words. I wondered, if I sat down, when I stood up again would the words be right way around on the arse of my cream satin dressing-gown? I shrugged and sat. Who cared?

The kettle was boiling over. I glanced up at Suzie. Her head was bent. Dick's note was in her hand. She turned to face me, tears in her eyes. "I'm sorry. It was there and I was here and I looked. It was just lying open. Maybe you didn't want me to see it . . . I'm sorry, Linda."

"I would have shown it to you anyway," I lied. This was my private grief even though I had called Suzie. I wanted her here but I wanted her to go home. Leave me alone but be with me. I didn't know what I wanted. I only knew it was too soon, the wound was too raw, for Suzie to go poking around in it. I was the only one who could feel the way I did. No one else could even guess at the isolation, betrayal and terror. The aloneness. All on my own.

"Tea or something stronger?" Suzie asked, trying to keep herself busy.

"Tea. I bought you a Peppermint Cream yesterday. It's in the fridge. I don't want anything."

It was unreal. Like you feel when you imagine what you'd do if you won the Lotto or something. You know, like when you make up the lists of all the things you'd do making sure to include a lump sum to charity. Hoping that if God was listening he, in his infinite wisdom, would most definitely let you win as soon as he discovered all the good you'd do with it. I was in an unreal place. If I spoke about it, it would be real. I'd never talk about it. Then I would never have to enter Deserted Wifeland.

"Linda, think. Where would he have gone? We'll find him. We'll make a few calls – he must be staying with someone. Think . . . you must know where he might have gone. We can get him to come back."

I knew Suzie was only trying to help. I lit on her. I needed someone to shout at. She was there. Dick wasn't. "Jesus, Suzie, you're so naïve! He says in black and white or blue and white that he doesn't want me. The bastard doesn't want me any more. He took the best years of my life and now he's putting me aside like a used-up lump and he's disappeared off to the arsehole of somewhere to find himself. Do you really expect me to crawl, grovel to him to come back?"

The phone rang. If a Martian had stood before us, requesting us to go to his planet, Suzie and I couldn't have been more surprised. We stared at the phone. Stop, stop ringing, I urged it. I didn't want contact with humans, happy humans. Suzie was just about all I could handle and even she was pushing it.

"It might be Dick," Suzie whispered, hoping not to be heard by the ringing phone.

I now hated Suzie. Suzie was in control. She handed me the phone.

"Linda?"

It was Dick. Dick was in control. Everyone was in bloody control except me. I was losing my head and all about me were keeping theirs. Good ol' Dessi bleedin' Derata. What did he know? He didn't know I was going to commit murder down the lines of a telephone. No one knew that. Murder by mental telepathy. Die, Dick, die, my brain kept saying. Then I heard his voice again.

"Linda, I had to talk to you. Did you get my note?"

Come home, come home, my heart said. I love you. I need you. Was this what it was like to have a breaking heart? I never knew it was such a physical pain. So sore. Until now.

"Yes, I got it," my mouth said.

"Linda, I'm sorry. I just need to be away from everyone, be on my own for a little while. Please understand. It's not you. I just need time to find myself. To be me. Not somebody's son, husband or father. Do you understand? I know it's hard but please try. Say you understand? I'm smothering. I feel I'm going to explode."

"No. I don't understand. I love you as you are. You don't need to find yourself. Come home and

I'll help you find you! We could find you together! We might even find me while we're at it. Dick, where are you? Let me come to meet you!" I was still crying. It had no effect on Dick.

"I'm in Heraklion, at the airport in Crete."

"Crete? Crete?" I couldn't be hearing right.

"I just need this time alone. I had to get far away. It seems nice enough here, quiet. It was the only place I could get. I'm so confused. I can't keep up with you and the children any more. I need to gather my thoughts and find myself. I promise I still love you and I'll ring you again. Soon."

I couldn't believe it. Dick in Crete. My thunder had been stolen again. I was sick of everyone stealing my thunder. I was going to protect it from now on. No one was going to steal anything from me again, least of all my thunder. I was meant to be telling him I was going to Crete with Suzie and here he was telling me he was actually in the feckin' country. The big bastard was in Crete. And how come he had to look for himself in faraway Crete? Surely he must have lost himself somewhere in Ireland. Most likely in Dublin.

Well, shag him to hell anyway! Who did he think he was? Something about divine justice kept popping into my head. I kept pushing it away. This was no time to be on Dick's side.

"Do you hear me, Linda? I love you."

"Do you? So do I. Love you, I mean."

He hung up. So I did.

"How is he?" Suzie asked, quietly. She didn't know what to say or where to put herself.

"How is he? How is he? He's bloody fantastic, off on our holiday! Swanning around *Crete*! Flushing toilets and admiring the plumbing, no doubt. How is he? I'll tell you how he is. He's fan-bloody-tastic that's how he is! The bastard! If he was here I'd kill him! The turncoat! The dirty rotten slimy snake in the grass has beaten us to it! The bastard is gone on our holiday. The nerve of him not to tell me! Who the hell does he think he is taking off into the sunset without a by-your-leave? Where's the money coming from? That's what I'd like to know. Who's he with? That's one thing I wouldn't like to know. Christ, Suzie, suppose he's gone off with a woman?"

"Don't be so foolish, Linda. Didn't he say he's gone off to find himself? How could he possibly find himself with someone hanging out of him, distracting him."

"How will I tell the kids their father, the bastard, has gone off to find himself?" I started to cry again. Gentle tears rolled down my face. "How can he do this to us? I never felt the need to find myself and I lost all of me years back. Lost it along with my virginity. I can't remember what me is meant to be like. What makes Dick think it's his God-given right to have a bit of himself for himself? That would be luxury in this house. Such selfishness. The man had flipped. Off his rocker. Two slices short of a picnic. Not the full shilling or even the 100%. Bats in the belfry. Screw loose. Let's face it, he's just plain mad."

If truth be told, I had noticed that Dick had been very quiet lately. I had been glad of the bit of peace. At least I didn't have to listen to him complaining. Dick was an expert at complaining. Usually about me. I had noticed there was something on his mind but I didn't force the issue. I assumed he would share it with me eventually. I never dreamed he would be sharing it with me on a telephone from Crete. The git.

How would I tell the kids? They would be devastated. How could I tell them their father had buggered off without hanging around long enough to say goodbye to them? He hadn't been a very active father but he had been there all the same. And a Dad in the hand is better than one in the bush. Especially not a bush in Crete. Chloe and Carl loved him. They didn't remember that he retched every time he saw a dirty nappy, ran for the toilet every time one of them brought back up the milk I had so diligently squeezed from my oversized breasts. Bodily functions and Dick didn't go well together. But that was the nature of the beast. It didn't mean that he loved them any the less. He got up to them once or twice in the middle of the night and handed them to me to be fed and changed. But he missed out on the nocturnal communion that went on in the depths of the night. The tiny creature sucking, nose and mouth pressed against flesh. Tiny hands curled around my fingers. But what you never have you never mourn. I mourned when my breasts became redundant. Hard and sore, aching to be needed.

As the children got older Dick found it harder and harder to cope. I loved my children through all the stages of life. From babyhood to adolescence. Now that they were both young adults I loved the rapport I had with them. The freedom their age brought me. The worries were still there, they were just different worries. Drink, drugs and rock 'n' roll. Watching the clock, waiting for the key in the door. The sheer bliss when everyone was safe in their beds asleep. It would be a long time before I had that peaceful feeling again.

Dick couldn't cope with the fact that his children were now young adults. He hated Chloe's hemlines, her experiments with make-up and hair colour. Carl's goatee, shaved head and ponytail – all at the one time. He didn't understand the importance of the plum rinse versus the blonde streaks debate. He wanted Chloe to ask him about making kites and dolls' houses, not how to put a plug on the hairdryer. He wanted to teach Carl football and show him how to knot a tie. But he had left it too late. They were gone past all that. He had missed it. I had answered all their questions a long time ago. Dick never noticed.

He was aghast when Carl stole his aftershave and everyone stole his boxer shorts. He hated all the pimply teenagers hanging around the house. I loved the buzz they brought with them. He only noticed the Bud. Even though Carl and Chloe had very kindly given Dick thirteen years to prepare for their assault into teenagehood, it still took him by surprise.

He nearly died when Carl brought a girl home for the first time. He sat staring at her. I expected her parents to call around later and accuse him of being a lecher. I had to distract him. Get him to come out to the kitchen to help me make coffee. He was purple in the face.

"What does she want with our Carl? He's only a young fellow. She'd buy and sell him. Did you see the outfit on her? Sure no full-blooded male would be able to keep his hands off her. She's tempting him, Linda. There'll be trouble!"

"Just because you can't stop leering at women doesn't mean your son is the same. Carl is a young man now and it is only natural that he's going to be meeting girls. I think she's a lovely girl, a bit like Chloe in fact. She's probably the first of many."

I carried in a tray with some tea and cakes. I left Dick to pour. I had forgotten the milk. Carl followed me out to the kitchen.

"What's up with Dad?" he screamed in a whisper into my face. "He's sitting like a stuffed image staring at Veronica. It's creepy, Ma. Get him to stop! What do you think of her? She's lovely, isn't she?"

"She's gorgeous." In this situation my true opinion was not really being requested. All he wanted was someone to agree with him. I obliged. "Don't mind your dad," I added, trying to be diplomatic. "He still hasn't adjusted to the fact that your voice broke and that happened years ago. Give him a chance to take in the fact that you're interested in the opposite sex."

Dick came in just as Carl left the kitchen. He had heard the tail end of the conversation.

"Sex? Jesus, Linda, what did you say about sex?

Surely he knows all about that sort of thing? Don't they do biology in school nowadays? I should have spoken to him about it a long time ago but whenever I broached the subject he laughed and told me he knew more than I did. I hope it's not too late. I'll talk to him tonight. You know about saving himself for that special day, waiting till he's married and all that. Maybe you should have the same chat with Chloe. God, Linda, you don't think Chloe's messing around with boys, do you? If she is, in that skirt she wears up around her bum, we're finished!"

"Dick, what makes you think Carl and Chloe are going to wait until they're married to have sex? What would make you think that they would be any different to us? Of course they'll have sex. I just don't want to know about it when they do. Ignorance, as far as my children's sex lives go, is bliss. I am acting on the need-to-know basis. Whether my children are having sex or not is something I do not need to know. Now that you've asked, I think Chloe is going out with that Dillon boy she keeps talking about."

"Dillon? What sort of a name is that? He's one of the second-name-or-a-first-name brigade, I suppose? Jesus, is there no end to it? Linda, you're taking this very calmly indeed. Our family is falling apart and you're just standing there peeling potatoes!"

"Our family is not falling apart. Our children are growing up. That means we'll have more time for each other. The reason I'm peeling potatoes is that even if the family were falling apart we'd have to eat. Calm down, Dick. You're blowing this up out of all proportion."

"Calm down! I'm informed that my two children are having sex all over the place and I'm to calm down. We are a dysfunctional family, Linda. I hope you realise that. We are the sort of family you read about in magazines. See on the *Oprah Winfrey Show*. Everybody sleeping everywhere and the mother peeling potatoes. Well, I can't handle it, Linda!"

"Since when have you been watching *Oprah*? I never have time to watch her. Anyway, I'm opting for the ostrich method of survival. Head down as far into the sand as I can get it. I can do nothing about the situation so I am choosing to ignore it. Hoping it will go away. They both know everything about precautions. That's as much as I can do. Running around like a headless chicken won't help matters."

I was sorry I said this. I caught a glimpse of the chicken I was preparing for dinner. Any minute now I was going to have to shove my hand up into the cavity and clean it. The mind boggled. I looked at the big lump of white plump flesh and then looked back at the chicken.

"Well, I think that's irresponsible." Dick started pacing. When Dick paced it was time to worry. He usually exploded after pacing.

"We might be but they're not. Stop pacing up and down, will you? You're giving me a headache."

"What?"

"Stop pacing. I think Carl and Chloe are being responsible."

"What do you mean?"

"Well, promise you won't lose it altogether? I really had promised myself I wouldn't tell you this but as you're so agitated . . . I'm only telling you this to put your mind at ease. I found condoms in both their bedrooms when I cleaned them last week."

"I can't believe it!"

"I know. The floors are carpeted in their clothes, clean and dirty. Dishes caked with leftovers all over the place. The wardrobes are vomiting more clothes out onto the floor and I happen upon their supplies of condoms. I could hardly believe it myself."

"I don't mean I can't believe that you were able to find them! I mean I can't believe they were there in the first place!"

"Sure, I'm just thanking God I didn't find used ones."

"Linda you're not normal. This is not a normal conversation for us to be having about our two children."

"But that's the problem, Dick." I tried to be gentle. "You keep thinking of them as children but they are adults – they can vote, drink and yes even have sex without your permission. They cannot however, use a washing machine or dishwasher with or without your assistance and that is where we have made our mistake. That is where we are not normal."

"How can you talk about dishes at a time like this? You're telling me there are no virgins left in this house. We are virginless and you want clean dishes."

"Yes, yes, I want clean dishes. I'm sick of being the only one who does anything around here. It's time we all grew up, Dick, even you. Time to face facts: your children are adults. The only reason they still live here with us is because it's free."

"Well, this is a real eye-opener for me!"

"Well, as your eyes have been opened to one fact, here's another. I'm retiring. I'm hanging up my apron and giving up the thankless, endless job of running this house. You can all feck off and do things for yourselves from now on."

"Jesus, what brought this on?"

"Nothing. Only I can't believe that you thought time had stood still. For years I have been a skivvy and now I'm all skivvied out. I don't care who has sex, I don't care where they have sex and I don't care how they have sex once they clean up after themselves. Now get out of my way till I peel a few carrots and make a white sauce."

Of course, nothing changed. I still did everything. I still felt no one could do it better than me. Not that anyone tried to compete with me. I had sort of gotten used to that over the years. Even the moaning about it was a habit I wouldn't have been able to drop. I was the only volunteer, so like the willing horse I carried the load and now Dick was getting the holiday, my holiday.

"I can't go to Crete with you, Suzie," I said.

"Why not?"

"Because Dickhead got there first. The bastard. I wish he was here."

"Of course we can still go! He'll be back in two weeks and the two of you will sort everything out then. Look, it's a month before we go so I'll pay the deposit tomorrow as arranged and we will just make our minds up to go. You're going to need a holiday after all this. Anyway, now you can go with

132

a clear conscience, sauce for the gander being sauce for the goose and all that." Suzie was determined we were going on the holiday I knew for certain we would never take.

"I suppose it'll be all right. Oh, Suzie, suppose he doesn't come back? Suppose he rings in and says he's staying there forever? What will I do then?"

"Well, let's not cross that or any other bridge until we come to it. Look at the positive side, Linda. He rang and told you he loves you. He'll be back soon and everything will be back to normal, you'll see."

She was trying her best. Keeping my chin up and all that. It was a thankless job. I forgot to say thanks. She went home to make Bill's dinner. I suspected she was making mine. I wished I was cooking Dick's.

The kids arrived home. I was lying on the couch. Pretending to read a book.

"Where's Dad? What's for dinner?" Carl shouted from the fridge.

"In Crete and Chinese." I shouted from the front room. I thought if I appeared calm they would think everything was all right, that I was happy their dad was off finding himself.

"Hi, Mam, when will Dad be home? I need

133

money for tonight. I'm going straight out after dinner." Chloe was her usual social self.

"He'll be home in two weeks. What time will you be home at?"

"What?" Chloe said.

"What?" Carl said.

"Chinese for dinner and what time will you be home at?" I looked from one to the other. Like peas in a pod. Tall, leggy and blond. Both had hazel eyes. Like mine. Dick's were blue. Carl was broad. Everything he had was large. Well, so he assured me anyway. He was tall, that I could see for myself. Six foot in his stocking feet. He had a smiley face and a rakish charm. He lived in 501s and wore lovely jumpers. Chunky polo necks. I bought all his clothes. Carl was a nice young feller. Chloe was just a little bit smaller than Carl, not much though. But she was very slight. Svelte even. She could have been a model but had no interest. Her hair could be any colour at any time but she was born blonde. She thought it wasn't blonde enough. Her skin was naturally tanned and though I say it myself she was one terrific-looking young woman. She didn't think so. She had the cutest dimples, she didn't like them. Chloe's favourite gear was short skirts, sloppy denim dungarees and little tops. I bought all her clothes. Chloe was a lovely young one. Well, if their mother didn't think so what hope had they got, children being like farts and you being just about able to stand your own? I thought mine were great, my kids that is. Soppy, eh?

"What did you say about Dad?" Chloe shouted.

"Where did you say Dad was?" Carl shouted at the same time.

"I said he'd be home in a fortnight and Crete. Could you speak one at a time?" I tried to keep it as nonchalant as possible.

"Me first!" Chloe was always faster than her brother who was standing open-mouthed holding a lump of ham in his hand. "Ma, I have two questions. One, where is my father? And two, when will he be home?" Chloe eyeballed me.

I took a deep breath and held in the tears. "Your father is in Crete and will be home in a fortnight."

"Right. I thought that was what you said. What business has he in Crete and why weren't we told about it? I am assuming, since Carl is standing with that stupid expression on his face and is not eating the lump of meat in his hand, that this is the first he has heard of this."

"Your father left me a note to say he was going away to find himself. Apparently the bit he's looking for is lying on a beach in Crete and it will take him two whole weeks to locate it." I kept it matter of fact. Trying to fool them into thinking everything was all right. It didn't work.

"You're joking?" Carl finally spoke.

"No, I'm definitely not joking." I couldn't keep up the pretence. "I never joke about the bottom falling out of my life. It is very serious for me when my husband of nearly twenty years takes off in the dead of night and just leaves a note. Had it been a suicide note I could have understood it better but there you are. That's life. You work your arse off trying to do everything to please a person and then he turns around and kicks you in the selfsame arse. So what do you want from the Chinese?"

"How can you think about food at a time like this?" Chloe's lip was starting to quiver.

"Our family is falling apart and you're talking about food?" Carl added. He was his father's son after all.

"We have to eat. Even if the family is in crisis we have to eat. It would be terrible for our three carcasses to be found by your father in a fortnight's time. He would feel guilty for buggering off and leaving us to die of starvation and worry."

I hadn't thought of that before. The smell would probably hit him first. Then he could find us holding hands, lying in pools of tears, his horrible little note clasped tightly to my heart. Of course, that would never happen. There was the Suzie factor to consider. Suzie would find us first. Force-feed us with some Hungarian omelette or other country's goulash.

"Listen, if we don't eat, Suzie will only cook for us. So what do you want?"

Suzie was not known for her culinary delights.

"Kung Po Special."

"Chicken Curry."

"Anyway, you can bet your father isn't starving himself to death – he's probably lurrying into an innocent little baby squid as we speak. Not happy with destroying our marriage and your family, he is no doubt causing some squid family the same anguish. Mr and Mrs Squid will be in the throes of depression. That squid family will be in therapy for years to come, seeing Psychologist Squid for yonks after their little babies have been eaten by your father. How can he be so cruel?" The thoughts of the little squid and my own two little squid made me want to cry.

Chloe came and sat beside me and held my hand. Carl hovered and made the ultimate sacrifice: he put the ham back into the fridge in case it was needed for tomorrow's dinner. Nobody spoke. Carl came back into the room and stood with us. A trio. We looked poised to burst into song. We burst into tears. Now Dick was missing we would never make a barbershop quartet. We held onto each other.

"I think this room could do with decoration." I try to distract my mind in times of extreme upset when the ostrich system fails me. The wallpaper was only three years old but it was dull. I loved this room. It was my second favourite, after my oasis, the kitchen. Earthy colours, rusts and dark greens. It had taken me ages to put up the plaster coving. Standing like the crucifixion waiting for it to dry. Glossing and painting. Stripping and papering. Sewing and mending. I couldn't re-do this room. I would have to look elsewhere for a distraction. I turned to the old reliable. Carl and Chloe.

"Ma, how do you know he's not coming back for a fortnight? Are you sure?" Carl asked.

"I'm positive. He told me on the phone. The slimeball left me a note and then rang me."

"Come on, Ma. Where's the note? Let me read it. I'm sure you made a mistake and Dad'll walk in that door any minute." Chloe was a real 'let me put my hand in the wound' person.

"If that bastard walks in that door it'll be a miracle! He's not to be let in. Do you hear me? Neither one of you is to let him in. Gone to find himself? Not if I find him first!"

The two children were upset enough and now I

was making it worse. They kept going behind my back gesturing to each other, muttering and shaking their heads. She's finally flipped, they signed to each other. Screwing their index fingers deep into their temples. Shrugging their shoulders. Contorting in any way possible that would indicate their complete agreement that their mother had finally lost all her marbles. They were in total agreement about something for the first time in years. It was scary. They were being polite to each other and whispering and going in and out of the kitchen together. Making tea and emptying the dishwasher without being asked.

I was flabbergasted. I sat, open-mouthed, watching them in silence. This only reinforced their marbles theory. My two children had been possessed. That virtue called unselfishness had finally managed to see an opening and had possessed them both. And at the same time. This was indeed extraordinary. How long would it last and was it worth sacrificing a husband for?

Dick rang again and I encouraged the children to speak to him.

"Tell him the doctor came and sedated me. Tell him you're both getting along very well without any parental guidance. Mention that all your friends, particularly the lager louts, are rallying around you. Calling with buckets of sympathy and plastic bags full of cans of beer. Say you're very worried about me. Tell him I haven't spoken since ten o'clock and that I might never speak again. Mention that I haven't peeled one carrot or potato since he left. Tell him that you both have sex on a regular basis. Make sure to emphasise that it is not with each other. But let him know you're not virgins. That'll scare the bejesus out of him."

"But I am," Chloe whispered.

"Me too," Carl joined in.

"Oh no, you're not. I found the condoms a few months back in both your rooms. You can't lie to me. Not now in my hour of despair, please!"

"What condoms?" In unison.

"The ones in your bedrooms. Come on, I found them. Please don't make an eejit out of me. Being made an eejit of once a day is bad enough. Couldn't you two wait until next week? I think I have a free slot then. How about Thursday? Yes, I don't think anybody else has booked in for Thursday. Say seven o'clock? How does that time grab you for the 'Let's make an eejit out of Mammy hour'? Is it a date?"

"Ma, we would never make an eejit of you. You manage that very well yourself. But you shouldn't be rooting around in our bedrooms. I don't have any condoms except the ones that were given to us in college. Handouts. I never used mine." Chloe sounded disappointed like she never got the opportunity.

"Me neither," Carl added, somewhat forlorn.

"Please don't tell me in this day and age that you are having sex with no condoms? Where have you been? Do you not practise safe sex?" Mother of God, do I have to go into the gory details of everything? Can no stone be left alone, unturned, imbedded in the grass, turning it bright green? Do they all have to be unturned and explained in minutia?

"I don't practise any sex." Chloe was embarrassed.

God, had she perfected it to such a standard that the practising time was long over?

"I don't either," Carl said. This was nothing new. Carl had never practised anything. I had wasted years and a small fortune on piano lessons. Finally after about three years he got the hang of 'Old McDonald'. Played in time to the Death March. We all had to sing as he played. The poor unfortunate animals on McDonald's farm all had speech impediments. One moo or baa took all of five minutes.

"Look, Ma, I don't know what idea you have but neither of us have had sex," Chloe said. It was like owing up to a great sin. A real mortaller.

"Oh God! I told your father you had probably had sex."

"Jesus, poor Dad!" they both had the gall to chorus. The worms were turning.

"Poor Dad? How poor can Dad be if he's lying on his back on a beach in Crete? What about poor Ma? What about me then?" I was thumping my chest. My voice was rising along with my blood pressure.

They sat on either side of me on the couch, their arms around my shoulders.

"The two virgins will always be here for you, Ma." Chloe was trying for a smile.

Another time I would have obliged. "Thanks," I tried.

"I don't want to be labelled a virgin." Carl was horrified. "And not for always anyway. I don't like it. I really don't think it's anybody's business. I wouldn't have told you only I thought it might cheer you up. Anyway, I am hoping to rectify the virgin situation any day now." He had a bit of a glint in his eye. I didn't like it.

So there it was. My husband had run off to find himself and I was to be cheered up by the fact that my children were virgins. The virgins did not cheer me up. They just got me to wondering if they were normal. What was wrong with them? Was Carl

142

running around desperately trying to get rid of his virginity, foisting it off on anyone who was willing to take it? Was Chloe only being nice to me? Had she managed to rid herself of it already? Was she trying to make sure it was really gone at every opportunity? I was getting so confused. I wished Dick was here.

CHAPTER SEVEN

I tried to keep Dick's disappearance act under my hat. A secret. The name Dick was erased from all conversation I had with friends and neighbours. Except Suzie, of course. I blabbered insistently about the weather, politics and the price of a pound of butter. Anything but Dick. When I was confronted directly with questions about his whereabouts I lied. Blatantly. Dick was on a business trip, I'd smile. Well, he was on a trip and it was his business. I moaned about how hard he was working and how sorry I felt for him. I found myself with verbal diarrhoea every time anyone rang me. I became an expert on politics and the news. If I kept talking and didn't let them get a word in edgeways then they couldn't ask about Dick.

A lot of people asked about Dick. He was a popular guy, was Dick. I couldn't get over how nosy some people were. Asking all sorts of questions like how he was. When was he coming home? Did he enjoy a drink? Did I think he was having a little breakdown or a big affair? It never occurred to me that they might just be concerned. I thought concerned people should keep themselves to themselves. The phone never stopped ringing. People came bearing gifts. Not jumpers or make-up or anything useful or exciting, more your cakes-and-sandwiches type of thing. Carl was pleased. He attended to the food. Chloe attended to the door. Making my excuses. Spreading the word that I was having a little lie-down. I lay by the phone having a little breakdown. I was tempted not to answer it every time it rang. But it might be Dick.

Word of my disaster spread quicker than wildfire. And we all know how quickly that spreads, don't we? I had really shook the place up all right. But I couldn't figure out how everyone seemed to know. Knew every gory little detail. Then I found out. The two big mouths I had for children were off crying into the arms of anyone and everyone who'd listen to their sob story about our dysfunctional family. They didn't like to talk about it at home. Apparently it would upset me. Upset me. Upset me! What more could upset me? As if I wasn't already the winner of the Upset Trophy. I couldn't get any more upset. I had perfected upset. Was the personification of it. If both my children had come to me in sackcloth and ashes with a suitcase of problems each I couldn't have been any more upset. I was as upset as it is humanly possible to get. I knew this because my nervous rash had taken up full citizenship on my chest and was spreading with the speed of Dick to Crete all over my body. Plenty of scope for it. This was the first time that my rash had stayed this long. Usually it was a social visitor. Arriving like a friend in times of great stress and then, when the dust settles, paling to pink and disappearing altogether. Now it was there all the time. Big time. Bright red. Beating like little hearts under my skin. I could see all the Christians who called to pay their respects looking at my chest. I had always wanted my chest to be a focal point. For my boobs, not my rash.

Shouting about our little problem all over the place was the only thing I could think of that might have caused me more upset, pushed me over the edge. I spent years giving my young adults lessons in the cloak-and-dagger routine. Classes in how to keep their mouths shut. They must have been absent for those lessons. If I was lucky maybe they had only shared our secret with a select few of our close friends and family. But I have never been lucky. No, luck was not my constant companion. In fact, lucky and me never made an appearance at the same time. No, when luck stepped in I was out.

I was the talk of the place, taking over completely from Doreen. I was the new centre of attention. The members of the "did you hear" club were running around all over our village. Busy passing on my news. Like Chinese whispers the story was passed on and on. It got longer and seedier as each one added to it. At least I was providing the entertainment. I was also getting the sympathy vote. I was known as 'Poor Linda'. Dick was known as 'that bastard Dick'. He was in the manure and good enough for him. Everyone thought he was a real shit. I nearly felt sorry for him myself. Nearly, not quite. I was in denial. I had convinced myself Dick was on a business trip. Everyone felt sorry for the poor shell of a woman rabbiting on and on about her husband's business. Not one of them realised that I was just being true to the club. I was keeping my own business to myself and trying to cover up the mess. I wanted to keep up the appearance of being the Superperson I had conned everyone into believing I was. Instead I had managed to convince them that I was the village idiot.

Suzie tried to cheer me up by saying that it was a nine-day wonder. I reminded her that Dick was going to be away for two weeks at least.

"They'll forget soon enough. They have to be talking about someone. It could be my turn tomorrow. Although I doubt my boring old life would be a suitable subject for any gossip. Take it from me, it will all blow over. By next week they will have forgotten all about you and Dick."

"Suzie, have you forgotten it took God Almighty seven days to create this kip of a world we live in, and we're still talking about it? A lot of damage can be done in a week, never mind two. What am I going to do? It's all very well for Dick – he doesn't have to suffer the faces behind the cheap net curtains and the nodding, tutting and smiling. You'll have to do my shopping for me, Suzie. I'm not crossing the door until Dick comes back. I am liable to do anything. I feel a surge of violence towards Dick and as he's not here I am liable to take it out on anyone. I could do something offensive with an aubergine, murderous with a mandarin or grizzly with a grapefruit and it's not only men I want to physically harm either, Suzie. Anyone would do."

Suzie backed away and I dropped the subject.

The doorbell rang. Chloe was in college. I was on door duty. I hoped it was Dick at the door. Cap in hand. It was a sheepish woman in a sheepskin coat. In this heat?

"Excuse me, I'm collecting for Deserted Wives. Would you have a few pounds you could spare?"

"Well, what have we here?" I said as she shook her plastic box in my face. She was smiling, actually smiling at me. "I'm saved." I stared at her. "A bleedin' heart from Deserted Wives has come to help the latest deserted wife. What do you mean calling here at a time like this? What do you do? Collect from the newly deserted and give to the old reliable deserted? Why don't you go and round up all the deserting bastards instead of letting them off the hook? Squeeze some of the money out of them for a change. I've got no spare money. Even if I had I would be better off keeping it. Cut out the middle-man or in this case middle-woman. If I give it to you it would be like donating to myself only I'd probably have to wait months to get it back. Do you not recognise a kindred spirit? Clear off with your do-gooder attitude! I am more deserted than any of you!"

I was shouting up the driveway. The woman was running up the driveway. Sweating profusely. Screaming at her fellow collector to 'Come on, come on!' and 'Get the hell out of here quick!'. I immediately felt guilty. I ran after her to apologise.

She kept running faster. Looking over her shoulder screaming at her friend to get her bloody ass out of this estate now. She ran very well even with the hindrance of the coat. I never caught up with her. Suzie came and dragged me back into the house.

"I'm a danger to society, Suzie."

"No, you're not. You haven't even been a tiny bit short-tempered with me."

"I keep holding back. I want to attack everyone. I will run amuck soon. I am a time bomb."

Suzie looked nervous. I think I had convinced her. I changed the subject again.

"I can't go in to work, Suzie. Suppose Dick rings when I'm in work? Or worse still, suppose I explode and kill my boss."

"You have to go to work. You'll lose your job if you don't."

"If I kill my boss I'll definitely lose my job. Anyway, I don't care. I don't even like my poxy job. Toadying to Uriah Heep morning, noon and night. Bending over backwards, for a pittance, to please him, so far backwards I have bloody carpet-burn on my forehead. Let him stuff his job. Anyway I rang him already and pretended I was sick but the slimy bastard knew what had happened. It must have been in the *Evening Herald* about me and Dick. Gerry Ryan and Joe Duffy were probably fighting to see which one of them would get to mention it on the radio. They probably decided to compromise and both got to tell the world. Start the ball rolling and the phones ringing. Bloody Pat Kenny is probably analysing the situation with some team of experts as we speak." I started to shout in the direction of the window. "Is there anyone out there that doesn't know about my life or lack of it?"

"Now, Linda, no blood has been spilt and no money has been passed in brown-paper bags or envelopes or whatever wrappings are in vogue this year so RTE won't be remotely interested in your little problem. Charlie Bird has enough to be doing chasing the proper Charlies of this country without starting on the Dicks. Of course your boss knows the whole story – doesn't his wife play bridge with Dick's secretary?"

"Oh yes, of course. The trump card! Hear ye! Hear ye! Come on, roll up, roll up, more exciting news on the Linda front! Her 'Shit Here' sign is in perfect working order! Shining and flashing, ensuring nothing but the greatest shit falls on her. Even her husband is a shit."

Suzie dared to laugh.

"I hope you're enjoying this, Suzie. Go on. Laugh your head off! You may as well. At least one of us can laugh. Unfortunately that's another little luxury I have been deprived of. I'm only glad that I could provide a bit of entertainment for you. Is there anything else I could do for your amusement? Perhaps I could bring a dose of piles upon myself and you could laugh till your sides split while watching me balancing on a rubber ring? Oh, bring on the clowns, why don't you?"

"I'm sorry, it just seemed funny."

"Oh, Suzie, I'm sorry. I'd think it was funny too if I wasn't right in the middle of it. Christ, I just had a thought! Suppose Dick hasn't gone alone? Jesus, Mary and Joseph, suppose he's gone with that snotty-nosed upstart of a secretary. I couldn't cope, Suzie. I'm for the lake if that happens. Large rock around my ankle and I'm gone. If I thought for one minute that upstart was lying there beside him in Crete with my thong on I'd just die."

I started to cry again. Suzie was used to this and handed me a tissue. She was pacing the floor.

"For the love of God, Suzie, will you sit down! You're making me nervous and as I am a basket-case already that might be considered to be the breaking of the camel's whatsits and all that."

Suzie plonked into an armchair and tucked her legs up under her. "Well, she can't be gone in your thong. That's upstairs under your bed in your suitcase, remember? But I'm just thinking, Linda, we could find out very easily if Dick took The Upstart with him."

"How?"

"Well, I could ring the office and ask for Dick and she'd answer his phone. What do you think? Will you be able for the shock if she is gone with him?"

"I'll break her neck. Immediately after I break his."

"Wait now. Even if she isn't in the office she could be out sick or something so we can't jump to conclusions. It will just be the start of investigations. Preliminary enquiries. So if I do ring we must bear in mind that we have to discuss rationally whatever information I come up with."

"Right, ring."

I listened in on the extension.

"Riess & Fortnam Solicitors, can I help you?"

Not The Upstart. I shook my head at Suzie and pulled a face.

"Hello, could I speak to Dick, please?" Suzie was excellent. Very businesslike.

"Who's calling, please?"

"A close friend. It's a personal call." Suzie was an artist. The drama course really coming into its own.

"I'm afraid Dick is on leave at the moment. Can I take a message?"

"Oh! Oh. Will you hold on?"

Suzie and me put our hands over the mouthpieces.

"What will I do? What's The Upstart's real name? Linda, what's her name?"

"Fleur. Wouldn't you know a shrinking violet like her would have a name like that?"

"Hello, could you put me on to Dick's secretary, Fleur, please?"

"Fleur is away from her desk at the moment. Would you like to ring back in a hour? She should be free then."

"Thank you, I'll do that."

We hung up.

"Now, now did you hear that, Suzie?" I started to pace. "Did you hear? Flirtatious Fleur is away. Away with my Dick!" I couldn't help it. I started to cry again. It's a funny thing about tears – we must have millions and millions of them. By this stage I should have been all out of them but they just kept right on a-comin'. Anything that is of no use to me I have lots of. Fat and tears. Just when I thought I was all cried out I'd find a new wetter, thicker crop. The type accompanied by the runny nose and the blotchy face. I am not attractive when I cry.

"Linda, stop howling! I understand you have to

cry now and again but you're crying for nothing. The Upstart is probably just having her lunch."

"At half past ten in the morning?"

"Well, her break then. Or she might be filing her nails or powdering her little snub nose or whatever she does. Anyway, we'll ring back in an hour and talk to her."

"I think it's delaying tactics, Suzie. I think she's in Crete with Dick and the company are involved in a huge cover-up. They are all running about now as we speak looking for a tape of The Upstart's voice or devising some plausible reason why she cannot speak to you on the phone. Like she has had her jaw wired to lose weight. If they say that I won't believe them because I know for a fact that she is only a size six and would like to put on weight. She feels her waist and hips are that little bit too thin and her voluptuous melons are that little bit too large. How lucky can an Upstart get?"

"Linda, this is not the FBI we're dealing with. There will be no cover-up."

The next hour was the longest in the history of the world, at least sixty-five minutes. I imagined Dick and the boobs-on-a-stick-insect Upstart on the beach making love, in the hotel lobby making love, in the pool making love, in the bar, yes, making love. If they made love in all the places and at all the times I imagined then Dick must be taking something. Then I began to wonder was I normal? Had I a one-track mind? Was I preoccupied with sex? Was this what I should be thinking about? Should I be worrying instead if Dick and fucking Fleur were, were – well, what else could they be doing?

Suzie was green when she rang for the second time. Give her her due in bucketfuls. I don't know if I would have done the same for her, especially with me sitting like a hawk poised to attack, my knuckles white, my beady eyes on her olive face. I was ready to pounce, squeeze my talons tight around her skull. One mistake and she was dead. I was ready to claw myself and everyone else to death if Fleur did not materialise.

"Riess & Fortnam Solicitors, can I help you?"

Again not The Upstart!

"Hello, I rang an hour ago," exactly, to the minute, "wanting to speak to Dick but as he is on leave I wonder could I speak to The Upstar . . ." she started coughing into the phone. You'd guess she was nervous. "Sorry, sorry, I have a frog in my throat."

"Better a frog than a prince!" the girl giggled.

"Could I speak to Fleur, Dick's secretary, please?"

"Just one moment and I'll see if I can page her."

I put my hand over the mouthpiece and whispered to Suzie. "There now, Suzie, I was right! It is a big cover-up. They will not be able to page Fleur because not if the pageboy shouted to the top of his lungs will the all-feminine Fleur be able to hear him in Crete." Particularly if she is in the middle of a large featherbed making mad passionate love to my husband.

"Hello, who's calling?"

It was her. Fleur. The Upstart herself in person. Was she speaking from Crete? Had they found a long-distance pager? Was it a recording of her voice?

"*Psst, psst,* Suzie, try to see if she's a recording!"

I used my loud whisper voice that works so well when reprimanding the children in a public place.

"Is this Fleur?"

"Yeeeas. This is she."

Stuffed Upstart.

"I believe Dick is on leave and I was wondering where he was and when he would be returning? I have a social engagement with his lovely wife and himself next week and I wanted to make sure I had the time right. The lovely Linda is not at home so I thought I'd give Dick a ring. The girl on the switch told me he was away. I hope he'll be back by next Wednesday?"

"Well, to tell you the truth we don't know. He's only gone an' flown the coop, scarpered if you know what I mean. They're calling it annual leave in here but between you, me and the wall he was acting a bit weird lately. Last I heard he was heading for Crete. We don't know who, if anyone, has gone with him. Poor Dick. He's such a nice guy. I believe Linda took it very bad. She's going around with eyes like cherry tomatoes and is living in a track suit with a baggy arse." She giggled. "It's not Linda's arse that's baggy. I mean the track suit is baggy around the arse. Although Linda could have a baggy arse as well for all I know!"

"OK, OK, I get the drift." Suzie cut short any further talk about my bum, eyeing me anxiously. A loyal companion is Suzie.

Fleur giggled again. Jesus, was everyone getting a laugh at my expense except me?

"It's the poor kids I feel sorry for," feeling-hearted Fleur continued. "God love them, apparently Linda's lost it. First their father, now their mother, losing both at the same time must be hard on them. I don't think Dick will be back for your function and by all accounts I don't think Linda will be functioning for it. Do you want me to get Dick to ring you when he returns? If he ever returns."

"No, I'll get him again, thanks."

"I wouldn't bet on it but I hope he comes back. He was great *craic* in here. I liked him anyway. He was always great at all the office do's. Participated in all the office don'ts."

"Goodbye, Fleur!" said Suzie abruptly with a sharp glance at me.

"Bye now!"

"Well," Suzie was pretending to be cheerful as she put the phone down, "we know that The Upstart didn't go with him."

"Did you ever hear anything like her?" I burst out. "She has the hots for him, Suzie, and what's wrong with this track suit? The nerve of her!" I pulled out the sides of the trousers to examine them. They looked good to me. "This cost me a lot of money when I bought it."

"Fifteen years ago?"

"Well, you could hardly expect me to wear my good clothes moping and crying around the house, could you?"

"No, but perhaps on Saturday we'll go somewhere nice. Just the two of us. Cheer us up. I'll pick somewhere nice. We'll have dinner out. A real treat. Then we could go on somewhere after and come back late. What do you say? It'll do us good."

I was staring into the mirror over the mantelpiece. I was hoping that the person staring back at me was not in fact me. I was hoping it was one of the Mirror People. You know, the horrible ugly people who live in mirrors. You can get a glimpse of them first thing in the morning or after a really rough night out. Sometimes when you're sick they arrive at all hours of the day and night. Well, there was one in my mirror now – the one with the plum eyes and alabaster face. Alabaster with cracks. I was hoping that any second now my own reflection would appear. But this Mirror Person was very persistent. It was wearing my hair, granted it was all sticking up at right angles to her head, like a very, very, old punk rocker but it was definitely my hair. She was also wearing my track suit and it looked dreadful on her. Raggy and baggy. I would never want to look like this Mirror Person.

"Suzie."

"Yeah?" Suzie was searching in her big black bag. Please don't let her produce a Peppermint Cream in this my most vulnerable moment! Surely she would be more sensitive than to start eating out of her bag. If she ate even one square I'd attack. Ram some down her neck. Bash the rest between my two hands and wipe them in her cheesecloth dress. She took out a tissue and started wiping the sweat off her upper lip. I was saved, for the time being at least. The phone call had taken a lot out

161

of Suzie. I also think she guessed what was coming next and didn't want to get involved.

"Suzie, can you come here for a minute?"

She stood beside me. I could see her beautiful reflection in the mirror. All smooth-skinned and bright-eyed.

I was pointing at the weirdo in the mirror.

"Suzie, is that a Mirror Person in there or is it me?"

"Well, Linda, you have been through a lot and you can't expect to look your best, now can you?"

"But I can expect to look like a human being, Suzie, can I not? That thing in there looks like one of the alien crew off the Starship Enterprise. Is that what I have become?"

"A bit of make-up and you'll be right as rain."

"A major operation is what I'd need to look right. A complete head transplant followed by the amputation of the track suit. Dick has done this to me, Suzie. I want you to take a photograph of me and I will send it to Dick tonight and let the bastard see what he has done to me. That will bring him back soon enough."

"Do you think so? Maybe if you sent him the photo he'd wonder what he was coming home to."

I was cut to the quick. Wounded by my pal. "*Et tu*, Suzie? Do you think I'm falling apart?"

"You're just not yourself. How could you be?"

"I'll show you. I'll show everyone. I'll show that git Dick. We'll hit the town, Suzie, you and me both. Prepare to be shocked. It's comeback time. I cordially invite you to the Comeback of Linda. I am going to rise again like that bird that comes up out of the ashes. You know the one? The one that always comes up out of all sorts of ashes. You've seen pictures of it. Well, that'll be me. I want you to be there when I rise, Suzie. You've got the best seat in the house. "

"It's a phoenix."

"Who's a phoenix?"

"That bird – phoenix, that's what it's called."

"What bird? Who? Jesus, what are you going on about, Suzie?"

"The shaggin' bird that rises from the bloody ashes, Linda, is called a feckin' phoenix!"

"Feckin' phoenix? Well, if you say so. Whatever you think, Suzie, I'm sure you're right. No need to get so stroppy about it though. I believe you."

I didn't really. I wasn't at all sure it was a phoenix. In fact, I knew for a fact that it was an albatross. Or was it? Maybe the albatross was the one that was constantly hanging out around my neck? As if it would be any fun there!

Poor Suzie didn't know what to do with me so

she hugged me. She was trying her best for me. No doubt about it, she was a real pal. I was in no condition to appreciate her. I knew I would later but not now. Now she was only a reminder of what I had once had and how wonderful her life was. How wonderful life could be. Any life but mine.

CHAPTER EIGHT

Another day. I hated days these days. I hated nights too. The weekend was the worst. It used to be my favourite. That was then. This was now. Then I used to go into town with Suzie and do what I do best – shop. We went to all the expensive shops in Dublin and then made our purchases in the usual cheaper chain stores. We stopped every now and again for tea. Saturday was Suzie's and my day.

Since the kids had grown up Dick and I always stayed in on Saturday nights. We had the place to ourselves. The kids went out doing their own thing. We never asked them what exactly their own thing was for fear it was exactly the same thing we used to do when we were their ages. Before we became settled. Into a Saturday routine. We had a good

Saturday-night routine going, Dick and me. We curled up in front of the telly, ate takeaway food and drank wine while Dick practised his flicking. Now I had no routine. I missed the run-downs. I was all alone on Saturday nights. I spent Saturday and every day looking out the window at all the happy people playing happy families. Except Larry and Doreen of course. No sightings of Doreen but Larry kept on with the ritual washing of the car so I reckoned he wasn't that devastated about Doreen's affair. Either that or he still didn't know.

At least I knew Dick wasn't having an affair. Lack of opportunity. Before all this shit I would have said he was also suffering from a lack of desire. Now I didn't know. Then again I didn't know Dick any more. How could I be expected to know him if he didn't even know himself? Particularly if some of him was missing. One thing was for sure: if Dick was having an affair he would have changed his underwear. Well, actually he changed his underwear every day, sometimes twice. I mean he'd have to change his style of underwear. If he was having an affair he would have gone for the brief sexy kind. Black. Not the bright colourful, tee-shirt material, boxer type with the Disney characters he was so fond of. I kinda liked them too. I suppose if I liked them and thought they were cute some other woman might think the same. No. Dick was not having an affair. I felt it in my waters. I wonder if poor Larry felt the same in his?

Suzie let herself in. She nearly killed me. For a minute I thought, hoped, it was Dick coming home. Until I heard her.

"It's only me."

"Suzie, I wish you wouldn't sneak in on me like that."

"I didn't sneak in. I let myself in with the key you gave me to save you having to get up and walk the three feet to the door. If you want the key back you can have it."

In a very rash moment I had given Suzie the key to my kingdom. She kept using it. So far she had walked in on Carl running down the stairs in the nude to get his boxers and socks off the radiator. Suzie screamed, he screamed and the two of them ran in opposite directions. Him back upstairs and her back to the safety of her own home. It took me ages to calm poor Carl down. He kept calling her a pervert and complaining that no one other than the people living in the house should have a key. Chloe agreed. Suzie had walked in on Chloe and the Dillon boy having a snogging session on the couch. Again, it caused poor Suzie to run for cover. Carl and Chloe wanted me to take the key back off

Suzie. They argued that none of their friends had keys to our house so why should Suzie? I suppose they had a point but it was handy for me to give Suzie the key. Some days I didn't even make the move from the bed to the couch.

But today I had thought she was Dick and I'd jumped up off the couch to greet him. Running my fingers through the grease that had built up from a week of not washing my hair. I was starting to look like Elvis. To make matters worse, Suzie, the bitch, looked lovely. Her clean, shiny, blonde hair was piled up on her head. Held in place with one of those claw clips. Soft little wisps were escaping. She was wearing a pale blue flowing skirt, soft cream suede boots, a pale-blue, low-cut, cropped top. She was carrying her best-shaped navy jacket. She looked terrific, alive, the exact opposite of me. Clean and with it. Ah feck her! She was making me feel awful again. I thought it was a bit mean of her to look so well knowing how awful I looked. Not the act of a true and loyal friend.

She made us both tea. She had brought two bars of chocolate with her. I still wasn't eating so she ate them both. She never put on a pick. Life is very unfair. Especially to me. Suzie eats like a horse. Eats anything you put in front of her. The more calories the better. She is still slim and svelte even after three pregnancies.

Suzie has had three children, all weird adults now – you know, all part of the arty farty set. A sculptor, a poet and something to do with films. They succeeded where their mother failed. They are all free spirits. Free-loading off Suzie every now and again. Suzie never puts on weight. Even when she was pregnant. She was like one of those women who give birth without even knowing they are pregnant. To be honest I never believed that was possible. Until I saw Suzie pregnant. She breezed through the nine months. She hardly looked any bigger. A small basketball-like shape grew slowly to her front. It was like a separate part of her. It invaded no other part.

To look at me when I was pregnant you would be forgiven for thinking my womb was just behind my face. I had a face like a balloon about to burst. You would think someone had got a bicycle pump and put the nozzle up my nostril. Blown my face up out of all proportion. Except that it wasn't. It was in horrible proportion to the rest of my humongous body. I looked like there were wombs housing children all over my body – at the top of my legs, in my two boobs, behind both my hips and of course in my belly. I looked like I was going to pop babies from all over any minute. Even my earlobes got bigger. I know this for a fact because Dick told me. He said nibbling my

169

earlobes had turned into a near act of cannibalism and if I didn't mind he would refrain from such a practice until after the birth. He refrained from a lot of other practices too. Even though he told me I looked lovely I never felt it. Maybe if he had touched me and held me I would have felt lovely. He was afraid. Amazed at the metamorphosis.

I got bigger by the day. I went to bed one size and woke up in the morning a full size bigger. This was very unfair considering I was sick at least three times a day and ate very little. Apart from pickled cabbage and gallons of ice cream with walnuts and maple syrup. Suzie on the other hand was never sick and appeared to lose weight while carrying a ten-pound baby inside the one womb she had exactly where it should be. Suzie's babies popped out after nine months. My two were dragged out, kicking and screaming after nearly ten months. They carried on kicking and screaming until they were five. Then they quietened down. I have been worrying about them ever since. Where's the justice I ask? Where I am concerned there is none.

Today Suzie looked extremely well. I wondered was she making the effort in the hopes that I might do the same. Was it Rehabilitate Linda Time? The new psychology course she was taking was starting to scare me.

"Get up off that bloody couch, Linda. You promised you'd be ready, willing and able to face the outside world today. It's half past four and you're still in your dressing-gown. It's a wonder you don't have rollers in your hair. Of course they would probably slide out on account of all the grease. Do you know your dressing-gown is filthy? What colour is it anyway? Dusky pink or dirty pink?"

"Actually it's cream."

"I hope you weren't even considering coming out in it. Call me silly but I would much prefer it if you put on some clothes. I don't think I could handle the attention you'd get wearing that thing. Come on, Linda. Shift yourself! You promised!"

Suzie was a bleedin' saint. A do-gooder. If there was one thing I didn't need it was either one.

"I know I promised but I can't. Dick might ring."

"I thought you didn't want to talk to him."

"I don't."

"Well, let the answering machine take the calls."

"I will but I'd like to be here when he rings. That is, of course, if he rings at all. The bastard probably won't even ring. I need to be here if he rings so that I won't answer the phone on purpose. If I go out and the bastard rings then I couldn't have answered it anyway so I won't be not answering it. I just won't be able to answer it. Do you see what I mean?"

Suzie didn't look like she understood at all. Sometimes no one understands me.

"Linda, get ready NOW."

The aggressiveness course being used rather than the psychology. I think I prefer it when she tries the psychology. She's so gentle when she does it. Particularly the reverse psychology.

"Of course you could always sit here wallowing in your misery. Moaning out the window. Doing your *femme fatale* bit. You could lie on the couch feeling sorry for yourself and while away the hours withering away. The children wouldn't mind. They could come in to pay their respects to you every now and again. They could give you couch baths and turn you, throw the odd bit of food in your direction. They would miss you being involved in their lives, I suppose. Then again they might regard that as a bonus. Dick would come home to find a frail little wimp where he had left a lovely attractive woman. I suppose I would have to go to the bother of finding myself a new best friend. Not an easy thing at my age. So, Linda, if you want to wallow in self-pity and ignore your children and me there's very little we can do. Perhaps I'll just head off and leave you here to rot. I might just see if Doreen wants to go out with me." She stared at me.

Was I meant to clap or something?

It was a much better approach though. I preferred it, the gentle coaxing approach. She knew using the kids and Dick would make me feel guilty. So she made the most of it. Turned the knife. She knows I have always suffered from the guilts. I have often felt it's an Irish thing. But as time goes on I begin to think I am the only Irish person who suffers from it. Dick never did. Another thing I am alone in. Suzie knew about this little frailty in my character. She was playing on it. For all she was worth. It was working. God damn her, the bitch had got me where it hurt.

"Oh. I hate you, Suzie. Why can't you bugger off to your own life and get out of mine!"

"Because you don't want me to," she replied. She knew me too well.

I stormed up the stairs and marched into my bedroom muttering about friends in need and all that rubbish. If truth be told I didn't really understand the friend in need bit. Lately I was finding more and more things that I didn't understand.

My bedroom was fresh and clean. I missed the mess Dick usually made. The bed was unmade but that was only a matter of pulling up the duvet. I didn't bother. It was one of those cream lace ones. It creased easily. The bedroom looked strange and felt empty without Dick.

He had decorated it for me the year before as a surprise. Just before his mother came to stay. Cream and pink. I had gone into town with Suzie one Saturday and come home to find the whole room revamped. Carl, Chloe and Dick had spent all day doing it. As soon as I left the house they got stuck in. Stripping and pasting. Suzie was under orders not to bring me back early. The carpet shop was given strict instructions what time to lay the carpet and some poor eejit putting in the wardrobes worked flat out all day. Cream wardrobes and dressing-table, pink carpet. Cream above dado, cream and pink stripes below. Even the bedside lamps were new and matched. When I arrived home it was finished. They blindfolded me. Led me up the stairs and revealed all. I sat on the bed and cried and cried. To this day they think I cried with joy. I will never tell them otherwise.

The old mahogany wardrobes, family heirlooms my parents had used and then passed on to me were gone. In their place were rows of cream, shiny doors, plain, lacking character. The old dressing-table I had scratched my name into as a child and where Carl and Chloe in turn had added theirs was missing. The headboard that my father had re-polished for me was now on some tip or other sharing its secrets, telling stories of my grandparents,

parents and myself. The old mahogany rocking-chair that I had rocked my babies to sleep in was relegated to the garden shed. Out of sight and out of place. All my old familiar bits were gone without even a goodbye. I missed them for months. I got used to the bedroom eventually – it did look cleaner and more streamlined. Dick's mother thought so anyway. She never stopped talking about her time in the room Dick decorated for her. But the character is missing. Gone. Like Dick.

"Get a move on! Come on, Linda! Time being of the essence, standing still for no man and all that. We have to go. Come on!"

Suzie was persistent. I hoped she wouldn't come up to dress me. That would be the final humiliation.

"Do you want me to come up and give you a hand?" she shouted up the stairs.

Jesus no.

"No, I'm nearly ready. Be down in a sec," I shouted back.

I had to go on a treasure hunt to try to find something to wear. I felt a wardrobe crisis coming on. All my trousers were in the wash. Most of my skirts were at the cleaners. They would sell them if I didn't collect them soon. Any skirts that were clean matched none of the tops that were ironed. My dresses were creased at the ends. Because I kept shoving things into the bottom of my wardrobe so the dresses couldn't hang properly. Would anyone notice a few creases around the hem? Would anyone notice if I was one big crease? Would anyone ever notice me again?

I settled on a short black dress. I cannot tell you the number of times I have been grateful to my mother for the little black dress advice. I have worn it everywhere, nearly worn it out in fact. Well, I have worn it out, but I mean worn it out on occasions as opposed to threadbare worn out. Another crisis looming. No tights. I bravely and slowly entered Chloe's room. I didn't know what I would find. Cups with green fur and white spots at the bottom. Plates with matching green fur all over them. Green fur inside half-full yoghurt cartons. I was sorry now I hadn't chosen green fur instead of the sunshine yellow as a theme for her room. Mould-coloured curtains and duvet. Rotten-coloured carpet, although the carpet colour really didn't matter as you never got an opportunity to see the carpet at all. I ignored the smell and the mess and stepped over all her clothes on the floor. I opened her wardrobe. It was empty. All the contents were on the floor. I rooted in one of her drawers. She had every colour of everything. The poor student had matching bra and knickers sets, vest and boxer sets, tangas and briefs with lycra, without lycra. All, I am glad to say, with gusset.

I stole a pair of my daughter's expensive stockings. They had denier and added lycra. Not like my two pairs in a box for two pounds. The working woman in the house just wore tights, plain ordinary tights. No added anything. I wondered did they look it. I made a mental note to compare price. The pair of stockings I robbed from Chloe had a silly price on the box. It must have been a mistake. I could have bought a jumper for that price. Must have been an error. I hoped Chloe spotted it before she handed over my hard-earned cash. 'Lace hold-ups' they were called. They must be the stockings used by robbers when they hold up banks. Imagine advertising that on the outside of the box! What was the world coming to when even the bloody thieves didn't have to do research on what stockings to wear over their heads? I wondered did the burglars hold up the shop for the hold-ups or did they have to pay for them? If they went to the same shop as Chloe they would be robbed. The stockings felt nice all the same. I could imagine someone feeling more comfortable with them on their face than my itchy tights. They were lovely and smooth, shiny even. I hoped they wouldn't roll down my leg at an inappropriate moment. Well, if that happened I would just have to do what I had done at the Christmas party, take them off and put them in my bag. On the other hand they could stay up all night but stop the circulation in my leg. I would get dead leg and start walking around like Basil Fawlty.

My eyes landed on a strappy pair of black sandals. We had the same size feet, Chloe and me. Eight. God help her, she got my feet. The sandals looked terrific on me, bordering on hookerish with the shiny stockings. I added silver jewellery to my neck and wrists. A pair of Chloe's large silver, dangly earrings. A good squirt of her CK1. My coffee jacket finished the ensemble and though I say it myself from the neck down I looked a stunner. The neck up would need work.

I thought of Doreen and borrowed some of Chloe's expensive creams that I had bought her. I cleansed, toned, exfoliated and moisturised my face. It didn't know what was happening to it. I wet my hair and put some more mousse into it. It went very well with the grease and gave me a soft shiny look. I layered on the make-up with the same care Michelangelo gave to the Sistine Chapel and created a fake me. All eyes and cheekbones. Brown, red and rust. The outside me looked like a normal person. 'Here look at me!' it shouted. 'I am a perfectly normal person. Who is the depressed person whose husband buggered off for two weeks? Not I! I am a confident happy person.'

The inner me was not fooled.

'Oh no, you're not!' it was shouting. 'You are a wreck of a human being living in misery with nothing but more misery to look forward to. You are the Queen of the 'Shit Here' sign. You are the first in the queue. The 'pick me for all things horrible to happen to' queue. The 'soc it to me' queue.' I wanted the outer me to take control. But the inner me was winning.

Carl put his head around my bedroom door and was obviously pleased to see his mother had returned to something resembling a human being. So what if he couldn't see that the inner Ma was still in bits?

"God, Ma, you look brill! If only Dad could see you now!"

"Thanks, Carl." I had reared a gentleman.

"Where are you off out to anyway?" he asked me.

"I don't know exactly where we're going yet. Suzie is taking me somewhere nice as a surprise. Will you ring the Chinese again for your dinner? I didn't cook anything. I don't know when I'll be back. Expect me when you see me." I smiled and hoped it showed more than it felt.

"Wherever you go you'll knock 'em dead. I hope you have a great time, Ma. You deserve it."

I had really reared one terrific young fella. He gave me a hug. He was towering over me, patting me on the back. Role reversal. I wanted to cry.

"Don't start crying, Ma. You'll only spoil your face."

"I know," I whispered. "Are you off out anywhere yourself? Big stud like you shouldn't be hanging around the house on a Saturday night."

"I'm going out later with the lads and eh . . ." He hesitated. "We're going to a party – it should be good."

"I love parties. It's ages since I've been to one."

"Ma, I know this is a really bad time but I wanted to talk to you." Carl sat down on my bed.

My stomach lurched. Heaved and somersaulted all at once. My outer self must have been fooling Carl into thinking I was back to my normal self all over and would want to listen to him. My inner self knew it would explode if it heard anything other than how wonderful everything in his life was. Except for the missing father bit.

"What?" My mouth was landing me in it again. Encouraging Carl to talk. And I was feeling ill again. The pit of my stomach was in turmoil. Churning. I am a glutton for punishment. There I was in the depths of despair asking my teenage son to confide in me. I wanted this lump of testosterone to tell me all his dark secrets. His innermost thoughts. Please let them be good and wholesome and happy thoughts. I knew what he was going to tell me would be none of those.

"Ma, I have met someone. I love her. I think she is the one I have always imagined I would be with for the rest of my life." Carl was speaking like a poet. Carl would never speak like that unless he was serious. Poetry and Carl are not really on first name terms. He was in love.

Well, that was all right. Teenage love. I could cope with that. Granted, I would have preferred to wait for another few years, say until Carl was thirty. But I could cope with a lovesick Romeo.

"That's lovely, Carl. I'm delighted for you." And I was. "What's her name? I bet she's fantastic. Do I know her? Why don't you bring her around for dinner or something?" I could never be accused of being less than enthusiastic or unwelcoming. Anyway, I wanted to suss her out.

"Well, that's the thing, Ma. Before she comes to the house I just wanted you to know something." Carl was fidgeting. He never fidgets unless he is very uncomfortable. I braced myself.

"Well, the thing is. You see. Well."

"Oh, get on with it for God's sake, Carl! Has she three heads or something?" I was hoping she had. I was sure I could cope with three heads. Anything else I wasn't so sure about.

"No." He laughed and stopped fidgeting. "Well, she's older than me. Quite a bit older actually. But I really love her, Ma."

I couldn't believe my ears. I had reared a fool, a gobshite. A thick. A romantic idiot. I would have to nip this in the bud. He was too young for this. I was too old for this. Another situation requiring my kid gloves. Where had I left them? I can never find the bloody things when I most need them.

"How much older? How long have you known her? It's a bit sudden, isn't it?" I fired questions at him.

"I knew you'd say that it was very quick but how long does it take to fall in love? I've known her for ages. I feel I've known her forever." He was back fidgeting again.

He started pacing around the bedroom. Fiddling with my jewellery boxes, picking things up and putting them down in the wrong place. Examining the family photograph beside my bed. Four happy smiling faces staring back at him. It seemed like a long time ago. He looked vulnerable. Hurt. Jesus, does the misery never end?

"I'm only thinking about you, Carl. You're very young."

"Ma, I'm eighteen." His answer to everything. Exactly my point.

"I'm a grown-up. You and Dad will have to get used to it. At my age you were married "

And look at me now. You big, big eejit, do you think it's a bed of roses? Wake up and smell the manure your mother is drowning in. Have you no brains getting yourself involved so young? I wanted to shout at him, give him a good shake. Knock a bit of sense into him. I wasn't an example for him to follow. Instead I put on the kid gloves that were lurking not too far away. If only I'd looked for them in the first place.

"Well, I'm glad that you're happy, Carl. That's the important thing." I nearly made myself sick. "That's all I want for you," I added. That and to be rich, I thought. "But give it a bit of time." Like twenty years. You can fall in love then. You should be able to handle it then. Maybe I'd be able for it then too. "Enjoy it now." I kept going on at him in an alarmingly soppy voice. "Don't take it too seriously. Stop thinking about the rest of your life." You big lummox, you! I was rabbiting on a bit. He was staring. I hoped he was taking it all in. "See the world. Have a good time, Carl." But preferably do it on your own or at least with someone your own age. "Don't rush into commitment," I was in full flight, "and children and obligations for a while yet. This girl might not want to be rushed." I was grasping at straws. "She might be frightened off if you take it too seriously." A little of Suzie's psychology wouldn't hurt. "Girls don't like to be rushed nowadays. They don't want to settle down and have children until they have seen a bit of life."

Please God don't let this older person be a ninnyhammer who wants the big white meringue bit before Carl's twenty-first birthday.

"She's not a girl, she's a woman. I am a man, Ma. We are serious. This is like a wonderful dream for me. Don't start preaching at me. I know what I want. It's her. You're always telling us to follow our dreams. Now it turns out we're only to follow them if they're the same dreams as yours. I'm not going to be living in this house all my life, Ma. Much as you might want me to. I will move on one day to start a family of my own. You'll have to get used to the idea. I think I've met the woman I want to do that with." He was passionate.

I always knew my children would fly the coop one day. Leave the nest and all that. I had thought Dick would be here with me when they did. I never for one moment thought that Dick would be the first to fly the coop. I expected Carl and Chloe to set up homes for themselves one day. I was hoping it would happen later rather than sooner. The natural progression from child to adult is hard for a mother to watch. Most people remember Padraig Pearse for his part in the 1916 rising. I remember him for the lines of one of his poems. *"Lord, you are hard on mothers, we suffer in their comings and in their goings."* I seemed to be always suffering.

"I'd love to meet this gir- woman of your dreams. Bring her around to dinner when your dad gets home and we can all get to know each other." Give your dad some suffering. Save some of your little surprises for him. How come it's always me gets the belt below the belt?

"All right, Ma," Carl said in a whisper.

Yes. Yes. It had worked. I would have to be careful. Suss out this older person. Then decide on a course of action. Think of a way to get rid of her. My stomach felt better, not much, but better. I rubbed the top of Carl's head. He didn't object. Maybe the boy was still there lurking deep inside the man.

"Linda!" Suzie was knocking on the bedroom door. Saved by the knock. A true friend.

"I'll talk to you again later, Ma," Carl said as he

stood up to open the door. He gave me a hug, more a tight squeeze.

"Fill me in when I come home, Carl. I'll be looking forward to it." I picked up my bag. He was back staring at the photo again. I wondered was he thinking about happy ever after, happy families. Wondering what had happened to ours. "Talk to me later, Carl. I'll be all ears," I said.

He laughed. "You better be. I've got a lot more to tell you."

"Great." I'll take a Valium sandwich and we can discuss the love life of an eighteen-year-old hormone.

"I knew you'd understand," Carl said as I left.

Understand that he was in love. That was the easy part. It was the 'lot more to tell me' I was worried about. Oh shit, there was probably lots more! Keep it coming at me! See how much I can take. Roll up, roll up, see can you smash this already broken woman! Keep the punches low. Use surprise tactics. I needed to get out of here.

Suzie made all the right noises. Ooooing and ahhing at me. She was definitely impressed by the outer shell. I felt like a million. A million drinks. Just as we were about to leave Chloe arrived.

"Off out somewhere nice then? You look brilliant, Ma. Do I recognise the footgear? They're great for dancing, you know."

She was a great kid. I had reared an angel. She reached out her arms to me and hugged me. She whispered in my ear. Out of earshot of Suzie.

"Can I get my nose pierced, Ma?"

The bitch. I had reared a gobshite.

"Of course," I replied. "We might both go together. Let the man pierce my heart. Everyone else has had a go. May as well let the expert do it. The amateurs are making a bit of a bags of it and it's hurting."

"Ah, Ma, come on! All my friends have theirs pierced," Chloe said.

"Their hearts?" I raised my eyebrows. Chloe laughed.

Everything I didn't want my kids to do all their friends were allowed do. I never heard that all their friends were allowed to study for eight hours a day, do their own washing or go out and earn a few bob.

"Come on, Ma. You have to move with the times. Nose-piercing is very common, you know." She had said the wrong thing and she knew it.

"Exactly, common. No daughter of mine is going around with anything common. I'm going out now. I'm going to try to have a good time. I will try not to think about your dad in far-flung Crete, Carl in love with an older woman or you

187

with your nose pierced and God knows what other bits that I cannot see. Goodnight. I love you." And I did but against all odds.

"I know. Me too!"

We both meant it. I wanted to cry again.

CHAPTER NINE

Suzie's Bill gave us a lift to the village.

"Where are you two off to then?" he asked me. Obviously Suzie hadn't filled him in.

"I don't know. It's a surprise. Suzie hasn't told me yet." I told the truth.

"Me neither," he said.

"I did. I told you, Bill. We're just going to call over to see Linda's friend, Jane," Suzie lied. I knew Suzie was lying because I don't have a friend called Jane. Suzie never lies. That is one of the things I love about her. She always tells the truth. She hates lies. Now she was lying. Everything was changing.

"We're going out to cheer Linda up. Isn't that right, Linda?"

"Well, I could do with some cheering up."

"So you can forget all your problems. For tonight at least." Suzie was smiling, chuffed.

"Is that a promise?"

"Yes. Most definitely and I always keep my promises."

This was true. Suzie did always honour her promises. I was glad she was back to her old truth-telling self. I couldn't handle it if Suzie started acting odd. She was the fulcrum I was balancing on at the moment. If she changed I was fucked.

"I'm very grateful to Suzie, you know, Bill. I'm just glad that you were kind enough to spare her on a Saturday night."

This last bit was a bit of a jibe at Bill. Suzie gave me daggers looks. Bill never, ever took Suzie out on a Saturday. He always went out for a few beers with the lads on Saturday night. Suzie watched *Kenny Live*. She didn't mind. She liked Pat Kenny. Suzie said that Bill worked so hard he needed time to unwind with the lads. He played golf and football and he had a great network of pals to draw from. Suzie adored the ground Bill walked on. Bill knew it.

"You can drop us here, love. We'll get a taxi home. Goodnight!." Suzie gave Bill a peck on the cheek.

"Bye, Bill, and thanks for the lift." I didn't peck his cheek or any other part of him for that matter.

"Have a good time!" he called as he drove off

"I'm glad you could spare her!" Suzie mimicked me. We linked arms as we strolled along the street. Laughing and chatting. To look at us you would think we were both happy. I was trying my best.

Suzie had booked a table at a new Italian restaurant. Pragas. It had only opened in the last few weeks. I had never been before. Mario greeted us at the door and showed us to our table. Mario was a bit of all right. His dinner jacket and crisp white shirt added to the effect. The place was packed. There was a great buzz. For the first time in ages I felt like a human being. Out doing normal things. I looked around at the other humans. They all looked cheerful. I bet none of their husbands felt the need to shag off and find themselves.

"Now I know this is Italian and we're going to Crete but this is the luxury we will become accustomed to for two whole weeks. Will we be able for it, Linda? Being waited on hand and foot?"

I prayed that no one would want to weight on either of my feet. They were killing me as it was in Chloe's shoes. Any bit of pressure at all, I knew, would hurt me deep down in my soul.

"I'm not sure if I will be able to go to Crete at

all, Suzie. I don't feel up to it at the moment. If Dick ever comes home I'll have to sort things out with him. I keep thinking that maybe he's met another woman. I'll have to fight to get him back, Suz. I don't want to lose him. You'll have to help me."

"Look, Linda, Dick will be back in a week. He wouldn't look at another woman. He loves you."

"I don't know, Suzie. Let's talk about it again when my head is clearer. Tonight I'm going to forget everything. Forget who I am. Pretend I am young again and out on the town. I'm going to enjoy myself like I did all those years ago. A long, long time ago." I was starting to feel maudlin.

"Right, hurry up and order – we've got places to go, people to see. We've been invited to a party. What do you want to drink?"

"A party. I was only saying earlier that I hadn't been to a party for yonks. That's great, Suzie. You're a real pal. Will we get a bottle of wine between us?"

We chose a middle-priced wine. Neither of us knew anything about wine. We reckoned wine was the same as people. Some were nice, others were horrible. We knew nothing of the colour or nose of wine. We were just as pleased. We had seen people sniff and snort into their wine over the years and we reckoned it was disgusting. The middle-price wine is always nice. It was so nice we ordered another bottle. That was a big mistake. My lips were numb from the first mouthful of the first bottle so I had to concentrate very hard on the glass-to-mouth action. I hadn't eaten for days and really didn't eat much of the meal. I ordered carbonara. I was sorry after. The one I made myself was nicer and cost less.

As the evening wore on and the wine kept coming, I kept thinking of Dick. Looking at him through rose-coloured glasses so to speak. The more I drank the better he looked. The food waiter had given up on us and the wine waiter was delighted that we drank everything he recommended. We were drooling. On account of the wine and the tight little Italian bum on the wine waiter. We kept calling him over to our table just to watch when he turned and left to get our drinks.

"He must have had some sort of operation to get a bum as good as that," Suzie said knowledgeably.

"Yeah," I agreed. "Most men his age have the fallen bum syndrome. I wonder did he get his lifted?"

"I never heard of a bum lift, did you?" Suzie asked me seriously.

"No, but you never know," I replied. "They lift

193

everything nowadays. I could do with a few lifts and tucks myself. Not that I'd ever let them near me with a knife. I'll tell you, Suz, even if my boobs were so big they were banging off my knees I wouldn't have a reduction. I'd sooner pick them up. Put a little bonnet on each one. Pop them in a pram and wheel them in front of me. Like twins."

"Pinky and Perky." She laughed.

"My face would have to drop off onto the path before I'd get it lifted," I added.

"I'm with you, Linda. Anyway, aren't we the perfect specimens?" She turned to the waiter.

"Garçon! Garçon! What's your name?"

He was the same guy that had shown us to our seats. Mario. He had said his name was Mario. She must have forgotten. Suzie forgets things when she drinks.

"Mario." He had a strong Italian accent.

"Well, Marrrio." She rolled her r's. Batted her eyelids and put her right elbow onto the table. It slipped off. She tried again and before it could slide she rested her chin neatly in the palm of her right hand to keep the arm in place. She batted her eyelids some more and smiled a weird sort of lecherous smile, very un-Suzie like.

"Me and my friend, Linda here, have been admiring your bum the whole night. Ever since we came in here in fact. We both agree that it is the best thing by far that we have seen tonight. Pity it's not on the menu. We were just wondering what your service was like?" Suzie was making a show of herself and me. The assertiveness classes and the wine were all speaking together.

"Qui, madam?" Mario started speaking French or Italian or something.

"We – that – is – my – friend – Linda – and – I – have – been – invited – to – a – classy – party – and – we – would – like – you – to – come – with – us," Suzie said very slowly, using a lot of pointing and arm movements. Miming. A touch of the Marcel Marceau school of English. She was cooing and purring. I think she was trying to speak pidgin English. Was this my friend Suzie? The shy retiring friend I confided in? I think not. This was an altogether different Suzie, brainwashed by course after course of aggressiveness, positive mental attitude and blatant randyness, it would appear. I couldn't believe that Suzie was picking up the waiter. Not physically granted but nothing would surprise me.

"I would be delighted, madam."

I didn't like the way he called her 'madam'. Like she was a madam if you know what I mean. Suzie was chuffed with herself.

"Yes! Yes!" She punched the air with her fist.

She was delighted. "I have just fulfilled one of my lifelong ambitions, Linda. I have chatted up a fella and asked him out. I feel wonderful. Yes. Yes. I did it." She was truly delighted and kept telling everyone. The couple beside us said they were delighted that she was delighted. They didn't look it. I thought Suzie'd never shut up. Shit, she was drunk.

"You did it all right, Suzie. What are we going to do with him now? You're a married woman and I'm nearly sure I am too."

"Mario!" Suzie called. "Who you like? Me or my friend?"

Jesus, Suzie was letting him have his pick of the two of us. She was having a brainstorm.

"Both you." Mario was a cute whore.

"Hava youa the amigo?" Suzie my friend obviously didn't want to share. What's yours is mine and what's mine is my own. She was definitely having a brain-attack and trying to speak Italian.

"I have Antonio friend. In kitchen, " Mario said.

"Bring on Antonio friend!" Suzie stood up beckoning to the closed kitchen door. I kept out of it. Didn't say a word. I couldn't. My whole jaw had gone numb with the wine.

"Antonio!" Mario shouted.

A massive Clooney came out of the kitchen. All man. Dark hair, dark eyes, dark.

"Mario, what do you want?" he rasped. Dark, velvety voice. Suzie and me drooled again.

"Ladies want you for a party." Mario was pointing from Suzie to me.

"Well, ladies, where's the party?" Antonio was even better-looking close up. He took my hand. I melted. A fireworks display started in my head. I was sure Antonio's surname was Banderas.

"A friend of mine is having a party – do you want to come? It should be a great night. Everyone who's anyone will be there." Suzie was doing all the talking. She was talking bullshit.

I couldn't talk. I was thinking. Thinking, 'Oh shit'.

"I'll come if I can take this brilliant piece of womanhood with me." He was pointing directly at me. Moi. He was taking the piss. Not by any stretch of the imagination could I be called a piece. But I appreciated his trying. I wanted to protest. I opened my mouth, at least my brain instructed my mouth to open. Nothing happened. The fireworks had moved from my head. They were exploding somewhere lower down.

"Ah ha!" Antonio pointed at me again. "You have numb lips and jaw? I have the perfect cure."

It dawned on me that Antonio wasn't Italian. He was Irish.

"He has a great cure for your problem," Mario confided. "He used to suffer from the same thing himself. He invented a cure. It's fantastic. You'll be speaking in a second – wait until you see."

Was it the drink or had Mario lost his Italian accent too? I needed desperately to check his bum to see if that was false. But I couldn't ask him to turn around. My mouth wouldn't work.

"Mario," Suzie whispered, "your Italian accent has vanished into the night. Give us a look to see if your bum has gone the same way. Let's see if you have an Irish bum. Wide and weird." We were both pleased to see that he still had the same tight Italian rear end.

Antonio came back from the kitchen. He was waving goodbye to all the happy customers who were leaving the restaurant fuller but poorer. He had a milky-like drink in his hand and he put it in front of me. I almost expected white smoke to rise up out of the glass. But it didn't. I checked out Antonio's smile. Looking for two very long teeth. Well, you never know. Vampires take on all kinds of disguises and it was dark outside. His teeth were all smooth, straight, square and white. Like a row in a crossword puzzle. Perhaps a bit too straight, methinks. Could they be false? I hoped not. I had a dread of kissing someone with false teeth. I always imagined that just as I got stuck in their teeth would also get stuck in. In my mouth. I would be left with the grinniest grin of all. Esther Ranson would sue. I'd have four lots of teeth. A two-up two-down mouth so to speak. Imagine the polishing and flossing on that lot. I know they could be removed. I also I know for a fact that they would not be removed immediately. Anything that embarrassing and hideous to me would take at least a week to set right. And if the 'Shit Here' sign was fully illuminated, showing the flashing arrow, pointing directly over my head it would take at least two to three weeks. I would have to go from doctor to doctor, they would pontificate on the importance of oral hygiene and would pass me on to a toothy specialist, and he in turn would send me to the hospital. There I would have to suffer through the humiliation of explaining my denture dilemma to every nurse, porter and brain surgeon in the building. Maybe it would be best if I went straight to a dentist or indeed a plumber. A plumber could tap into my problem immediately, sink all his resources into it, use his plunger to suck the extra set from my jaws. In fact I don't know who I'd go to. I made a mental note to find out. It could be valuable knowledge for future reference.

"Now you must close your eyes." Antonio held my hand. A goose walked over my grave. A whole gaggle of them in fact. "Don't look at the glass," he instructed. "I will put it in your hand. You must drink it all in one go. Knock it back."

My face was totally numb by now. I couldn't blink or smile. I tried to nod but my neck wouldn't let me. I was prepared to take the drink even if it was poison. I was prepared to let this stranger, albeit a very, very, very handsome stranger, give me some hemlock or other. For all I knew this could be a wicked ploy from a wicked boy. Mario and Antonio could have millions of women locked in the basement. All these women could have one thing in common – numb lips and face. In their dire need for a cure these women could have taken the drink I was about to take. When these poor dumb, numb women had taken the chalky drink the boys would have their wicked way with them. Then throw them in the cellar. Visit them from time to time. Instead of the drink removing the numbness it might freeze it totally. Even after the alcohol had worn off they might be left numb. Rightly numbed. Numbed all over for the rest of their lives. Unable to scream for help. Unable to eat yet able to smell the aroma of all the culinary delights being cooked above them. Absolute torture. Then the boys would visit for other delights. Did I want to join these poor, half-starved, numb delightful women? I still had a choice, I could say no. Well, I couldn't. I couldn't actually speak. But I could shake my head. Well, actually, I couldn't do that either. So I had no choice. I felt I was going into a coma anyway. One way or the other I was doomed. Fecked if I took the drink and fecked if I didn't.

I tried to close my eyes as instructed. No luck. They were, after all, numb. I sat staring. A foolish grimace on my face. Like someone holding in a fart at a function.

Antonio put the glass into my hand.

I knocked the drink back.

It burnt the mouth off me.

It burnt the throat off me.

Finally, it burnt the innards off me. Lethal with the fireworks.

Had I had a fire alarm inside it would have been ding-donging merrily on high. Two units of the fire brigade would have been dispatched. Gallons of water wasted on my flaming gizzards. Suddenly, it all settled. No need for an extinguisher. I felt great. I blinked. I pouted and smiled (not at the same time). I turned my head right then left. I think my head could go around even further than it could before. Not all the way, thank God, but well over each shoulder. I don't think that's quite normal but it was a great achievement.

"Thanks." Words were inadequate but I tried.

Suzie was astounded. She had often suffered from my not being able to speak to her after I had consumed a few beverages. She was always left talking to herself of an evening. I always sat grinning at her making gestures of conversation. She was delighted with the suddenness of the cure.

"What was that?" Suzie pounced on Antonio. "It's terrific stuff. Can I have the recipe? This will have a very positive effect on my life. Do you understand the importance of this cure, Antonio? It must be worth a fortune. We could market it. We would be overnight millionaires." She started rooting in her velvet bag for a biro and page.

"I can't give you the ingredients of the mixture. It's a secret."

Later, as we waited on the steps for the lads to lock up, Suzie told me to worm the recipe out of Antonio.

"Find out what was in that mixture, Linda," she said as she pulled me towards her. She was wearing her long white trench coat. The collar was up and she was peering all around as she spoke. She leaned forward and grabbed my arm, looking over her shoulder as she spoke. "Do anything he asks, Linda, anything. Just make sure you get that recipe."

Mission Impossible. I watched, open-mouthed, waiting for my pal Suzie to self-destruct.

CHAPTER TEN

We flagged down a taxi and headed across town to the party. I felt a bit weird. Guilty I suppose. I desperately wanted to go to the party, in fact I needed to go, but I knew I shouldn't. It was like sneaking a bit of chocolate during Lent and convincing myself it wasn't sweets. Antonio was very attentive. You know, insisting on opening the taxi door for me and paying the fare. That only made me feel worse. I knew I was using him. It was strange to be on the other side of the fence. Me using someone. It didn't feel half as good as I had thought it would.

The party was a house-warming of a friend of a friend of someone Suzie worked with. She knocked on the door and we got in when she mentioned the bookshop. I expected a lot of bookish people all discussing the latest publications, talking about genres and all the Johns: Banville, McGahern, Le Carré. I was trying desperately to remember the last book I had read. Paul Wilson's *The Little Book of Calm*. 'Millions Will Envy You' was the title of one of his many little wiseisms. It had stuck in my mind. "No matter what your circumstance or position, millions would give anything to be in that same position." Not my position they wouldn't, I thought. I am the exception that proves Mr Wilson's little rule. Unless of course someone wanted to be guaranteed lots of toil and suffering in this life in order to be sure of endless rewards and pleasures in the next. After all my suffering on this earth, I was guaranteed a really wonderful place in the next life. I would be exalted then. Too feckin' late. Come to think of it, I thought, maybe that's another con job. Maybe this is it. All there is. After all the rot there is nothing to look forward to, only rotting away. No, God could not be that cruel. I really did need to calm down. Thoughts like that could damage a person. Calm. Think calm. Poor ol' Mr Wilson had met his match in me. His advice 'to strive to appreciate the positive aspect of your life' is all very well if you can find one. I looked, honestly I searched high up and low down for positive anythings in my life. I came up empty. There are none. Calm was out for me. It was just as well because I don't think I could have handled any new emotion at this time.

I needn't have bothered racking my brains for titles. Nobody cared what I had read recently or indeed if I even could read. I doubted the literacy of any of the party-goers. The room was in semi-darkness. Candles and dimmer switches. Muted yellow paint on the walls added to the glow. There was very little furniture. A big, deep, soft couch was covered in yellow and orange throws and cushions. Bright coloured bean bags were scattered all around the place. Either the guy was big into the minimalist theme or was broke. I suspected broke. Then again I suspected everyone.

All the guests were younger than me. Much. All wrapped around each other in group gropes. Bodies were everywhere, all looking like the socks in my house lying around in pairs, but odd pairs. This was a party for free spirits. Vodka, whiskey, gin. Ramona, Tuesday, Zen. All well on the way to being drunk – trying to forget their names no doubt. It was the first party I had been to without Dick in twenty years. Except of course the odd hen party.

But then aren't all hen parties odd? They don't

count as real parties. Not one member of the opposite sex. Just loads of giggly girls wishing the latest sucker well. Plying her with gifts of underwear, crotchless lacy black knickers she would never wear, suspenders two sizes too small, red bras with black lace and more than its fair share of lift-and-separate techniques. Chocolate willies she would never eat – well, I assume they are never eaten. Maybe some girls do, some girls don't. And fruity flavoured, super-sensitive condoms with ridges that that would never see the light of day. All the materials needed for the nocturnal hobby the bride was about to embark on. Legally.

The highlight of these parties was always a strippergram. Always a let-down. The stripper strutting his stuff was never the well-built sexy young hunk you had imagined. The stuff that they strutted was always less exotic and over much quicker than you would have thought possible. They never ever did the full Monty. This was a particular bone of contention with me because I was always on the quest of comparing wobbly bits. I was always disappointed at hen nights. The wannabe stud always got the would-be bride's name wrong. They sang congratulations to Irene at my friend Imelda's hen night and Anita at Annette's so I guessed that there was some logical reason for this. I couldn't see it but then again I wasn't a stud or logical. They never got the name of the girl who was to pay them wrong. An even more logical reason for that I suppose.

There was plenty of drink at the literary party. Antonio assured me that the effects of his cure would last for a long time. I could drink without anything going numb. I made the most of it but I suspected the cure hadn't reached my brain yet. Because it was most definitely gone way, way beyond numb – in fact it was dead. I was glad I was suffering from dead-brain syndrome. That way I could not be held accountable for my actions.

"Dance with me?" Antonio asked.

"But nobody is dancing." My brain may have been in a state of rigor mortis but at least it still knew enough to warn me, in no uncertain terms, that I was not the right age or in possession of the right figure or faculty for an exhibitionist.

"Does it matter? Pretend we are the only two people in the room." Antonio, of the young muscular body and bulging pecs, had an answer for everything.

"Unfortunately, it does and we're not." I looked around me at the bodies lying on the couch and floor. Antonio and me were the only two humans that were still standing. We were also the only two that were fully clothed and able to stay in an upright position. Apart from Suzie of course and some fella she was talking to.

"You must dance with me," Antonio insisted. I like a man who takes the lead. Antonio had a strange way of looking at me. Like he liked me. It was a whole new experience for me.

"When I finish this drink I might dance." I took a large slug from the glass. No, not a snail type of slug. A big mouthful type. Had there been a real slug in my drink I would have run out the door immediately ringing a bell and shouting unclean, unclean. So it's a pity there wasn't a dirty big garden-variety slug in the glass. That way I would, by now, have been tucked up, in the safety of my own home. Curled up in bed. Alone. Again. I poured myself another drink. Any minute now I was going to be dancing around the bodies like a bloody fool. Showing my age and my state of being. Ah, what the hell! Dick was far away in Crete acting like a kid and the kids were off acting their age somewhere else so why couldn't I act their age as well?

I looked for Suzie. I wanted her to talk sense to me. She was talking sense to some fella she worked with. He was all brown corduroy and check. In fact, he looked a bit staid and out of place. Suzie did too. I think she had sobered up and was regretting coming to the party at all. But it was her idea. They came over to me.

"Linda," Suzie said, "I'm not sure this was such a good idea. I think we should go home. Ken said he'll give us a lift now if we want."

"And who is Ken when he's at home?" I knew there was an edge to my voice. I couldn't help it. She was hellbent on spoiling my fun. Well, what was supposed to be fun.

"Hi, I'm Ken," the staid sober-looking fella introduced himself. "I work with Suzie. We've done one or two courses together as well. You must be Linda. I've heard all about you."

A lot of people had heard a lot about me. Lately.

"Hi, Ken," I said. "Suzie's told me all about you too. I assume it's all true." Ken smiled a boyish grin. Suzie had indeed mentioned a Ken to me. I had got the impression that he was seventy-five years old and given to wearing string vests and braces. Suzie had lied. I wondered why?

"Come on, Linda. Ken'll give us a lift home," Suzie said again. "I think we should leave. I don't like it. It's gone a bit weird." She looked around the room, taking everything in. The couple in the corner lying on top of each other. The girl was being the dominant partner. On top of him. Her tights were in a roll around her ankles. Like some sort of bondage apparatus. She was still wearing her high-heeled shoes. Her top was pulled up over her boobs that were hanging down like two plucked turkeys waiting for Christmas. The fella underneath her was hidden. His face buried in her turkeys. Another fellow was staggering around in the middle of the floor, like a two-year-old. A bottle of vodka stuck in his mouth. There was a group standing by the door chanting something about love conquering everything. Give them time, I thought. They'll learn. Love never conquers the bills or puts food on the table. Maybe love wasn't all it was cracked up to be.

"Come on, Linda." Suzie was close to tears. "Let's go now while we have the chance of a lift with the only sober person in the room. Ken hasn't been drinking. Come on, Linda. Please let's go home."

"God, Suzie, you're such a kill-joy. What's wrong with you? It's all very well for you, you have a home to go home to. What have I? My home is empty. My life is empty. At least here I feel alive like somebody wants to talk to me, listen to me even."

"Are you sure that's all he wants?" Suzie asked

"You could come back to my house for a cup of tea and a chat. We could ask Ken too."

"There's plenty to drink here, Suzie, and Antonio is chatting to me very nicely thanks. Please, Suzie, I can talk to you tomorrow. Please, please, Suz, stay. This is important to me. Nobody knows who I am here. I love it, I'm anonymous. I love being anonymous with Antonio. Where's the harm in a little dance?"

"It's what will happen after the dance that I'm worried about. That's why I want you to come home, Linda. I thought this party would be full of people our age, having a bit of a sing-song and a dance. I thought we could have a bit of fun and then go home. But they're all just drunk and on the verge of an orgy. I don't feel comfortable. It's all very fine for the rest of them but we're married women, Linda. If Bill knew I was here he'd kill me and everyone else in the room. He would go ape, throwing these puny little bodies all around the place. Jesus, Linda, he'll kill me if he ever finds out. Let's go home."

"I won't tell. Anyway, I'm not going. You can do what you like. You're so staid sometimes. I'm not going back to that empty house or empty bed for that matter. I'm enjoying myself. Where's Mario gone?"

"He's with some bimbo or other over there in the corner telling her that he's a doctor. I think she actually believes him."

"Well, why don't you talk to Ken? Live a little, Suzie! Put your positive mental attitude into practice and make the most of the evening." Suzie was becoming such a stick-in-the-mud.

I could see Antonio coming back from the loo. He was talking to a brassy young girl in a bright red topless dress. It was very short and very tight. She was wearing black platform boots, suede and leather patches. An interesting combination. Her long white-blonde hair was arranged like a veil over her face. She kept blowing at it through the corner of her mouth. She was going for the windswept and interesting look. She had a figure that could only have been achieved by corsets and Wonderbras. Everything pushed in and up. Her legs went all the way up to her neck. I felt a pang of jealousy. I wished Suzie would leave me alone and go and talk to someone else. She looked very pissed off. I knew she would piss Antonio off. Lucky for me Ken went over to get his jacket and started rattling his keys and making his goodbyes to his friends.

"You'd better go over and tell Ken that we don't need a lift. Unless of course you want to leave me here all by myself," I told Suzie.

"I wouldn't be so worried if I thought you'd stay by yourself!" Suzie's tone was bitchy.

She smiled a weird sort of smile, showing no teeth and stormed over to Ken. I saw him put his arm on her shoulder and sympathise with her. I knew Suzie was giving him the full story about my vulnerable state, about my life being rotten and me not being compost mentis. He started shaking his head slowly from side to side, tapping Suzie on the back and looking over at me. He took off his jacket. It looked like he was going to stay. He didn't look too upset and seemed to enjoy being Suzie's confidant. Lapping it up, in fact. I left them to it and went over to Antonio and the lady in red.

I put my arm around Antonio's waist, stretched up on my tippy-toes and whispered into his ear, "What about that dance now?" The moment of jealousy had made me brave and daring. I took him by the hand and led him away into the middle of the floor. He wrapped his big strong arms around me and held me tight. I put my head on his big strong chest and my arms around his waist, resting on his lower back. Just about then the fireworks started going off in my head again. Multicoloured, vibrant lights, flashing. It was bliss. Better than any other display I had ever seen. Then again I'd only ever seen one fireworks display in my life. It was on the weekend before Patrick's Day, down on the quays in Dublin. Me and the kids went. Dick stayed home to watch it on telly. Crowds of us gathered from all over to ooh and aah! It was brilliant. But this was even better. My own private display and this time a fine hunk of a man was holding me.

Since Dick left I had ached for someone to hold me. Touch me. But Dick was in Crete. My need to be held grew stronger as the days passed until it became a physical hurt. I was in pain. Antonio wasn't getting rid of my pain but he was trying. I liked it. No one had ever bothered trying before. He made me feel vulnerable. He started to stroke my hair. I hoped the mousse and grease combination wouldn't put him off. He leant back and I lifted my head. We looked at each other. It was magic. Like what you see all the time in films but never ever happens in reality. Well, it was happening to me. This was real. I could see my reflection in his dark, dark eyes. He smiled. I could see myself smiling back. I pulled his body towards me, nestled in again tight against his chest. I could smell the freshness of his white shirt mixing with the Hugo Boss. I felt the steamy warmth of him, the heaving of his chest and the pounding of his heart. His handsomeness was overpowering. I was heady. I knew he was going to want more of a fling than a fling around the floor. I didn't care. I was content, bordering on happy. This was second-best and I was happy to settle for it. Why change the habit of a lifetime? He held me tight. Electricity flowed through me. My body ached for him to touch me. I nestled in tight against him. He took my hand and interlaced it between his fingers. He held it softly against his chest. Slowly, softly his hands moved over my breasts. I felt like a woman again. Like this was the first time. I felt my nipples harden. Thanks be to God everything seemed to be in working order. I wriggled slightly to let his hands fit neatly around my boobs. Thank God he had big hands. I suspected he had big everything. He was an expert. Knew exactly what to do. For one fleeting moment I wondered how many others had there been. With Dick I was the only one. Was I still the only one? I wanted Dick, I wanted Antonio, I wanted someone, anyone. Antonio was there. My eyes were closed and the room was black. Inside my head was on fire. I slid my two hands down into the arch of his back. Tucked my hands in under the waistband of his 501s. I felt his flesh. It was smooth and soft. Not like a baby's. Stronger. Muscular. We moved very little, just swayed.

Toni Braxton was singing 'Unbreak My Heart'.

Not in person, it was only a CD. Then again she could have been giving it loads on the floor and I wouldn't have noticed. I wondered would Antonio have noticed her though? I hoped not. I wanted Antonio to unbreak my heart. I was lusting for him. I wanted him to kiss me. I started singing along with Toni. Antonio lifted his head; automatically I lifted mine. He bent down towards me. For a moment time stopped, we stood still, then I kissed him. Holy shit, I kissed him. Not a kiss of love but of lust. I put my hands around the back of his head in through his black silky hair and pulled him hard against me. His hands were all over my body. I was like an animal on heat. Unleashed. I felt his hot tongue touching mine. Rolling around. I wanted him, all of him. In a frenzy I was devouring him. We pulled away for air and looked at each other. I could feel the tears roll down my face. He wiped them away and then kissed my lips again. It was magic. I was dizzy. He was wild, uncontrolled. His hands ran all over my body. He felt every inch of me. I could feel every bit of my body tingle against every bulge of his. I wanted to stand before him naked. Never a thought for the cellulite or stretch-marks. I didn't care. I could feel him breathing hard against my neck, kissing it, biting it softly. Running his tongue along the side of my chin. Finding my mouth again. I marvelled that worthless ol' me had made this happen to a vibrant, handsome man. I wanted more. I wanted everything he could give me.

"Antonio," I whispered his name.

"Linda, let's leave here now. Come back with me to my place. It's years since I have felt like this. Do you believe in love at first sight?"

"Maybe. I don't know." Love, lust did it matter?

"Come back home with me, please!"

He bent and kissed me again. Not soft, gentle loving kisses but devouring, hard loving kisses. I loved it. Rockets and sparklers all exploded together.

Please God, don't let this be a dream. If it is, let me stay in it till the end. The climax.

I reached down and opened a button of his 501s. My fingers found a second button. I popped it open. He was breathing hard. I was breathing hard. Everything about him was hard.

"Ma! For fuck sake what are you doing?"

I nearly jumped out of my tingling old skin.

Carl was shouting at me. Pulling me by the shoulder.

Please God let this be a dream.

"Carl." I barely got the word out of my mouth or my hand out of Antonio's fly. I couldn't believe it. Of all the parties in all the world Carl had to walk into mine.

"Who the fuck are you?" Antonio was having none of it and this was no dream.

"Get the fuck off my mother, you horny bastard!" Carl was shouting and pushing Antonio in the chest. His beautiful broad chest.

Toni Braxton stopped singing. Her heart taking second place to the entertainment I was providing. All the bohemian types stood around. Gaping.

"Carl. Carl. Carl." I was only capable of the one word. So I kept repeating it over and over. I could feel the tears again. The floodgates opened. I started to wrack and sob in front of everyone. Carl of course thought it was because Antonio was attacking me and started poking and prodding him in the shoulders again.

"Do you hear me? Get your fucking hands off my Ma, you big bastard!" Carl was purple in the face. Veins popping all over his forehead and neck.

Antonio dropped his hand from my waist. Tried to defuse the situation. He tried to block Carl's punches. I was terrified. Carl looked deranged.

"Who the fuck do you think you are? Come on, big boy, let's see what you're made of!" Carl was ranting and raving. He curled his two hands up in front of his face and started flaying more punches.

He is not very good at boxing so he only succeeded in looking foolish. I felt sorry for him. He was trying to defend his mother's honour. Just as she was about to give it away for nothing.

"Carl, it's all right. This is a friend of mine." Well, after all that touching and feeling he was, sort of.

"A very close friend it looks like!" Carl was having none of it.

"Carl, this is Antonio – he is a good friend of your dad and me." Well, I was in a sticky situation. If lying could get me out of it, I'd lie.

"This is your son? You have a son who is this old?" Poor Antonio couldn't take it all in.

"Who the fuck is he, Ma? What about Da?" Carl kept asking questions. I wished he'd shut up.

The party-goers were standing around us. Forming a circle. Anticipating a great show. Waiting for blood to be spilt. I hoped it wouldn't be Carl's. Or Antonio's.

"Shut up, the pair of you!" Suzie came to the rescue. "Can't you see you're upsetting Linda."

Staid Ken physically stood between Carl and Antonio.

Carl calmed down a bit but was still dangerously close to killing someone. I knew exactly who it would be. So did Antonio. He stood well behind Ken.

"Who the fuck is he?" Carl was pointing over Ken's shoulders at Antonio. If points could kill, Antonio would have dropped down dead.

"He's a waiter in a restaurant," Suzie said.

"No, I'm not! I own a top-class Italian restaurant!" Antonio was indignant.

"He owns the restaurant Suzie and me had a meal in earlier on. He went to school with your dad. We go back a long way. He was only saying hi. Being friendly." I tried to rescue the situation and my good name.

"Too fucking friendly by the looks of it! Oh God, Ma, you were all over him! What's got into you? You're behaving like a slut. You're supposed to be my mother! Mothers don't do things like that even with family friends. Do they, Suzie?"

"Of course they do. All the time. Lighten up, will you, Carl!" Suzie turned from Carl to Antonio. "Dick will be delighted we met you. We'll be sure to tell him." She reached over to shake hands with Antonio and at the same time drag her best pal out of the swamp I was drowning in. Thank God for Suzie.

"Who the fuck is Dick?" Antonio had to spoil it. Open his beautiful big mouth.

"You know Dick. The one you went to school with?" Suzie said winking her eye and nodding her

222

head at the same time. She looked like someone with a very serious medical complaint.

"My husband," I whispered.

"Let's hear it for Dick!" Some smart Alec in the crowd shouted. Everyone cheered and clapped.

"You are married?" Antonio was looking around, inching his way away from me, waiting for the husband to make a grand entrance.

"Yes, she bleedin' well is married! She's married to my da! You bollocks!" Carl was at the pointing again.

"You have a husband? First a son. Now a husband. Why not bring out the whole bloody family?" Antonio was not making this easy.

"You remember Dick? You knew him as Richard," Suzie said keeping up the twitching and blinking. Overdoing it a bit in fact but I was eternally grateful to her yet again.

I linked my handsome son and moved as far away from Antonio as I could. Poor Antonio was left scratching his head, staring after me, wondering what had happened. The crowd rallied around him, clapping him on the back and congratulating him on his conquest.

"I'm sorry, Carl," I said. It sounded feeble. But I was truly sorry. Sorry that he had seen me on the verge of whoring about with an Italian impostor but I was not sorry for wanting to. That was Dick's fault.

"Come here, Ma." Carl put his arms around me and for the first time in years I heard him cry. There is nothing as pathetic as seeing a young man cry. It is even more pathetic if the young man is your son and you are the cause of his tears.

"Is dad coming home at all?" he asked.

"Yes." I was sure. "Soon."

"Do you want him to?" My son can be very perceptive and wise.

"Yes. I think I do. I can't let twenty years be wasted. What was the point of it all if I don't make the most of it when he comes back?"

"You know me and Chloe are all right, don't you? We want you to be happy. We'll go along with whatever you decide. We don't know what to do. Half the time we wish he'd come back. The rest of the time we wish he'd stay as far away as possible. We know he was mean to you sometimes. I tried to stop him. Chloe and me talked it over with him a few days before he left. Chloe thinks it's her fault he's gone. She had a right go at him. She asked him if he ever hit you. She kept on and on at him. Shouting that she had seen bruises and that if she ever found out that he had hit you she'd kill him with her bare hands. I told her she was crazy. I said we'd know if he hit you. We would. Wouldn't we, Ma? You'd tell us? If he ever does, if anyone ever touches you, Jesus, Ma, I'd kill them myself. Do you think that Da left because me and Chloe had a row with him? I'm sorry if we chased him away. We didn't mean it. I feel so bad. We were only trying to help. Maybe me and Chloe shouldn't have interfered. It's hard to sit around and do nothing. Maybe we should have. You always say we're good at doing nothing."

"You know I don't mean it," I said, shaken. "You and Chloe were right to do what you did if you felt you needed to. You're all grown up now, Carl. You have to make your own decisions. I do love your dad though. Sometimes I don't like him very much. Now and again he flies off the handle but he doesn't mean to. He's always sorry after. He never really hit me. I hope he comes back soon."

Out of the corner of my eye I spotted Antonio. Suzie had had a good chat with him. He was staring at me, smiling. He looked a bit forlorn. He smiled again and winked and I knew there and then everything was going to be all right. I could rely on him to keep tonight our little secret. Carl put his arms around me.

"Would you like to dance with your son?"

"I'd love to." And I did.

"Em, em –" Some woman was hovering. Trying

to interrupt this mother-and-son bonding time. I ignored her. Carl was holding me, swaying, rubbing me on the back, telling me that everything was going to be fine. I was doing the same for him.

"Em, em –" The tall leggy woman in a black skirt and black strapless top showing more than her fair share of skin and cleavage was still trying to edge her way in. She kept looking at me, smiling. I gave her a dirty look. Even under all her make-up I guessed she was thirtyish. She had long chestnut hair. A colour that was enhanced with bottles and sachets. She had the greenest eyes I have ever seen. She was a stunner. Carl saw her. His face lit up. He reached away from me and put his arm around her. He kept smiling at her.

"Ma, this is Kyrstie." He was delighted with himself.

"Kyrstie?" I was back to the one-word sentences.

"Hi," Kyrstie said.

Suzie came over to make sure everything was all right.

"Kyrstie?" I said again. I turned to Suzie and introduced them. "Kyrstie," I said pointing.

Suzie, the Judas, put her hand out and shook hands with Kyrstie.

"Hi, Kyrstie." Suzie at least was able to use two words. Then again this was not her crisis.

"Hi, Kyrstie, I'm Ken. I work with Suzie." Even the unknown Ken was able to form a sentence. Everyone was acting grown-up and articulate except me.

"Kyrstie?" I asked again.

"Ma, what was really going on with that guy?" Carl asked.

Even if I wanted to tell Carl that his mother had a human need for some adult passion and affection I certainly wasn't going to in front of this Kyrstie person. This very old Kyrstie person.

"Nothing at all. I just gave him a little kiss because we hadn't seen one another for so long. That's all, no big deal. You know the way it is?" I was getting irritated. I was sorry I wouldn't be able to see Antonio ever again. I was surprised by myself. I really liked the Italian impostor. I might never see him again.

"Whew, I thought for a minute that you'd picked someone up, Ma. Stupid, eh? But none of my friends ever kiss me like that."

Mine neither, I thought. I wished Antonio would walk up and sweep me up off my feet and carry me off into the sunset. Or anywhere else for that matter. As soon as I wished it I felt two inches tall even in Chloe's six-inch heels. I felt like a heel. I had lied to Carl and he had believed me. Because I was his mother. Children can be fierce gullible: Santa Claus, tooth fairies and long-lost friends. But what about this Kyrstie business?

"Is this the woman you were telling me about?" I whispered to Carl, foolishly hoping it was his girlfriend's mother or aunt or even grandmother – she was old enough to be any one of them. I was grasping at straws. The way they looked at each other could mean only one thing. I didn't like it. What did she want with my child? She was too old for him. This old person was the woman Carl thought he was going to spend the rest of his life with. Fat chance if I had my way. All my animal instincts were now centred on a new target, far away from the passion of sex and directly to the passion of murder. Like a lion defending her cub, my claws were out. But this woman was no naïve eighteen-year-old. I would have to be careful. Subtlety was going to be the keyword here.

"Isn't Kyrstie divine?" Carl asked me.

Divine? Divine? What sort of a word was that for a chunk of a man like Carl to be using. I had never heard him use 'divine' before. Next he would be calling her pet and asking was she warm enough. This was worse than I had feared.

Carl turned to Krystie and put his arm around her waist. "How are you for a drink, pet?" he asked. "I hope it isn't too chilly in here for you?" he added. Who was this person? Where had he put my son? The one who would never ask you had you a mouth on you even if you were in the desert sporting a tongue made of sandpaper.

"How are you?" the Kyrstie person rudely interrupted my thoughts. "Carl has told me all about you."

Was everyone being told everything about me? Was there anyone left out there that didn't know all about me?

"I'm fine, thanks." As fine as any mother could be in my situation thank you very much, cradle-robber. "I hope it was all good." I gave the usual reply.

"Carl told me you and his dad were going through a bit of a rough patch. I've been helping him get over it. Giving him a bit of moral support and a shoulder to cry on," Kyrstie said.

The bitch. Who the hell did she think she was, adding to my rough patch. Turning it into a rough field. If Carl was going to cry on anyone's shoulder it would be his mother's. After all, he had been whingeing into it now for eighteen years without complaint. At this stage I am a veritable sponge.

"That's very kind of you but I'm sure Carl is fine," I said as pleasantly as I could between clenched teeth to the child-snatcher.

"Yes but he needs someone to talk to. I am there for him. You don't have to worry. He confides in me." Kyrstie rubbed my arm in a consoling, condescending way as she spoke.

The little usurper. Usurping my authority and taking over my role. Letting Carl confide in her. Being there for him. Who the hell did she think she was? His mother? She may have been old enough but it would be a long time before I would be relinquishing my most favourite post. She was talking again. On and on.

"Carl has told me everything. You know, about his dad disappearing out of the blue to find himself. I think it's splendid. It's wonderful that you have the sort of relationship that allows you both a bit of space from time to time. When your husband comes back he will be whole again. All the stale dead wood of your relationship will be burnt out."

What was she on about? Barbecues and bonfires? There was no stale wood in my relationship and if there was I would, at this very moment, be using it to burn this Kyrstie one at the stake. Was she for real? What else had Big-mouth told her?

"Oh. Yes. Carl's dad is just taking a bit of a break," I said trying not to let my annoyance show in my voice. "He'll be back in a few days. You must come to the house for a meal when he returns. He'd love to meet you, I'm sure." It'll be enough to send him packing to some other hole in the world. I tried my best to sound civil. "We must have a lot in common, us being near enough in age." I failed.

"That's great. I'd love that." As she spoke she turned to Carl. She looked at him as though he were a god. She kept touching him. Nowhere in particular. Just tapping and rubbing his arm and hand. It was sickening. Acting as if she loved him.

"Carl and I would love to take you out for a drink one night. Take you out of yourself. Wouldn't we, Carl?"

"Yeah. Ma, that would be great."

"I'd like that." In a pig's eye but for Carl's sake I had to be nice. I knew if they took me out of myself the danger would be I would never go back to myself again. Wouldn't I be the right eejit if I did? Once I had been taken out of myself there would be no going back. 'Way hey!' I would shout as I made my escape and 'Thanks a bunch for taking me out of that horrible self and now I'm out I might just as well bugger off and stay well well out of myself for many a long while, thank you very much indeedy'.

"We'll do it then. Maybe next week?" Carl was enthusiastic. God help him.

"Well, let's see how the week goes then we can

arrange something. How come you're here, anyway, Carl?" I said. Upsetting your mother and wrecking my fun and momentary oblivion.

"Kyrstie's friend is a friend of the guy throwing the party. So we decided to give it a try. We don't know many people here though," he said.

I might have guessed that the Kyrstie person was responsible for spoiling my fun and ruining my family. She would definitely have to go. But when? That was the key question. How soon would I be able to get rid of her? And how? Could I put something in her drink? Slip her a Mickey Finn. If I knew what a Mickey Finn was I might do that. I wonder would Suzie know how to make a Mickey Finn? Even if she did I couldn't have asked her. Suzie was in deep conversation with Ken. I only just noticed that Ken was in fact a Clooney. Antonio would have known how to make a Mickey Finn. Where was he when I needed him?

I could of course frighten her off. Tell her horrendous stories about Carl. Invent tales of him having such a hairy back that we had to shave it twice a day. But then there was the danger that she may have already seen his back. She looked like the type of person that had seen more than just his back. I'd say she sussed out the goods long before she made the purchase.

I should know how to get rid of her. Hadn't I been thinking of murder for days now? I had come up with some great ideas. Foolproof. Every time I thought of Dick I thought of a terrific way to kill him, just as soon as he came home. Some were a bit too drastic to use on this Kyrstie person, like the reaching down into her throat and hauling out all her innards and stomping them into the ground. Anyway she looked like she had a thin neck and it would be very messy. Lots of cleaning up for me. I didn't think Carl would help. No, it would be best to reserve that 'hands on' one for Dick. I needed to set up a killing with very little chance of my being caught. I didn't want Carl to blame me when his new girlfriend's body was found. Well, actually his new but aged girlfriend.

I had thought of hundreds of plots. Now when I needed to remember them I could only remember one. The best one. The Ruth Rendell of murders. The one I had decided was sure-fire guaranteed to work without any asparagus being cast in my direction. I was going to re-wire the plug on the hedge-trimmers. Shock Dick into oblivion. Then swear blind to the police that before Dick went out to cut the hedge he had changed the plug on the electric saw himself. I would confide in the police that Dick was no good at DIY. This would be said through the valley of tears of the grieving widow. I would relate how I had begged and pleaded with him not to change the plug, how he knew nothing about plugs. There was only one problem. How in God's name was I going to get this tart Kyrstie to offer to cut our hedge? And even if she did offer wouldn't my thicko of a son offer to help? I'd have to discuss this with Suzie in greater depth. I would have to enlist help.

Maybe Oprah or Sally or Ricki would cover the 'My son has an older girlfriend' subject tomorrow. I would make sure to have a notebook and pen beside me all day in case one of them said anything useful. I had been waiting for days for the 'My husband went off to find himself' programme. It had never aired.

A huge number of people with every variety of problem make appearances on these programmes. Yet, not once had any of my problems been discussed by any one of them. The guests on the shows are usually led to the slaughter. Wolves in sheep's clothing. They must be paid. Particularly the ones who go for the make-over. Want to get rid of the sheep's clothing. Jenny Jones is the lady for them. People come on complaining about the state of their friends or partners and Jenny waves her magic wand. Frumpy, lumpy, friends sit whingeing.

"My friend is an exotic dancer and tends to wear her work clothes going around the supermarket. Can you make her look more demure?" The exotic dancer struts out. All boobs and bum in the shortest shorts and a bikini-top oozing tits. Her face veiled by her big blonde hair. Her lips outlined in some red or brown lip-pencil that has not been blended. She has a permanent pout. The poor thing is sent off to the 'team of experts' who turn her into a bigger frump than her frumpy friend. I'd say the new look lasts as long as it takes to get out of the studio with the big cheque.

Lately, I had taken to studying talk shows the way others study on the Open University. I lay on the couch with my duvet and soaked in all the advice. I could cure every problem. Except my own. None of the shows ever even touched on the disappearing husband subject. I wondered if that was because only one husband in the world actually wanted to find himself – mine? I could be a show all by myself. Weeping and wailing over my absent husband. Then when Dick came back I could make another appearance. A survival special. Dick and I could wax poetic about our marital experience: "I am so grateful to my darling husband for having the courage to go off" – to feckin' Crete for two bleedin' weeks – "in search of himself," I could say. "I am so happy with what he found. A wonderful, witty, sexy self. I am glad he found himself. Fair play to him. We are all delighted with his new self" – particularly the bank – they are delighted with the interest we're paying on the loan he took out to finance his search – "I recommend that every husband go off and do the same. Praise the Lord, halleluia, we have been saved!" I would wipe a tear from the corner of my eye and then Dick and I would embrace. At this stage I would be caught out, snared. The audience would guess that I was less than genuine. The game would be up just as soon as Dick turned around and they all saw the knife sticking out of his back. Right between his shoulder blades.

I don't know which show I would choose to make my first public appearance on. I suppose whoever offered me the most money. Might as well make a few bob out of my disaster. Usually I lose money. Lots of it. Maybe this time I could make a fortune out of my misfortune. Go on all the chat shows. Do the circuit. Although judging by that day's performance I didn't think any of them would want me. So, what's new? Today started off with Kilroy on prostitution, then on to Ricki doing a make-over, Sally on bonding or was it bondage, Vanessa on self-worth, Jenny on self-mutilation, back to Ricki (she has two slots a day), Geraldo on gay relationships, Montel on the multiple orgasm, Jerry Springer and the bouncers doing referee while some guy told his wife that he was sleeping with her mother, sister and best friend. I ended up with the Queen of chat – Oprah. She advised me how to get financial independence. Leave the doors open and allow the money to come in, she said. I shouted back at her that when I left my door open my money disappeared out the same door and my husband wasn't long about following. There is only one route to financial independence. Only one way for the average parent to gain this most desirable position. Financial independence can only be gained when your children get jobs and leave home. There is nothing more draining, financial and otherwise than being parents to eternal students.

Once a week I had the pleasure of the Duchess of York in my living-room. At least Oprah and Sarah (well, if she's invited herself into my home I'm entitled to call her Sarah, Duchess seems a bit formal) have some knowledge of what they're talking about. After all, between the two of them they have had every misfortune known to woman. They have both been fat in their time and if you have the willpower to conquer fat you can conquer anything. Of course neither of their husbands went off to find himself.

Unless Andrew did the Houdini trick and we were never told about it.

The audience on all these shows are direct descendants of the audience that enjoyed the Christians being thrown to the lions. They enjoy all sorts of problems. My wife is a prostitute, my children are on drugs, my husband wears my clothes, my children hate me, my parents hate me, my partner hates me, my friends hate me, the whole world hates me, I hate myself. Never a thing about disappearing Dicks.

Inner peace was discussed a lot. I wanted some of that. There was a war waging inside my innards. My stomach was in a knot and rebelling against nourishment of any kind. My heart, broken and all as it was, was still thumping but had moved from the safety of my chest to the base of my neck. I felt sick constantly but I was afraid to get sick in case I hurled my heart, still pumping and broken, into the toilet bowl. If that happened, not recognising my own heart, I would flush it down the toilet. Thinking it was the remains of last night's barbecued ribs. I would be rendered heartless. Maybe that would be a good thing. I wouldn't be hurt any more.

But I was hurt. For tonight I would just have to grin and bear it. Grin and bear Kyrstie too. Be nice for Carl's sake even though it would stick in my craw, wherever that was. Guess I'd know pretty quick when I felt the pain in it. Maybe I could get something to stick in Kyrstie's craw and she could choke on it. No Heimlich Manoeuvre for her.

Ken suggested he'd drive us all home from the party. As I had no chance left with Antonio I agreed. We stopped on the way for some Chinese.

"Can Kyrstie stay the night, Ma? It would be miles out of Ken's way to drop her off," Carl asked me when we were back in the car.

"Do you think she'll be safe, dear?" Jesus, my mouth was running off at it again. How could I have let my thoughts of murder out to Carl.

"What? Would she be safe? What do you mean?" He sounded puzzled. I was not surprised.

"Well, what I mean is, will she be safe if she sleeps in the spare bed in Chloe's room. It's such a mess. God knows what would happen."

In our family we are convinced that only Chloe can sleep in her room and survive. Anyone else, like the dreaded Kyrstie, would need a course of injections or die of the fumes and mould inhalation. Problem solved. She could stay overnight in Chloe's room.

"Ma, you can't expect Kyrstie to sleep in Chloe's room. I wouldn't let a rat sleep in there. In fact, the rats wouldn't lower themselves. No, Kyrstie can have my clean room and I will kip on the couch."

Feck, Feck, Feck.

We all barrelled into the house. Kyrstie stood in the hall hanging up her jacket and taking everything in. Shoes, coats, bags and baggage. The huge roll of carpet that I was planning to put down in the bathroom. It had been lying there for at least three months. I hoped Kyrstie would assume it had only just been delivered.

"Still haven't got around to putting the carpet down in the bathroom then, Ma? It must be there lying in the hall for the last three months at least. I could give you a hand with it now that Dad's away." Carl beamed, being the dutiful son and showing off to Kyrstie.

Feck him.

"That would be great." I said.

"Hi, what's the story?" We heard Chloe coming in. She was in good form. The Dillon boy was with her. I felt like running from my own home. I was outnumbered.

"I caught Ma in a necking session at a party and brought her and Suzie home." Bigmouth Carl confessed all my sins for me. He added, "By the way, this is Kyrstie."

"Hi, Kyrstie! I've seen you around the college, haven't I?"

"Yeah. I've seen you around too. Social Science, isn't it?" Kyrstie replied.

Chloe was indeed doing Social Science. She loved anything social. We weren't too sure about the science end of things though. I only hoped she wouldn't end up an expert on Social Welfare.

"What about you, Kyrstie? Are you a mature student?" I asked.

"Yes, how did you know? Did Carl tell you? We're in college together." She smiled at me, then at Carl. A wide open smile.

"Just a wild guess." Feck it to hell, I knew college was a bad idea for Carl. He just wasn't cut out for the freedom of it all. The choices. This was one bad choice he had made right here.

"I'm doing law," Kyrstie said. "I worked in a solicitor's office as a typist and I just got interested in the subject. I loved my job but I was going nowhere fast. There was no ladder for me to climb. So I decided to go to college and study law."

Ladder, I'd give her a ladder, with a rung or two loose.

"I hope to get into some big law firm when I graduate," Kyrstie added.

Oh, I'm sure you do and it just so happens that Carl's dad works in the biggest law firm in Dublin. Earning a pittance for working his guts out. Was she job-hunting or child-grabbing, I wondered.

Chloe pointed at the tall lanky chap who was shuffling awkwardly beside her. "This is Todd or, as Ma would say, "the Dillon boy". Everyone giggled. Except me. My children seemed determined to cause me the most embarrassment they could manage.

Another first. Meeting the Dillon boy. I had been wanting to meet him for months. Any night would have done. Chloe had to pick tonight. Thank God the youngfella looked normal enough. All denim and the right numbers. I wondered if his shiny black hair was dyed. It was too black, like his eyebrows and the dark shadow around his face and upper lip. Even his eyes looked black. I had never seen anyone with black eyes before. Except Carl, of course, but that was only around his eyes and only after a football match. I know very little about football. I have made a point not to learn too much. I knew enough to know that the ball is only used as an excuse to beat the crap out of the opposing team. That was enough for me. Any more and I would be in danger of getting hooked. Wearing very unbecoming scarves and chanting about people who walk alone. Now that Chloe was walking out with the Dillon boy she never walked alone. She was always hanging out of his arm. She said he was Italian. He looked it right enough. Trust

Chloe to pick a feckin' foreigner. What would he know of our culture? Cornettos and bolognese aside, what could they possibly have in common? I suppose Chloe thought he was some sort of stallion. I was praying to Jesus she never asked him to prove it. Could that be a tinge of the little green eye? He was definitely a gift in the looks department and to listen to Chloe he was God's gift. Especially to her. She saw him morning noon and night. Saw no bad in him. Well, sometimes, some nights. The nights when she had to sit in and watch telly. They were the nights he slaved away part-time in some Italian dive. Whenever Chloe talked about him she became sort of foolish. You got the urge to shut her up before she made a complete fool of herself and shared that he had the cutest little toe or something. Everything about him was cute apparently. His laugh, his walk, his smile. I had to hand it to her, though, cute was a very appropriate word. All over cute I'd say. Something about him made me warm to him immediately. Probably his proximity to Chloe's age and the fact that he hadn't brought Chloe to a party tonight. The party. First impressions of the Dillon boy were good. First impressions are always important. I decided to welcome him into the bosom of our family in the hopes that he'd stick around and distract Chloe while I was going through all my traumas.

"Hello, Todd. Nice to meet you. How's your mother?" I asked. Trying my best to remember what Chloe had told me about his mother. There was definitely something she told me to say. Either the sun shone out of her on a regular basis or she was sick or something.

The chap shuffled his feet, his eyes misted over, he ran his hand nervously through his hair. I waited with bated breath for the soliloquy on the goodness of his mother. When he spoke it was very quiet, almost a whisper. I leaned over to listen.

"I thought you knew." He hesitated. I felt sick. "I thought Chloe would have told you. My mother died about six years ago." He was on the verge of tears.

Jesus Christ. That was it. Now I remembered. Chloe was giving me daggers. She had warned me not to ask about the mother. She had said it so often that I got confused. I thought it was the father I wasn't to mention. I made up my mind to keep quiet in future, ask no questions. But my mind forgot to tell my mouth.

"I'm awful sorry. I thought it was your father that was, well you know, was there something about your father? Is he sick or dead or something?" Chloe was standing with her hands on her hips staring more like little darts now than daggers. But loads of them. I don't think she appreciated my welcoming speech.

"No, my dad's fine, thanks. In fact Chloe and me were supposed to have a meal in his restaurant tonight. We decided to wait until tomorrow night. It should be good." The child was enthusiastic.

"I didn't know your dad worked in a restaurant, Todd?" I was on safe territory now. I knew about restaurants. I would be able to manage a harmless conversation about them at any rate.

"Where is it? Did we ever eat in it, Chloe?" I asked smiling. Chloe was ignoring me.

"It's not open very long," Todd said. "We only moved to Ireland a while ago. My mother was Italian, you see. So we lived in Italy. My grandparents own a few restaurants over there. My mother was a brilliant cook. My dad is Irish but my mother taught him all her secrets. He's nearly as good as her at cooking now. Nearly but not quite. Anyway he decided to come back to Ireland and open a restaurant here. At first it was terrible. I knew no one. I wanted to go back. Then I met Chloe. So I guess I was meant to come here." He looked at Chloe. She looked at him. If looks were love they were in it. Up to his dark Italian hairline. "The restaurant is doing very well. He's delighted with himself. I'm glad for him. He's had it tough. He's the best. Why don't you come for a meal with me and Chloe? I'm sure my dad would love to meet you."

Chloe started to stare at me. The invitation was not coming from her. Romantic meals were only for two. I made three. A crowd. I could take a hint. I could even take a direct, but silent, command.

"Well, thanks for asking but another time maybe. Where's the restaurant? It would be nice for all of us to go maybe in a week or so."

"In the village. Pragos is the name of it. You've probably heard of it. If you want to book a table or anything just ask for my dad, Antonio. Well, it's really Anthony but he changes it when he's working. His assistant Mark changes his to Mario. Makes it more authentic. They're both very dark. You'd be amazed at the number of idiots who fall for the Italian line."

We all laughed. Some of us a bit louder and more hysterically than others. Like idiots would, I suppose.

"If you ever want to book a table just let me know or give him a ring and tell him you're Chloe's mother. He'll look after you well, give you a great service."

I felt weak. I didn't like to tell the young fella that his father had been all set to look after me very well indeed thank you very much and give me a great service into the bargain. The room started to spin. Holy shit. I had been going to have sex with my daughter's boyfriend's father. Something definitely odd about that. Near incestuous.

Suzie was enjoying the sideshow. Only short of breaking out the popcorn and directing everyone to seats with a torch. I know she was thinking about just deserts, and tiramisu was not the dish of the day.

"Let's get this food sorted out. I'm starving." Ken got stuck into the egg-fried rice. Less egg on that as on my face. Suzie dragged me into the kitchen to get plates and forks and something non-alcoholic for us to drink.

Once inside the safety of my kitchen I lay against the door.

"Shoot me now, Suzie. Please! Don't bother with the blindfold. Just shoot me quick and clean. No one will bother to mop up so make sure it's clean. I haven't left a will but let it be known that I leave all my worldly goods to Carl and Chloe to fight over – you can have my thong, Dick is to get my Visa bill, and my 'Shit Here' sign is to be given to Kyrstie."

"I can't shoot you. I've no gun. If I had a gun it would give me great pleasure to use it. But first I'd want to shoot Bill. I don't know why but I have this yen to shoot him. I suppose I could do the two of you together and say you challenged him to a duel and you both got shot in the process." Another great murder scheme. Not much use to me for the Kyrstie situation though.

"Come on. Take these plates in," Suzie said as she handed me a pile of clean plates.

Chloe burst in the door. It banged me on the head. I felt much better. "Ma, are you gone mad or what? I told you not to talk about parents in front of Todd! For God's sake, get a grip. Is what Carl's saying true – you know about you being all over a bloke at some party or other? And how come this Kyrstie's here?"

I caught a grip of the table and braced myself.

"I'm sorry about the mother thing. I got confused, and no, it's not true. Carl's just teasing you. Kyrstie's his girlfriend." I knew the last part of the sentence would deflect from the first.

"His what?"

"His girlfriend," I said. "Here, bring these inside." I handed her the plates and added a roll of kitchen towels and a bottle of mineral water to the pile.

"What? She's your age! How can she be Carl's girlfriend?" Chloe was gobsmacked.

"You'll have to ask Carl that," I said.

So she did. She went back into the telly room and asked straight out.

"How come Kyrstie's your girlfriend, Carl? She's nearly Ma's age."

Suzie and me nearly choked on our chicken balls. Only Carl did the ordering we wouldn't have been eating balls at all. I have great difficulty in ordering chicken balls. I always think some poor cock is going to get his come-uppance just because I fancy a snack.

We were in luck. Carl was so busy tucking a paper towel into Kyrstie's ample boosom that he didn't hear Chloe's question.

She asked another. Louder this time. "How did you two get together?"

"Actually we met at a concert," Carl started. "Remember the one I went to in the Point Depot a few months back? I had no money for a ticket and Ma treated me. Well, I sort of bumped into Kyrstie at that and we hit it off immediately. Love at first sight. So really it's all thanks to Ma." He gave Kyrstie a little squeeze on her very shapely knee.

I tried desperately to choke on a chicken ball but couldn't. I wanted to fling myself onto a barbecue rib. Impale myself. I was to blame. Dick would kill me. Any hope I had of his returning vanished. He had asked me not to give Carl the money for that bloody concert. In fact they were the very words he had used.

"Don't give him the money for that bloody concert, Linda," he had implored me. "I have bad vibes about it. There'll be trouble at it."

I had ignored him and given Carl the money unbeknown to Dick. I had also given more warnings than usual about safety and drugs and drink. I mustn't have mentioned girls. Dick was so happy to see Carl return sober and safe from that concert. He had laughed at himself for being like an aul' one worrying over something so silly. Now it turned out he had every reason to be worried. There had been trouble. Her name was Kyrstie. I made a mental note to listen to Dick from now on. That was if he ever came home and if he stayed long enough to say anything when he heard his son was going out with a girl my age, well nearly, and that his wife was feeling up any man that happened to be handy.

"How old are you, Kyrstie?" Chloe's curiosity got the better of her.

Carl dropped his fork, curry sauce all over the creamy-coloured carpet. Chloe started to giggle and Suzie jumped up and said she had to go home. Ken said he had to go too. In the middle of his crispy duck. Deserters.

"So how old are you, Kyrstie?" my daughter repeated, feck her, as soon as the others were out the door.

"Thirty-two," said Kyrstie proudly.

Jesus. Seven years younger than me with a figure like that. She hadn't had children though. Her body clock must be a time bomb.

Now Antonio's son had had enough for one night and decided to bid a hasty retreat. Before the bomb exploded. There was a lot of giggling and smacking noise at the door. Chloe came back into the room. Mischief all over her face along with the smudged lipstick.

"I hear you're staying the night, Kyrstie. What are the sleeping arrangements? Will you be in with Carl or do you want to take the spare bed in my room?"

I could have killed her. She was obviously paying me back for my earlier little faux pas. What would she do when she found out about my even bigger one?

"It's all right, Chloe. Thank you for taking such an interest but Carl will be sleeping on the couch tonight and Kyrstie will have his room." If I wasn't having nocturnal delights tonight then no one was.

"Are you sure you don't mind me staying?"

Kyrstie asked. "I have to be up very early in the morning to get back to Chrissy."

"I'm sure. It's no problem." I said. Then it sank in. What she had said. Chrissy? Who's Chrissy? If I was lucky and my 'Shit Here' sign was turned off it might be her brother or father or dog. If I was really, really lucky it would be her husband. But no. I have never had any luck with luck. Lucky and me are not compatible.

You know the way people talk about raffles? If there was only one ticket they'd lose. Well, that actually happened to me. Due to lack of interest the raffle was cancelled. I was the only one who had forked out the £100 for a ticket. The prize was a car and a holiday. The proceeds of the raffle were to go to a very worthy local charity. My name was plastered all over the local newsletter as the only person who had been good enough to participate in the raffle. The charity would go bust if it gave me the prize. I was obliged to let them keep the prize and my money. Every now and again when I'm short a few bob I remind myself of that hundred pounds and think of all the things I could have done with it. I often wonder did the charity put it to such good use. I decided to let my bad luck go with it. It didn't. No, bad luck must have liked hanging around me a lot. I must be a great person to hang out with because even after all these years it was still lurking around.

"Eh. Who's Chrissy?" I know it was a stupid question given my state of mind, but it was because of my mind being in such a state that I asked it. I didn't really want to know the answer. I sort of knew it already. I just hoped I was wrong. I am usually wrong. I always want to be right. But not this time. This time I was looking forward to being wrong.

"My daughter." She smiled as she said it.

I was right. Ten out of ten. Sometimes it's a terrible thing to be right. This was definitely one of those times.

"She's four and she's adorable," Kyrstie prattled on. "I must bring her around to you to show her off. She loves Carl."

I'll bet she does and I bet he's nearer her age than yours. Me and Chloe were staring. Doing the same sum. Fourteen years between Chrissy and Carl and fourteen years between Carl and Kyrstie. A right mess we've landed in here. The 'Shit Here' sign was on again.

"Where's her dad then?" Leave it to Chloe. She was always one step ahead of me and the posse. I was still reeling with the daughter news and here was Chloe bringing on the whole shagging tribe.

"He died," Kyrstie said. Jesus, was everyone dead or dying? Where did my children pick these people from? I wished I was dead.

"He was very young when he died," Kyrstie continued. I wished she'd stop. I felt a wave of sympathy welling up inside me and I was not prepared for it.

"He drowned," she continued, completely ignoring my wish. "He was out fishing in a boat in Briarstown lake and fell into the water. He wasn't wearing a life jacket. He hated wearing them. Said they restricted his casting style. It was horrible."

"I'm sure it was." Old and all as she was she was too young to have been through such tragedy. I started to feel sorry for her. I am a gobshite.

"God, it must have been horrible. I can't even imagine it." Chloe was a bit of a softy at heart.

Carl held Kyrstie's hand. I wished he wouldn't do it in front of Chloe and me.

"How old was Chrissy?" Chloe asked.

"She was only one at the time. She didn't understand what had happened. She missed her dad and she was sad because I was crying all the time."

Tell me about it. Maybe we could compare notes. See who could cry the most.

"My parents were great. They helped me over it.

My dad's retired so they're able to help me with baby-sitting and stuff. I put Chrissy into the crèche when I'm in college."

"It must be hard all the same, financially as well as everything else," I said, near to tears. The bladder was very near my eye these days.

"Well, no. That's one area I don't have to worry about, thank God. When Sam died he left me very well off. He and his father were into property and, well, you know how that's gone over the past few years."

"Property is always a sound investment," Carl said wanting to change the subject. He squeezed Kyrstie's hand again then leant over and pecked her on the cheek.

My nerves couldn't stand any more. I excused myself and went upstairs to Carl's room to change the sheets on his bed. His room wasn't as bad as Chloe's. You could say it had a lived-in look. Very lived-in. Carl had great intentions. His clothes were always piled high on his bedroom chair. Other belongings were piled everywhere else. His books and notes were the only things that were kept neatly stacked – on his desk. They looked new. No dog-ears here. Whether he ever opened them or not was another thing. They seemed untouched by human hand. Strange to think I used to worry about Carl's study habits – or lack of them – and Chloe's excessive sloppiness. That was before I had a missing husband, a near-adulterous and near-incestuous relationship, a prospective daughter-in-law as old as myself with a four-year-old child to dwell on.

I did a quick bit of tidying, shoving boxer shorts and shirts into the bottom of the wardrobe. Picking up used cans of Lynx deodorant, receipts and bits and pieces of paper off the floor. I went to empty the wastepaper bin. It was empty, clean as a whistle. The only clean thing in the room. I hung up his dressing-gown, practically blindfolding Jennifer Aniston in the process. She was behind Carl's bedroom door. Well, not hiding there in the flesh. That would have been the answer to all my prayers. I could have asked her to distract Carl away from Kyrstie. I'm sure she would have been delighted. I could hear her now: "Because he's worth it," she would say. But it was just a life-size picture of her hanging on the back of the door. Maybe her picture would do. I took the dressing-gown that she was now wearing back down and folded it into a drawer. Leaving Jennifer fully exposed.

A few years ago Carl had painted his room red and white. The paint cost a small fortune. As soon as the paint was dry he covered every inch of the room with pictures of footballers. All dressed in red and white. Then, suddenly last year, all the footballers were relegated, dropped. Substituted by girls in varying modes of undress.

Kyrstie knocked on the bedroom door.

"Come in. It's safe," I said.

She was amazed when she saw the collection of young women staring at her from every angle. Not amused, I'd say. I lent her one of Chloe's nightdresses. It had taken me ten minutes to find one that would cover her bum and boobs at the same time. Whatever happened to the good old-fashioned winceyette nightdresses? Buttoned up to the neck and curling in under your toes? Passion-killers. I could have done with one of those for Kyrstie. Instead I came up with a black, knee-length, plunge-neck piece of satin. Half a yard of material. But it had one saving grace. It wasn't see-through. I worried myself sick that she wouldn't put it on and Carl would go walkabout during the night. Having a right royal time for himself.

"I hope you have everything you need," I said. Including your chastity belt and contraceptives, I wanted to add. "If you want anything just give me a shout. Goodnight, Kyrstie."

"Thank you. I might use a towel and some shower gel from the bathroom if that's all right?"

"Help yourself." Go on, take everything you

can lay your hands on. Why ask my permission? Who am I? You've already helped yourself to my son without asking, why not take anything else that's going? I might have an extra pint of blood lying around in my veins doing nothing if you fancy. I was being bitchy and I knew it. I couldn't help myself. I hoped it didn't show. I wondered was there something I could take to stop the bitchiness. Maybe they had Bitchorette patches. I'd need to get in a whole consignment. Maybe there was just one big full body-patch I could put on in the morning. I must make enquiries.

"Linda, I know you don't really like me." Kyrstie was soft-spoken.

If she had attacked me, been on the defensive, I would have been well able for her. But she was being nice, matter-of-fact. I was disarmed and I was tired.

"I know you're not too happy about me being with Carl. Is it me you don't like or the age difference? Or maybe it's both?" I couldn't believe it. She had me well summed-up. She wasn't finished. "I know he's much younger than me. But the age doesn't matter to us. We love each other. You needn't worry about him tying himself down too young or him getting hurt. I would never do anything to hurt him. I respect him. I don't know where all this will lead to with Carl and me but I will tell you this much. I love him and he loves me and Chrissy. He loves you too. Don't make him choose. I'd like to think that you'd give me a chance but I can understand if you can't."

And there it was. She had put her finger on it. Who did she think she was to be putting her finger on it? Make him choose indeed! Who was she to be so reasonable? I looked at her flaming unruly hair and her bright green eyes and saw something in there that I hadn't seen before. Me. She feckin' well reminded me of me. But she looked nothing like me.

"I won't lie to you." I finally found my voice. "You're right. I won't make Carl choose. I wouldn't be that foolish. I'd be afraid to find out which one of us he'd favour. But I have nothing against you as a person. I'm sure you're a lovely woman. Look, there is no nice way to say this but putting it bluntly I think you're too old for my son. But he seems happy, so you and I will just have to put up with each other." I was amazed at myself.

Try as I might I couldn't dislike this girl. She had been through so much in her short life even if it was that bit too much longer than Carl's. It was obvious Carl was happy with her and thought he was head over heels in love with her, maybe he was.

Even Chloe who was prepared to label Kyrstie as the Wicked Witch of the West was at ease in her company. At least there were no airs and graces about Kyrstie. She spoke her mind. I hoped she wouldn't speak it too often. If only she wouldn't hurt Carl I might be able to accept her. Let nature take its course. Let them tire of each other naturally.

"You've got me all wrong, Kyrstie," I continued. "If you were twelve to fourteen years younger I'd be welcoming you with open arms. But you're not and I'm just worried that's all. But I do like you more than you think."

I smiled when I saw the relief in her face. She had been dreading meeting me and this evening was sprung upon her. Upon all of us. We were unprepared. I should have given the girl a chance. Fat chance. To think if I'd known what a Mickey Finn was she could be dead by now.

"Will Chrissy be all right without you tonight?" I was curious.

"My parents take her one night a week for a stay-over. They love having her and I know she's safe with them. I worry about her all the time. I know it's foolish but it's the way I'm made."

"Me too. Goodnight, Kyrstie."

"Goodnight."

When I went back downstairs Carl was struggling,

trying to open the zip on his sleeping-bag. I took it from him. There was a knack to opening it. Curse a few times under your breath and pull. Hey presto, it opened.

"What do you think of Kyrstie, Ma?" he asked. "She's lovely, isn't she? She reminds me of you sometimes." Would that be her age? I wondered. He yawned as he climbed into the sleeping-bag. He lay down on the couch. Just a head exposed. He looked lost.

"I like her." I meant it. "If she makes you happy, Carl, then I'm happy. But she might not be your life partner so go easy. Don't get too involved. Have a good time. Don't get into a rut. She's a nice girl but you should have told me about her age and Chrissy."

"I know, Ma, but I didn't think we'd be bumping into you tonight. I wanted to ease you in gently. Bit by bit. I would have told you everything eventually. I was biding my time. Waiting for the right moment."

"I don't think there ever would have been a right moment," I said.

"I know. Maybe it's good it's all out in the open. I hated not being able to talk to you. I want to ask you lots of things. I never felt like this before, Ma."

"Must be love or else all that chicken curry you

stuffed your face with. Goodnight, Carl. I love you. You know that, don't you?" I ruffled his hair the way I had always done. He smiled the way he's always done.

"'Course I do, Ma. Oh, by the way, I have a funny feeling that the Dillon boy is Antonio's son. We must tell him that his father went to school with Da." Carl yawned again.

"Well, let's not mention it just yet, Carl. Leave it for a while."

Carl raised his eyebrows and smiled at me. Just before he turned over and fell asleep. "Good night, Ma."

I peeped in at Chloe. She had fallen asleep before I got to say goodnight. She looked like an angel. I pushed her hair out of her eyes and she moved.

"Love you, Ma."

"Love you too."

I was crying again.

CHAPTER ELEVEN

I woke early the next morning for one reason only. Suzie and her bloody key were in at the crack of dawn. I thought it was a bit insensitive of her to interrupt my first good kip in ages. I had slept all night for the first time since Dick left. Not the peaceful sleep my body longed for but the toss-and-turn kind that left me more exhausted when I was woken up. So early.

I put on my dressing-gown and went downstairs. I was itchy and couldn't stop yawning. My head felt as though it was too big for my body. So it felt enormous. So big that a lonely drummer had found his way inside it. He seemed lost. Beating and banging away on the inside of my skull. Trying to escape. Over and over again. A muted throbbing, building to a nice crescendo every time I moved. The wind section in my stomach joined in. Churning and groaning. The chicken balls must have been off. I had probably got a dose of food poisoning. It had to be something I ate. Couldn't have been anything I drank. Even though I drank a lot more than I ate.

I found Suzie in the kitchen filling the kettle with water. She looked lovely, again. I thought this was even more insensitive of her. I didn't think it would have killed her to look awful just once.

"Hi, Suz," I said in between yawns. "Jesus, look at this place."

The kitchen was a tip. Silver cartons everywhere. Blobs of congealed curry sauce all over the white worktop. Dried-out tea bags vying for space among the chip bags. Dirty plates and cups piled high. Balancing. Waiting for their turn in the dishwasher that was full of even dirtier dishes. That's the trouble with dishwashers: someone has to fill them and empty them. It's always me. I pushed the button and the clean-up started.

I surveyed all I was master of and I didn't like what I saw. It would take me years to get everything back to normal. The kitchen would be the easiest place to start. I would leave the rest of my life till later. Much later. I doubted if I could ever make it a bacteria-free zone again. The kitchen, not my life. My life has never been free from bacteria. The kitchen was, once. But now millions of little bacteria were well settled in. Squatters. Enjoying the freedom I had given them. They were probably partying every night. Having a ball. Bonking and breeding at a great rate. Oh, well, I supposed someone might as well be having fun. I was only jealous I was getting none. I pulled up a chair and sat myself down among the happy bacteria. Maybe I could learn something from them.

"I was going to bring you up a cup of tea," Suzie said, dipping a tea bag into the scalding water. She was using the wrong cups. I was getting Chloe's. She was using Dick's. I said nothing. Change was as good as a rest and I was tired. Very tired.

"Sorry, I let myself in again but I thought I might have to help shift a few dead bodies. Particularly a more mature female, well over the age of eighteen by the name of Kyrstie. Now I want a blow-by-blow account. I'm sure you came to blows. Leave nothing out. Start with her age. How old exactly? You keep talking. I'll make us some toast."

"We've no bread."

She ignored me and continued searching in the press. She found a stale heel off a sliced pan. Very

stale. Even without the benefit of a best-before date
I could see it was too old to be of any use to anyone.
It was hard and crusty, yellowed with age, curled at
the edges. I empathised with it, felt sorry for it, knew
exactly what it was going through. It reminded me
of me. Suzie unceremoniously dumped it into the
already overflowing bin. At least it would be with
friends. More happy bacteria.

Then Suzie hit the jackpot. She found a packet
of unopened Cream Crackers. She started to butter
them. Another little find, a pot of strawberry jam.
I caught her looking carefully for green mould
spots in the jar. It must have been spotless because
she started lashing the jam onto the buttered
crackers. The red gunge oozed out from the sides
and through the tiny pinholes when she sandwiched
them together. I felt sick. The drummer in my head
was on overtime. I think I recognised the *Lark
Quartet* by Haydn being beaten out over and over
again. Whatever it was, it was for the birds.

Suzie pointed a sticky finger over towards the
worktop.

"There's a note here for you and before you ask
I didn't read it this time. To tell you the truth, I was
afraid after the last time." She stuck her thumb in
her mouth and sucked the last of the jam and
butter off it.

The note was folded over and on the outside printed in very precise, neat handwriting was:

To Carl's Mom.

Thanks for the Chinese and the chat. I hope you don't mind me leaving so early but I have to get back to Chrissy. I'll bring her over to see you very soon. Thanks again, Kyrstie.

Leaving notes was getting to be a bit of a habit around here. At least this one didn't have bad news. Although it did confirm that Kyrstie was coming back. Very Soon. She was obviously planning to be around for a while. I brought Suzie up to date on the Kyrstie situation. I added in the Chrissy bit for the shock value. It was well received. Suzie was stopped in her gallop. She even stopped running her tongue around the edge of her cracker sandwich. A small droplet of jam hung from her upper lip. Stretching. It was a full five seconds before she flicked out her tongue and caught it just as it was about to fall.

"Jesus," she said. And that was all she said. What more was there? We sat in silence drinking the hot tea. It was black. I hadn't bought any milk. I hate black tea.

Suzie started licking the sticky red jam off her fingers again. Making mouth noises. I wished she'd stop. I felt very sick. It was probably guilt. About the party and the rest.

"God, if Dick ever finds out about last night I'm dead. Carl is sure to have discussed last night with Chloe. He will need someone to confide in and Chloe is the only person in the world that will have the same views on his mother as him. Chloe might put two and two together. Chloe was always good at maths. She'll get the right answer: four play."

Chloe would find out all about Antonio and the rest. I felt even more guilty because I had enjoyed the rest a bit too much. Chloe and the Dillon boy would get into deep meaningful discussions about their oversexed parents. Chloe would possibly be in therapy for years when she found out. I made Suzie promise never to tell Dick. Or Chloe. Or anyone else for that matter. I wondered what Antonio was thinking. Was he thinking about me? If he wasn't now he would be in a few minutes. I was going to have to ring him. Beg and plead with him to keep his lovely juicy, sensuous mouth shut.

Suzie felt lousy too. She was worried in case Bill found out. She was all right though. She needn't worry. She had done nothing wrong and even if she had her son couldn't be called as the prime witness to her infidelity. Me and Suzie made a pact never to speak about last night again.

"Anyway, Bill was asleep and snoring like a pig

when I got home." Suzie broke the pact as soon as it was made. "I just slid in beside him and fell fast asleep. He got up early this morning to play golf. I pretended to be asleep. He never got a chance to ask what time I was in at or where I had been. If he asks I'll just say it was a quiet night. He's so pre-occupied at the moment he probably won't even ask. I am seriously worried about him, Linda. When he went to play golf this morning he never took his golf shoes with him. He never came back for them either. He must have borrowed a pair at the club. His mind is miles away lately, Linda. Every time we are together in the same room he makes some excuse or other and hightails it off somewhere. I don't know what's wrong with him."

"I told you. He's probably just tired. Overworking." I told her what she wanted to hear. I had never heard of anyone going to play golf without their shoes. Bit like going for a drive without the car. I didn't tell Suzie that. I imagined Bill running around in his stocking feet chasing the little white ball. I was restless. Sitting in the grotty kitchen was only a reminder of how grotty everything else was getting. I plucked up the courage to ring Antonio.

"Pragos restaurant."

"Hi, Mario, is that you? It's Linda, from last night,

the party, remember? Could I speak to Antonio please?"

"Oh, hi, Linda. Brilliant party. Great entertainment. Hang on and I'll get him."

"Linda?" As soon as I heard Antonio's voice a firework that must have been lurking around, lying low since last night, went off in my head. Firework can be very dangerous.

"Antonio. How are you? I'm sorry about last night. I'm going through a bit of a bad patch and I don't know what got into me. I'm mortified. I hope you're all right. Carl got a bit carried away. It was a shock for him to see me with a strange man. Well, not that you're strange but you know what I mean. I really am sorry."

"Don't worry about it. I understand. Suzie told me all about you and your husband. It was a shock for me when your son appeared out of nowhere though. But I actually enjoyed last night. Have you and your husband split up or is he coming back? I don't know about you but I really felt something for you. I meant what I said about love at first sight. I'd like to see you again. Please."

"Oh. Antonio. I'm sorry. It was lovely but I am married. Dick only went away for a few weeks. He'll be back soon. I enjoyed last night. But I love my husband. I'm sorry. I don't usually behave like that and I should have told you I was married and everything but I was trying to forget. I certainly succeeded in that, eh?"

"Yeah. But it was wonderful before Carl turned up. I thought I'd never meet anyone again after my wife died and then you walk into my life. You can't just vanish now. Maybe some time we could meet up?"

"No. That's impossible. I just rang to apologise and," I took a deep breath, "to tell you that your son is going out with my daughter. It's all very complicated but I need you to keep to the story about going to school with my husband. Please!"

"Chloe is your daughter? She's fantastic! Todd is mad about her. If she's anything like her mother I'm not surprised he's so crazy in love with her. I promise I won't say a thing to upset you. Can I keep in touch with you? Just as friends. What would be the harm in that? Now that our children are dating we might bump into each other anyway."

It would be great to bump into him, naked in a room with soft music, not a drum in sight. Candles glowing. Showing my cellulite off to its best advantage. There'd be plenty of harm in that. I hoped. But I knew it could never happen. I had a longing for him that was too strong even for me to ignore. It would be best for me never to see him again.

"All right," my mouth said, speaking for my heart. "We can be friends. Maybe even good friends. There'd be no harm in us being friends. Friends would be lovely. No one could complain about us being friends, could they? Thanks, Antonio. I'm sorry again for last night."

"I'm not. Last night was the best night in a long, long time. Goodbye, Linda."

I don't know whether it was the hangover or what but I swooned. There and then in the hall on my own. I had to hold onto the pole at the end of the stairs to steady myself.

When I went back into the kitchen Suzie was sitting with a notebook and pencil. She had our day mapped out for us. Museums and art galleries. Away from any harm.

"I have a better idea. Let's go for a walk." I was in no humour to appreciate dead things or other people's talents. I would only end up comparing them to my own unique talent for cocking everything up. No one ever appreciated my talent. There was no market for it. "Come on, Suzie. It will do us both the world of good." I wasn't so sure about the world of good bit but I hoped I sounded convincing. I wanted a bit of fresh air to settle my stomach. The Bisodol wasn't working any more. I was hoping the drummer would finish his recital as soon as I hit the streets. I wouldn't be asking for an encore. I rubbed my stomach. Something was stirring. I was in danger of bringing up last night's supper and not as a conversation piece.

"You should go to the doctor, Linda. You might have an ulcer or something," Suzie said and she was right. I would have to go to the doctor. I was feeling sick more and more often and I had put it off long enough. I was just afraid he was going to tell me I was dying. I wasn't in any shape to be told that. Although if I was going to die I might as well be told sooner rather than later. We could use it as leverage to get Dick back.

Speak of the divil. The phone rang. I forgot to let the answering machine take it.

"Hi, Linda. It's me, Dick."

"Hi, Dick, how are you? Have you found yourself yet?" I hoped he had. His voice sounded lovely and I wanted him home.

"Oh, Linda, it's great to hear your voice. I was ringing for ages but the phone was engaged."

That was me onto my wannabe lover. "Chloe was talking to one of her college friends."

"I thought I'd never get you. How are things?"

Shite, just shite, I thought.

"Great, just great," I said We're all having a great time here. I'm picking up men and whoring about. Carl has a new girlfriend my age who happens to have a four-year-old child and Chloe is madly in love with an Italian fella who has a father I'd like to sleep with. Well, not just sleep with. "We're all fine, Dick but we miss you. We all love you and want you home with us." I was pleading. The exact thing I had said I wouldn't do. I started crying into the phone. Another thing I had promised myself I wouldn't do. But I was very vulnerable after the party and all my willpower and good intentions had vanished. Replaced with remorse and guilt. The old reliables.

"Linda, I love you. I'm coming home. We'll have to sort everything out. I'll talk to you when I get home. I have something important I want to tell you. I have made a very important decision about my future."

"What is it?" I was afraid he'd tell me.

"I'll tell you when I get home."

"Did you find yourself, Dick?"

"Yeah. I think so." I wondered would I like the bit he had found.

"I'm glad."

"Tell the kids I love them."

We were cut off.

Suzie held me while I cried again. She should

have been demanding a fee for this new full-time occupation of holding me and patting me on the back. I owed her a hundred boxes of tissues. She went home to change from her flowing white dress into a pair of trousers to go for the walk.

I knew there was no danger of either of the kids waking up but, just in case there was a nuclear explosion and the bright lights roused them from their sleep, I left them a note. The note-leaving was really catching on. I assured them that I would be back in a while and that Suzie and me were gone for a walk. That would give them a laugh if nothing else. They would get great mileage out of Suzie and me going for a walk. Dick would be told when he came home.

"Something weird happened to Ma while you were away. She went for a walk without the car. We were awful worried about her. It was terrible, so out of character that we thought she was having a breakdown."

They would all laugh and maybe I would laugh too, then again maybe not. I would probably not be laughing for years and years. I put on my black evening trousers, not because I wanted to look particularly glamorous but because they were the only clean ones I had. I lathered my face with make-up and applied more mousse to my hair. This made my hair go very hard and sharp in places. I made a mental note to warn Suzie in case my hair hit against her and she cut herself. I had one pair of flat shoes so I wore them. I only ever wear high-heeled shoes. I fool myself that they take inches off my legs – not in height, in width. They also add inches to my legs, not in width, in length. In flat shoes it's a case of beef to the heel like a Mullingar heifer. Not that I have ever seen a Mullingar heifer but it's on my list of things to see some day. It must be a great tourist attraction. Well, in Mullingar anyway.

I took a long tee-shirt with buttons down the front, yellow and black, out of my suitcase that was still hidden under the bed. The suitcase had all my best tops and shorts and of course the thong neatly packed for my trip of a lifetime. I was set. We decided to walk along the coast. Blow the cobwebs away.

"I still can't believe how close we came to madness." Suzie insisted on referring to the subject she had promised we would never refer to again.

"Read any good books lately?" I said.

"OK. I get the message – change the subject right? Well, here's a change. The latest on Doreen is that she's getting ready to fly the coop. Guess she's leaving poor Larry. News on the grapevine is that the guy she's having the fling with is a local.

Apparently he's married. He's all set to leave the wife but he's afraid that she'll fall apart and try suicide or something if he does."

"I wonder who the hell it is. At least we know now it's not Carl. I still think it's that fella that goes in to service her boiler. I'm telling you, it's more than her boiler she gets serviced. Honestly though, how many times can a boiler break down in one year?" I was hoping it was the boiler-man. What I was really thinking was too frightening to contemplate.

"Well, it can't be him because he's Roger's brother. Remember, Doreen told us that months back."

"Wouldn't be the first time a family member let loose with his member, Suz."

We walked along quietly, both of us picturing Doreen with the boiler-man. If she felt anything like the passion I felt with Antonio I wished her the best of luck. It was a pity it all had to come out though. It would have been best all around if no one knew. Then Doreen could go on having her bit on the side and being married to Larry. But it always comes out. Someone always has to tell, spoil it.

"I wonder did she tell Larry yet? No sign of him this morning arsing around with the car."

Suzie had a good view of Larry and Doreen's

house from her bedroom window. She had been keeping a close eye on things since the news broke. Every movement or change in routine was noticed and reported back to me. It was a bit of diversion.

"Well, that certainly is suspect." I had to agree.

We walked along quietly, both of us picturing Larry. His head in his hands crying the rivers of tears I had shed over the past week. I wondered did men and women cry the same amount of tears once they started crying. Would Larry only be capable of a small pond as opposed to my large lake?

"Will he kick her out do you think?" I asked Suzie.

"I don't know. Would you if it was Dick? I think I'd kick Bill out."

We walked along quietly, both of us picturing Suzie, small little Suzie, kicking big Bill in the arse so hard that he went flying out the hall door and landed on the road. We looked at each other and burst out laughing.

It was a great day. Other people had problems. I was not alone. I think I was coming out of my depression. Antonio wanted to be my friend and Dick had rung and it appeared that whatever part of him he found loved me. The sun was shining, the sky was blue, birds were singing. I felt a thump on my shoulder. One of the singing birds had shat on my good tee-shirt. That's the thing about the 'Shit Here' sign: dumb birds see it and take it literally. I felt the wave of depression return.

Children were out cycling on bikes. They were happy and laughing, shouting at each other to catch up. Suzie and me looked lovingly at them. We remembered our own kids doing the same. The little kids cycled nearer. And nearer. Straight for us. The smiles were wiped off our faces as the little gits almost knocked us down.

"Brats!" I shouted childishly after them. It felt good.

A young mother pushing a high pram passed us by. The child in the pram was screaming, its big round face turning almost blue with the effort. Before I had my children I used to feel sorry for babies that cried. Now since I have had children of my own I feel sorry for the mother when a baby cries. There was this poor unfortunate woman, doing her best, pushing the heavyweight of a baby along the coast. Giving him a bit of fresh air. She could have been sitting at home reading a book, watching telly, even twiddling her thumbs for all the kid cared. She had muffled him up and made the effort to bring him out for a walk and what thanks did she get? None. Just the humiliation of the little git screaming. I smiled sympathetically and nodded to her.

"What are you looking at?" she shouted at me.

"Nothing," I muttered.

Maybe this walk was a bad idea. It was destroying my faith in human nature. The milk of human kindness, I was discovering, was all dried up. This walk was meant to be therapy for me. Instead it was destroying my faith in everything.

"Where have all the good guys gone, Suzie? Are there any nice people left in the world, except for you and me?"

"Well, there's Antonio and Ken – they're nice. And our families, they're nice too. Well, our children are nice anyway. Sometimes. They will go forth and multiply and the nice people will get the upper hand again."

"I hope they don't multiply too soon or too often, Suz."

"I'm glad for you that Dick is coming home. It'll be great. You'd better get the fattened calf ready. You'll be as happy as Larry." This was a bad choice of person. We both knew how unhappy Larry must have been.

"I don't think I'll ever be happy again. Every time I feel happy coming on some little shit-head crops up and gives it the elbow. No, happy is not for me, Suzie. It would be too much to expect. From now on I'm going to strive for content. I might manage content."

"You should do one of my courses. There's a new one starting soon – Positive Thinking. Will I put your name down?"

"No."

"Are you sure?" she asked again.

"Yes. Positive." Emphatically.

"All right."

"Can we turn back now, Suzie? I feel sicker than I did at the start and I'm beginning to feel more and more depressed. Jumping into the sea with a rock around my ankle is beginning to look like a very attractive option."

We turned for home and that's when it happened. I heard a loud crack. Then I heard a scream. When I turned around Suzie was in a pile on the ground. Her arm was twisted in a funny position – well, I certainly couldn't get my arm to go like that, bent up under her. She had stumbled off the grass verge and fallen flat on her face. To break her fall she had put out her arm. Bit of mistake that. I tried to help her to get into a sitting position. She was very unco-operative. Writhing and screaming. Finally she managed to manoeuvre herself upright on her hunkers then finally fell back onto her bum. There she sat on the ground holding her arm. Rocking to and fro. Writhing in agony. Making a holy show of us.

"For God's sake get up off the ground, Suzie! People are staring at us." I was mortified.

Suzie just kept screaming. Doing the dying swan. On the path. The audience was gathering at a great rate.

"Jesus, Linda. I think I've done something to my arm. Did you hear the crack? That was me."

She started crying. I didn't blame her – the arm looked very peculiar – but I wished she wouldn't be so public about it. The little brats on the bikes appeared again. They must have had radar. Knew when there was a performance worth hanging around for.

"What's wrong, missus?"

"Did you fall?"

"Is it bad?"

"Is she crying?"

They gathered around in a group, pointing at Suzie and talking all at once.

"Clear off the lot of you! Go home!" I shouted. One of them started wailing.

A larger crowd of children gathered. If I started a collection now Suzie and me could make a fortune, I thought. Suzie looked a serious shade of green. I ran to the edge of the grassy bank and started to puke. The crowd dispersed.

"Are you all right, Linda?" Suzie dragged herself over to me on her bottom. She had green marks all over her trousers.

"I'm fine," I said as I crossed my arms over my stomach. I puked again. "How are you?"

"Grand, grand," she lied. "I'll have to go to the hospital. Remember that First Aid course I did? Well, if I was paying attention and the instructor was right then I think I've done something to my arm. I don't think it's meant to be this size or colour."

I knew she had lied about being grand. I puked again for good measure. Suzie retched in sympathy.

"We need to get to a phone and get an ambulance." I tried to take over the situation. I failed. I got sick again.

"Linda, why are *you* getting sick?" Suzie asked.

"How the hell do I know? It could be the bird shitting, the shitty husband leaving, the son with the old shit of a girlfriend, the daughter going out with my would-be lover's son going to land me in the shit, the shitting bank balance, the size of your arm. Take your pick, Suzie, any or all of the shitty reasons above."

"I only asked." She howled in pain.

"I'm sorry. I feel useless. I think I'm going to faint." I said it so I did.

I was lucky a jogger was out doing his thing and just as he was slowing down trying to get past Suzie who was still sitting on the ground I fell into his arms. He recognised Suzie's face. Thank God we were not relying on him to recognise her by the arm otherwise he would have jogged off into the sunset. Had there been one. Even Suzie didn't recognise her own arm. He recognised Suzie because he knew her, worked with her even. They were book pals. He was her boss. Ken again. I was well out of it now. I was in a pleasant, quiet black place. I could see nothing and hear even less. It was a very nice place indeed. I fancied hanging around for a while in this no place in particular. It suited me. I could get very accustomed to it. It was all quiet. Peaceful. Sweetness and light.

Luckily enough, Ken had a mobile phone with him. I asked Suzie later where he had kept it. There were no pockets in his tight little shorts. She said she didn't know and she didn't want to. She was so grateful he had a phone with him at all that had he been Maxwell Smart and made the call from his shoe she wouldn't have questioned him. Except maybe to ask why his work colleague, Ninety Nine, was called after an ice-cream cone with a flake. We had both always wanted to know that.

Since Ken had a mobile phone he did the decent thing and rang for an ambulance. He waited with us for the twenty minutes it took to arrive at the scene. Suzie used the waiting time wisely to ring my house and hers. She told Carl that she had had a fall and I was taking her to the hospital. He never asked why the injured party was making the call and she never mentioned that his mother was lying in the arms of yet another strange man. She couldn't reach Bill anywhere.

I came out of my faint calling the roll.

"Dick, Carl, Antonio?" I knew I was being held by a man. It is not something you confuse. Strong arms around you. I just didn't know which man. I was hoping it was the last on my list. I could hear someone screaming. Suzie. Shit. I was back out of the dark place into a darker place, my life.

"Linda, are you all right?" Suzie was concerned.

"Yes, Suz, I'm fine." Lies again. "How are you?" I was worried. Her arm looked like a leg.

"Fine." All lies. "Would you believe it, Linda? Our knight in shining armour is Ken."

"Of course, Ken, I didn't recognise you with your clothes off." He looked better than the other night. Very casual. Less staid.

"Hi, again." He shook my hand which seemed a little bit formal since I discovered that he had opened the buttons on my tee-shirt and slapped me around the face a couple of times after I fainted. All on Suzie's instructions but none the less actions that would surely merit the bypassing of the hand shaking.

We heard sirens. I made a conscious decision not to look at Suzie's arm and broke it immediately – not her arm – she had done that all by herself. I looked at the offending limb. I knew it was broken. I felt sick again. Ken held onto Suzie and me. He insisted on coming with us in the ambulance. He said it would be handy for us to have a healthy adult and a mobile phone. I didn't like the way he was looking at Suzie. He was a bit too concerned about her. Staring into her face and holding her all the time. My God, he fancied her. Ken had the hots for Suzie. I doubted if Suzie knew, I doubted if he even knew. Well, well, there's a thing.

The ambulance men insisted that Suzie be put on a stretcher. They tut-tutted a lot and spoke of the damage people do out running in the wrong clothes. They took one look at the bird-shit on my top and told Ken to help me into the ambulance. We took off at the speed of light with the siren blazing. The little bike brats tried to race us. We won. I wanted to give them the fingers out of the ambulance window but realised it would be no use.

They wouldn't be able to see me. I would be just standing at the window with my two fingers raised in the victory sign for no one to see. The ambulance man might even assume that I had hit my head and was off my rocker. He, not having the benefit of knowing the traumas I had been through lately, would be forgiven for suggesting to a doctor that I be admitted to the psychiatric wing of the hospital. Ken would be too pre-occupied making doe-eyes at Suzie to notice. Suzie would be so embarrassed at the antics of me in front of Ken that she would deny all knowledge of our beautiful friendship. She would betray me before the cock crowed three times. I would be locked up for days. Even weeks. Maybe it wouldn't be too bad. A padded cell with no birds or people. I could do with a bit of peace and quiet. It could be another bit of leverage to get Dick home. If I was really lucky they wouldn't allow visitors. Maybe just Dick and the children. They could hold my hands and cry over me. Dick could blame himself. The children could blame Dick.

CHAPTER TWELVE

We skidded to a halt at the hospital door and Suzie was rushed in. I followed in hot pursuit with Ken bringing up the rear. The place was like a war zone. Men and women were limping and bleeding all over the place. There was weeping and wailing everywhere. Gnashing and grinding in every corner. And that was only the overworked nurses. I thought we had missed out on some big disaster but the nurse assured me that this was the normal day-to-day routine in the Accident and Emergency.

I had to push my way through the heart-attack victims and the bleeding and broken limbs. I ran after Suzie but was stopped in my tracks and dispatched in no uncertain terms to a little window at reception. A middle-aged woman who took an unhealthy interest in me asked me lots of very personal questions: what was my name, where did I live, had I a phone, and the jackpot – what was my VHI number. I swear if I had been dead they would have resuscitated me, given me a blood transfusion and put me on life support until they got my VHI number out of me. Luckily I know my number off by heart. Don't laugh – I have a thing about numbers and you never know when you might need it. Like today. They wanted me to give them twenty pounds. They were not impressed that I hadn't any money on me. Learn from my mistake: as well as the clean underwear always carry your VHI number and a twenty-pound note with you in case you're knocked down by a bus. It will save some time when they rush you to Casualty to sew you back together. It would not be a good time for you to be rooting in pockets and counting out pennies, particularly with limbs missing.

The woman typed all my details into the computer including the fact that I was a bad debt. She told me to take a seat. As they were all bolted to the ground I assumed she meant to sit down. I asked could I go in and see Suzie.

"Who's Suzie?" she asked taking off her little round silver-framed glasses.

"My best friend," I said.

She put her glasses back on again. "Yes, I'm sure that's lovely for you to have a friend but why do you want to see her here?"

"She's in there." I pointed to the closed doors. The ones that mobile phones couldn't be used beyond. Feckin' Ken had gone in with Suzie and his phone. He was probably ringing all and sundry, relaying the latest calamity to befall Suzie and me. The ECG machines and life-saving equipment were probably all gone to hell, bleeping and flashing. God knows how many people would die if he made a long-distance call.

"Why is she gone in there?" Ms Prim in her bottle-green twinset and mousy bun asked from the safety of her 'Register Here' office. I could see now why they kept her behind glass. She was an animal.

"She fell and the ambulance men brought her in there," I answered as nice as I could muster.

"Has she given her details?" The glasses were on again.

I was afraid, very afraid. Suppose Suzie hadn't given her details? Did this mean they would refuse to treat her? Would she be turned away with a flea in her ear or somewhere else for that matter? Well, the beds had that lived-in look. A flea and a broken arm would be too much for any one person to handle in any one day.

"I'm not sure. They just rushed her in there. I don't think there was too much time for details."

"Well, you give them to me then." Her voice was raised. She was only short of taking a packet of matches from her pocket and shoving them, one by one of course, under my nails.

I chanted off Suzie's details. I didn't know her VHI number. I only have a thing for the numbers in my own life. Black mark against Suzie. Black mark and bad debt.

"Which arm did this best friend hurt?"

"Her own."

"I assumed it was her own arm, dear. Let me rephrase – which one of her own arms did she hurt?"

"Hurt? Hurt you say? Easy known you haven't seen it. Hurt is a very, very mild word to use while describing the present state of Suzie's arm. Mutilate is a more accurate word. I can't remember."

"Was it her right arm that she mutilated?" She looked at me, taking the glasses off again.

"I think so."

"Well, was it the left arm?" Glasses on.

"Yes, yes, the left. I think."

"You have a choice of two, right: right or left?" Glasses definitely off and being pointed at me. Up until this moment I had never regarded glasses as an offensive weapon. Broken pint glasses, yes, but reading glasses?

"Left."

"Left, right?"

"No left."

"Now let me get this right. She hur – sorry, mutilated her left arm – is that what you're saying?" Ms Prim lifted her left arm high into the air. I ducked. Well, I thought she was going to take a swing at me through the hatch. How was I to know it was only to emphasise her choice?

"Yes, right, her left." Who was I to argue?

She put the glasses back on and left them there.

I was wrong, so was Ms Prim. It was the right arm.

"Twenty pounds please," she said. I thought it was a bit too much for getting a question wrong.

"I just told you I didn't have the twenty pounds for myself, so where do you suppose I would get the twenty pounds for Suzie? Pickpocket some of the other casualties? Magic it from behind my ear? Or click my fingers and hey presto – forty pounds for the little lady in the hatch!" I knew I was losing it.

"No need to be so rude. I'm only doing my job." A little too well, I thought. "Would your best friend not lend you the twenty and pay for herself while she's at it?" Ms Prim said, delighted with herself.

"WE HAVE NO MONEY!" I shouted. I heard a distinct "Aaah!" from the injured and wounded behind me.

Finally I was allowed to let myself into the inner sanctum.

Suzie was crying. Sitting on a trolley crying. It was a sorry sight. Ken was holding her left hand. That was a sight to behold. He was holding it a bit too familiarly, I thought, even if her injured arm did look mutilated. It was the size of a very well inflated football. Black and grey and blue and green and brown. Quite a nice mottled colour really. I was thinking the colour would be nice in my hall under dado, a brighter colour above dado and a border at ceiling height. Her arm was huge.

"Does it look bad?" Suzie asked me.

"No." I was lying again.

"Do you think it's broken? I do." She answered her own question but she wanted me to disagree with her. I obliged. "Not at all." This lying was catching on. "Go away out of that, would you! Broken? Sure, why would you think that? There's no way it's broken. No way. Not at all. Not even a tiny weeny break. Think positive. What about that positive thinking class you go to? Use some of that."

"It's not starting until next week."

"Well, get in a bit of practice for next week then. Just think 'My arm is not broken, my arm is not broken' and it won't be."

"Eh. I think maybe it is," Ken volunteered. And who the hell asked him? Ken was one of those honest types. He obviously did not know the difference between being honest and frightening the shit out of my pal. I wouldn't say Ken had an over-abundance of friends. Although judging by the way he was drooling over Suzie he would be counting himself among hers from now on. He would probably want to come on Day Release with us. Well, he has a penis so he can't.

"Eh, I think you might be as well to keep out of it," I whispered to Ken.

"Oh. Ken, do you really think it's broken? Didn't you do the First Aid course last month? What am I going to do, Linda? What if they put me in a plaster? I won't be able to drive, will I? How will I manage?" Suzie started slobbering again.

I didn't like to tell her that she couldn't drive anyway. "Wait and see what the doctor says, Suz." I patted her hand. The one Ken wasn't holding onto for dear life.

"What about you? What did they say?" Suzie asked.

"Nothing. I wasn't bleeding all over them, carrying one of my limbs or even my head under my oxter. They said they'd see me later and I have a funny feeling that means much later. Like next week."

A Clooney arrived in a white coat. Suzie and me stared; Ken didn't.

"Well, well, now, what did you do to yourself?" he crooned at Suzie. She certainly wouldn't be able to complain about the lack of attention. She was soaking it up. I hoped she was enjoying it. I don't care if she was in agony – two fantastic-looking men touching her at the one time is a rarity. It would be such a pity not to enjoy it. I had noticed that Ken was indeed very Ken-ish. Big, broad, blond, hunky in his own way. He was still wearing his shorts and his legs were nice. Very tanned. He looked concerned for Suzie. It showed deep in his deep blue eyes.

"I was out walking and fell," Suzie said. I admired the way she never even blinked an eyelid. She gave the impression to everyone that this was a frequent pastime of hers. Walking. She hadn't even walked to the shops in five years. I was wracking my brain trying to remember the last time we had gone for a walk. I couldn't.

"It looks nasty." Clooney was an obvious-stater,

obviously. For whatever reason best known to himself he prodded Suzie's arm with his index finger.

"*Ah, aah, Jesus, dear Jesus!*" she screamed.

"It's sore then." A definite obvious-stater. "Well, we'll get you to x-ray now."

"Is it broken?" Suzie was sobbing.

"We'll know more when the x-rays come back."

A man burst in the door. Someone had bitten the nose off him. I suspected the woman at the hatch. He was probably short twenty pounds and had no VHI number. But no, he had been involved in some fight with a gang and they had bitten the nose off him. They hadn't just given out to him. They had actually bitten his nose off his face. His face was all red. Not with embarrassment, with blood. The blood was everywhere all over his shirt and hands. He was carrying a small plastic sandwich bag. It didn't hold his lunch. It held his nose. He had put his nose in the bag. A nosebag so to speak. He ran around the room waving the nose and dripping blood. His nose was running and dripping. I couldn't help wondering if he could smell the awful hospital smell? Did he smell? Well, he did smell actually, as we discovered when he came over to Suzie and me to show us the nose.

"His nose, you know." Suzie looked at me,

knowingly tipping the side of her nose with her left index finger.

The noseless man ran over to the doctor shouting. "I kep me dose clean! Any chance of dowing it back on?" He sounded like he was talking through his nose but that was impossible. He kept asking for anyone who could sew. As if the doctor was none other than the Tailor of Gloucester; a stitch and tuck here and he'd have the nose patched up in no time.

As the nose passed me by I passed out. By the time I was conscious again Suzie had been x-rayed. Once again I had let my best friend down at the time of her greatest need. She had to rely on Ken. Ken looked as if he was enjoying being relied upon. Suzie was wheeled into the cubicle beside me. They took blood test, heart tests, lung tests, algebra tests and that was of Ken who was the only healthy one of the three of us. They kept coming in to me, nodding and smiling. I could sense impending disaster. The 'Shit Here' sign had stayed fully lit through all the collapsing. It was still shining brightly now. I had hoped it wouldn't be allowed into the bedded area. I was hoping it would have to stay out in the waiting area. I was really hoping it would find some other poor sucker to latch onto. No such luck.

Suzie was writhing in pain. I could hear her beyond the pale faded, green curtain.

"Can we pull back these curtains?" I asked a little blonde nurse. "She's my friend."

"Yes, pull them back. I can't see what's going on!" Suzie was assertive.

"When's it due?" the little blonde nurse bubbled as she did what we asked and pulled back the curtain.

"I don't know," I said.

"You don't know?"

"They only took the x-ray a few minutes ago. It's due back shortly, I suppose." How the hell was I supposed to know? She was the one in the white uniform. If anyone knew surely it would be her.

"Not the x-ray. The baby."

"Baby?" Suzie said.

"Baby?" I said.

"Baby?" Ken said.

All together now.

"Suzie, you bitch, you never told me!" I was very upset. I couldn't believe that Suzie would keep that secret from me. I was her true and loyal friend and she had never told me! I hoped she had not told Bill before me – that would be too much. "You're a dark horse, Suz! Keeping a secret like that! No wonder Bill's a bit preoccupied. But I'm delighted for you, Suzie." And I was. Rather her than me. Jesus, a baby at her age!

Suzie was speaking over me. Saying the same thing only different. "Linda, you never said! You bitch! I'm delighted! No wonder you were so upset at Dick disappearing. Is that why he went?"

"Who's having the baby?" Ken was fascinated.

"Her," I said, pointing at Suzie.

"Her," Suzie said, pointing at me.

"You," the nurse said.

She was pointing directly at me.

I nearly died. Now I know people often say that and they don't mean it. I nearly died when I got an increase in my wages cheque, I nearly died when I won the Lotto or I nearly died when Johnny proposed. The fact is none of these situations call for nearly dying. Being told you are pregnant when you are thirty-nine years of age and you've no husband to your name calls for nearly dying. I nearly died.

"I can't be. I just can't be. I already have two children, big children. I have my quota. I'm too old. I'm in the middle of the menopause. So it can't be me."

"Hi!" Another doctor, a gynaecologist, was beside me. Not a Clooney. More your Boris Karloff type. Gynaecologists are never Clooneys. "We did a few tests and, apart from the pregnancy, you seem to be in perfect health. We'd like to keep you in overnight for a few more tests, make sure everything is in order."

"Keep me in? Me stay here? Right, I get it. This is a joke right? So where are they? Come on, the game is up! There have to be cameras, right? Suzie and my children have set this up early for my fortieth birthday. I'm not pregnant at all, am I? Suzie did the falling and hurting her arm just so you could play this silly little joke on me. Well, the joke's over, folks. So where's the video camera, then? This is one big elaborate joke, right?"

"Wrong. I'm afraid there are no cameras. Your friend has broken her arm and the rabbit died. The tests are positive. You must have known. You've had other children. You're about three months gone." The doctor was very serious indeed.

"Gone, I'm not the one gone! You're gone, gone in the head! I am an unhappily married menopausal woman." Turning into a dangerous woman.

"Congratulations," Ken said. I forgot he was sitting listening to my every word.

"Don't you dare congratulate me!" For no reason I blamed Ken.

"Are you sure?" I whispered to Dr Fingers.

"Positive."

"Christ, Suzie, I'm pregnant!" I looked at my pal. "I don't know whether to laugh or cry. Wait till Dick hears about this. I was looking for something to bring him back. Reckon this might do the trick. Suzie, this means I'm not the dried-out prune I thought I was. Men needn't pause any more. God, Suzie, I'm pregnant!" I started to laugh, quietly at first. Then louder and more raucously. I looked over at Suzie again. She was joining in. The two of us were laughing hysterically. Tears rolling down our faces. If you had asked me that morning what was the worst thing I could imagine happening to me I would have numbered getting pregnant among my list of answers – fainting in public and being shat upon by birds would also have featured on the list.

This must be Anti-Christmas Day – I was getting my list of things I mostly didn't want in all the world. It looked like the Anti-Santa or Anti-Christ was being very generous this year. Picking out just one worst thing for me would have been too stingy. I could just hear the Anti-Christ: "Give her the full list! Such a long, long, list! Let's be generous this year – after all, Santa will give her diddly-shit so we'll give her everything. All her worst possible fears. Spare nothing."

There was no way I was leaving a bottle of brandy or a few sweets for him, I can tell you.

Though if I'm to be completely honest, bare my soul even, I was sorta, well, kinda happy. To tell the truth, I was really delighted in a weird sort of way that I was pregnant – with child. Months of eating anything I liked without getting fat. Well, I knew I'd be getting fat but people wouldn't point the finger and say: "Look at the big, fat, obese pregnant woman." It would be rude. They would assume I was carrying a big baby and a lot of water, not a lot of fat. But I couldn't stop laughing. Me pregnant, again. I was seriously worried now because I was still laughing. I must have been laughing for five solid minutes. Could I harm the baby by over-laughing? I tried to stop. I needed to go to the loo. But I couldn't stop laughing. I was losing my breath, getting a pain in my stomach and chest. My face was sore. I wanted to stop laughing. Dear God I needed to stop. It was going, as my mother would say, "just that little bit too far". Suzie was snorting with laughter beside me. Ken was muscling in on the act too. We were all hysterical. Suppose we never stopped? Suppose we were sent home from here still laughing? I would miss our chats. We would only be able to laugh with each other. Never chat. Ken and his penis would have to join us as he would have nobody to laugh with. Suzie and me looked at each other again, then we started crying.

"Linda, I'm delighted for you," Suzie said. Her face was blotched from crying and laughing.

"Guess what, Suz? I'm delighted for myself."

"I'm delighted for you too," Ken said. He was just glad it wasn't his new pal Suzie.

"I wish I was pregnant," Suzie said. "Instead of lying here with an arm that's taking over my whole body. The arm is bigger than my head, Linda. Look!"

Her wrist was indeed bigger than her head but her head is very small.

Clooney came back with the x-rays. He patted Suzie on the hand.

"Well, you've broken it all right. The wrist is definitely broken." He looked under his eyebrows. Well, he didn't lift up his eyebrows and look underneath them exactly. He put his head down, chin-resting-on-chest type of down, then he looked sympathetically at Suzie giving the impression he was looking under his eyebrows. Take my word for it. I was there. I saw it.

"Well, bandage me up and let me out of here." Suzie was being just that little bit too jolly, a little bit forced, I thought.

"I'm afraid it's not a matter of bandaging it. It's a bit more serious than that."

"Look, just put a bit of plaster of Paris on it and

it'll be fine. I'm not an athlete or anything so I'll manage."

"Well, I know you're not an athlete but you would like the use of your arm again, wouldn't you?"

"That would be nice, thanks."

"Well, then we'll have to manipulate it back into position."

"Oh, no you can't do that. No one can manipulate me. That's completely out of the question."

"What's the problem?" Clooney asked.

"Sheer terror." Suzie was shaking. Emphasising her terror.

"It'll be fine. We'll put you asleep." Clooney was trying his best.

"Oh no. I can't go asleep."

"Why not? Allergies?"

"No. I'm afraid I'll never wake up."

"Look, you have nothing to worry about. You need some manipulation and a plaster to keep the bone in place while it mends. You have to be asleep when I do it."

"Oh. God, Linda. They're going to put me asleep and pull and chuck at my sore arm. Will you stay with me?"

"Of course I will!" I'm pregnant. I couldn't help thinking about it. I was a bit preoccupied. Pull at her sore arm. Well, now. There's a thing.

"So will I." Ken was holding Suzie's hand again, pledging himself to go the distance.

"How long will we be? How long will it take you to fix my arm?" Tears were flowing down poor Suzie's face. She was trying to stay in control.

My God, I am with child.

"It takes an hour."

"Linda, they'll be an hour pulling and chucking at my arm."

An hour. Well, now, and I'm pregnant.

"Linda, are you listening to me?" Suzie was still crying.

"Of course I am. That's terrible. All that pulling. I'm sure it won't be that sore. Did you hear that I'm pregnant, Suzie?"

Suzie completely ignored me and turned to Clooney. "When will you do it?" She seemed anxious.

"As soon as I can. We have to wait for a free theatre."

"Don't let's wait for a free one. Let's get it over and done with. I'll pay for a theatre," Suzie said, in between blowing her nose.

"I don't mean a theatre free of charge. I mean available. We have to wait until the theatre is available."

Suzie went into a complete cry. Loud and wet.

"I'll be back and give you more details in a while. The nurse will come in and get you ready." Clooney scarpered. One glimpse of tears and he was off.

The blonde nurse came in.

"Who's for the chop then?" Obviously absent for the Bedside Manners lesson.

"Me!" wailed Suzie.

"Her." I was glad to point at Suzie. "I'm pregnant." The nurse went to pull the curtains.

"You can leave them open," Suzie said. Her face looked green, nearly as green as the colour her arm had turned.

A porter came in and took a heart machine out of our cubicle.

"I'm pregnant," I shared.

The nurse asked Ken to wait outside. She took out two white gowns, gave one to Suzie and one to me.

"Will you put these on." More an order than a question.

We took off our tops. Both nodding appreciatively at each other's snow-white bras. Neither of us had been caught with the near-grey ones. Suzie put on the gown. Wide-open space at the back. I could see her drawers. I didn't want anyone to see mine.

"*Psst!. Psst!* Suzie!" I called. "Ask for two gowns."

"I'm bad enough with one."

"No, Suz, we'll put one on frontwards and the other on backwards."

"Linda, you're a real pal."

We asked and it worked. No peepholes for us. No thrills for Ken. We sat smug on our trolleys in our negligée sets.

I'm pregnant, I thought.

I'm going to die, Suzie thought. I caught her vibes.

"Suzie, you'll be fine. I'll stay with you as long as they let me."

A man in a silly green hat and trousers arrived. He had his feet in two plastic bags.

"I'm pregnant," I shared again.

"Congratulations! Who's for theatre?"

"Me," poor Suzie whispered.

"Her!" I shouted for fear they'd pick me.

I got off my trolley with the confidence of a woman whose bum is not on display and put my arms around my best friend. We cried again and I told her she'd be fine even though I hadn't a clue whether she would be or not. I was a real friend. Ken gave her a peck on the cheek. He looked like he wanted to give her much more. I think he was impressed with the gown. I watched as they wheeled her off into the distance. I was glad it was not me.

Then it was my turn. They came for me. A bed

was free on one of the wards. I was frightened. I had never been in hospital before except to have Chloe and Carl. That time I was in such agony that had they tied rope around the babies' legs and dragged them out into the world I wouldn't have cared. I would be back for more of that in six months. A glutton for punishment. But now it was different – I was worried about my children. Would the ones at home be able to cope on their own and was the one with me going to be all right?

Ken kissed me on the cheek and said he'd make the list of phone calls I had given him. I swore him to secrecy on the pregnancy front. I wanted the pleasure of telling everyone myself. Yesterday I knew nothing about Ken. Now I numbered him among my closest friends. He was kind and attentive, gentle and fair. He was single and a few years younger than Suzie and me, but just a few years, nothing worth writing home about.

"Just tell the kids that they decided to keep me in to do a few tests but that there is nothing wrong." That will keep them happy. I had visions of Ken giving them the bald facts and the kids running around, tearing their hair out, fighting over who'd have to give their room up for the baby.

"I'll call to see them in person and come straight back." Ken was a nice man.

There was still no sign of Bill.

A young man in a casual jumper and jeans came to bring me to a ward. He was pleasant enough but not a great conversationalist. I thought of different topics I could discuss with him. The weather, illness, his work, was he busy? I tried out a thousand mundane subjects in my head.

"I'm pregnant." I finally settled on one.

"That's great," he said. We travelled the rest of the way in silence.

I was worried about everything. I started to pray. Prayed on that journey like I had never prayed before. I took the easy option and decided to leave it all up to God. Put everything in his hands. There was nothing I could do anyway. I had three special intentions: a) let my baby be all right b) let my young adults at home be all right and c) let Dick get his arse back to me as quickly as possible. All carried equal importance.

I hoped God would recognise me. I used to talk to him a lot before life had gotten in the way. At night I always intended to have a bit of a chat with him but I always fell asleep in the middle of our conversation, a thing that would have annoyed me if anyone had done it to me. It was a long time since we had spoken properly, me and God. I was hoping the story about the prodigal son was not complete fiction.

CHAPTER THIRTEEN

It was very late when I was finally wheeled onto the ward. The middle of the night. The porter parked the trolley up beside an empty bed and the nurse told me to get into it. This was some feat. The young porter and the nurse eventually rolled me off, like a piece of pastry, and while I lacked the skill and grace of the principal ballerina of the Bolshoi Ballet Company I finally managed to get onto the bed with no major trauma and some degree of decorum. Even though the ward was in darkness I could make out that there were three other beds there. Two of them were occupied. The one opposite mine looked empty, either that or else there was a very, very quite flat person asleep in it. There were snoring sounds coming from the other two beds. Home from home.

Another nurse came in.

"How are you feeling, now?" she asked kindly.

"I'm fine. I think."

She tore the plastic covering off a disposable thermometer and stuck it in my mouth. The thermometer of course, not the wrapper.

"Do you still feel sick?"

"Doe." Why did she have to ask me now? Did she not know it was rude to speak with your mouth full?

"Are you at all faint?"

Faint-hearted, I wanted to truthfully reply but I just shook my head. She seemed nice. She had chocolate-coloured eyes and very black hair. The white uniform made her skin look tanned. She looked a little older than my Chloe. She held my wrist. She kept looking at her watch as though she was late for a very important date.

"Don't let me keep you," I said, not wanting her to take all my vital signs if she was rushing off somewhere. Some gorgeous Clooney waiting for her no doubt. Someone she would give her heart, body and soul to and who in turn would rip them all out and stomp all over them. A lamb to the slaughter.

"I'm not going anywhere. I'm not finished here until eight o'clock in the morning. Even then I will only be fit to drop into bed."

But whose bed?

"I'm just taking your pulse." She smiled at me.

"Well, I knew that." I didn't want to make a complete eejit of myself.

She took my blood pressure. I expected the machine to 'ping'. I was sure the silver ball would climb rapidly up the machine and explode out the top with a roll of drums and a pouring forth of confetti and streamers. I thought I would win the prize for the highest blood pressure ever. The nurse told me it was normal. Not normal to have these thoughts but my blood pressure was normal.

"Are you sure?" I couldn't believe that my blood pressure was not up to ninety. I assume ninety is high, otherwise why would we use the up to ninety expression? So as it was normal I was left with two possibilities: either the nurse was lying to me or the machine was broken. It could have been both. I knew that there was no way that any part of me was normal.

There was a great crashing sound as another trolley made an entrance into the ward. Not on its own. My porter was pushing it.

The poor woman in it was in a terrible way. Singing *'Crazy'*. It must have been Patsy Cline. Joy of joys, I was sharing a room with my hero Patsy Cline. But I thought she was dead. I hoped I would

313

not be sharing the room with a dead person. That would be most unhygienic. There was bound to be a smell and a depressing atmosphere.

"... *myself worry? Wonnnnndering what –*"

Maybe it was just the only other woman in the world who could sing that song exactly like Patsy.

"Suzie? Is that you?" I asked.

"*– I should doo-oo-oo?*"

"Now, now you'll wake everyone up!" The nurse tried to shut Suzie up. "You try to get some sleep. You should be feeling a bit dozy."

"I hope you're not referring to me as dozy," Suzie slurred. She could pronounce all the words in the song perfectly. It was speaking she had a problem with.

The nurse was trying desperately to stop her singing. I wished her well. Suzie couldn't really sing so she rarely did. But every now and again, on her once-a-year day, she sang in public. Usually at a party. When she did warble there was no stopping her. She has been known to go from 'The Fields of Athenry' straight through to 'Jerusalem' in one evening.

Suzie was in full stride with 'Crazy' now, lying on the flat of her back with her right arm propped up on pillows. The other arm was stretched wide open for the finale. She was giving it her all.

Fulfilling a dream. I guessed she was in Carnegie Hall. I wanted to applaud. Applaud her singing and the fact that she was all in one piece. I hoisted myself up on one elbow.

"Suzie!"

"Linda? Linda? Is that you?"

"Over here, Suz!"

"I can't see you, Linda. I can hear you but I can't see you."

"Suzie, I'm over here in the bed opposite you – here, Suzie!" I waved vigorously at her.

"Linda? I can see nothing. I think I'm dead, Linda. I knew if the bastard manipulating me didn't get me, the other one with the stuff to make me sleep would. I think he gave me too much of the stuff, Linda. I don't think I'll ever wake up. I feel weird – all light-headed – my eyes are open but the whole place is in darkness. There was a lady all dressed in white a few minutes ago but she's gone now. I think she was an angel. There's nothing now. There isn't even a tunnel with a bright light. I must be going to hell, Linda, to hell in a basket. There's no light, just darkness! The road to hell is not paved with adequate lighting."

I reached up and tried to put the light on over my bed. I banged my funny bone off the locker. Not so funny. The pain was woeful.

"I hear a noise, Linda. The devil is coming to get me, Linda. I knew I'd be going to hell. Just my luck, a few impure thoughts and I'm for the hot zone. If I'd known Old Nick was going to get me anyway I'd have done a few good mortallers before I fell. Robbed a bank, lied on my tax return, left the lid off the toothpaste. I could have done anything. It's not fair. I think a person should be warned when they have used up all their chances of redemption. If I had been told months ago that it was pointless even trying to be a good person any more, that I was destined to go to hell one way or the other then I wouldn't have bothered being nice. I could have been as obnoxious as I liked."

I finally managed to switch on the light over my bed. I could see her lift her head up. I waved over again so she could see me. She sat upright. Well, as upright as she could with her right arm in plaster. Her blonde hair was forked out from her head. I wondered if she had had an electric shock in theatre.

"Linda, it's all right! I can see the light now! It's just ahead of me. I'm one of the chosen, Linda. I'm going towards the light!" She burst into song again. "*Walk, walk in the light! Walk in the light! Walk in the light of God!* Linda, tell the kids I love them. Tell Bill to fuck off!"

She was deranged. She lifted her arm off the pillows and sat to the side of the bed. She pulled herself as near to the edge of the bed as she could. I leapt out of my own bed and in one step caught her just as she was about to overbalance and take a nosedive onto the floor. I rang the bell for the nurse.

"Get me to the light, Linda. Don't let me rot in Hell!"

"Suzie, you're not dead! You're in a ward in the hospital."

The nurse breezed in. She wasn't best pleased. She glared at Suzie. "Now, now, what's all this? You can't get out of bed and you can't sing either!"

"Don't take that tone with me, young woman," Suzie started. "I can so sing! I am a perfectly good singer. *Sing, sing a song*! Come on, all together now! Join in!" Suzie tried to show the nurse just how good a singer she was.

"Of course you can sing, Suz, just not here. The other inmates are asleep – you'll wake them up." I wished Suzie would shut up. It was getting embarrassing. One thing getting up at a party and belting out a few bars but this was something else.

"Later you can sing all you like." The nurse was copping on fast. Defusing the situation.

"We'll have a bloody good singsong later, Suzie."
I meant it.

"Linda, is that you? Thank God! What went
wrong, Linda?"

"Well, you didn't die so everything went right.
You're grand, Suzie."

The dark-haired nurse must've felt she was on a
roll. Being nice seemed to be working – but she just
had to go that little bit too far. "By tomorrow you
won't know yourself." She patted Suzie on the arm.

"Why? What else are they going to do to me?
What can they possibly do that will make me
unrecognisable to myself? It's only my bloody arm
that has a problem! Don't let them touch any other
parts of me! Please!"

"No, no, dear. You'll feel much better tomorrow,
that's all. Nothing more to be done with you." She
turned to me and rolled her eyes to heaven. I didn't
even blink. I was not going to join in any rolling or
tutting behind my best friend's back. "It's the
anaesthetic," she said as she tucked Suzie in. She
told me to get back to bed and left, promising to
look in on us again soon. As soon as she was gone
I went back over to Suzie.

"Suzie, it's Linda again. I'm here." I stroked her
forehead. Pushed back the wisps of damp hair from
her face.

"Linda, thanks for being such a brilliant friend, for being there for me in all my hours of despair. All my trials and tribulations."

"You never have any tribulations, Suzie." I touched her face gently. I hoped I wasn't turning into a 'touchy-feely' person. That would be more than I could bear. "None compared to mine anyway."

"Listen, Linda. If I tell you something, a really big something, will you promise not to remember it tomorrow?"

"I promise."

"There is something odd about Bill."

"Well, that's nothing new. Aren't you saying that for as long as I can remember?" I laughed.

"No, this is new. There is something not quite right lately. I don't know what it is."

"Oh, you're probably just imagining it. Bill is the same twopence halfpenny he always was. "

"No. I think he might be only in the penny place now. I think the business might be in trouble. He seems preoccupied and he's always working. He works so hard. All hours of the day and night. He deserves to do so well. He should be seeing the benefits of all his efforts but I don't think he is. He won't even talk about it and I don't know where to turn. You always thought Bill and I had the perfect life. But we have our troubles as well, Linda. Oh, nothing as drastic as him buggering off to foreign parts or anything. But lately he's been acting different. I don't know what's wrong. I feel useless, Linda. What am I going to do? I'm not happy any more."

I knew it. I feckin' well knew it. I knew my friend wasn't happy. I had suspected it for a long while. Every time I asked her about it she denied it. But she was worried about that bastard Bill. He had most likely run the business into the ground and she had been putting on a brave face for months. She had him on a pedestal – didn't we all have the bastards on pedestals? Suzie's eyes were closing. No sweet dreams for her tonight.

"Suzie, try to get some sleep and we'll have a good chat tomorrow."

"Will it all look better tomorrow, Linda? Will I be happy?"

"Yes, I promise."

We were a right pair, Suzie and me, and we had picked a right pair. I was husbandless and pregnant, she had a poxy husband and she was armless. I trundled over to my own bed. I was cold and I felt very lonely. I would ask the doctors if there was any way of removing our 'Shit Here' signs tomorrow. Get a signectomy. That would solve all our problems. I tried to sleep but that was another luxury I was to be deprived of. Along with the mink coat and the Hope Diamond, sleep was another thing to add to the list of things I could only desire from afar. Years ago I would have aspired to them all but now that I was joining the wrinkly brigade in a few months I knew there was no hope of the Hope.

I wished my fortieth wasn't looming in the distance. The timing was bad. It's hard to cope with being forty when you're forty. I wished I could turn the clock back. Far back to before I was the custodian of the sign. I wanted to be young and single again and have no worries. Would I be worryless if I was single? Well, to all intents and purposes I was single now but not by my own doing. I didn't even have the satisfaction of making that choice. It was made for me. Like all the other choices in my life at the moment. I was not running the show. I was only a spectator. I had been conned into thinking this was my life. But I was only a puppet. And I didn't even know who was pulling the strings. Well, I was going to cut all the bloody strings. Take control. Grow up. About time too. Nearly forty is as good a time as any to do that. I was going to change my lot. Change it all.

Starting now. Take action. First I would make a

decision on Dick. Did I love the bastard or not? Did I want him back or not? Had I a choice? Maybe that was a bad subject to start with. After all, I really did love him and I had little or no control over whether he came back or not.

Maybe I should never have married him in the first place. It was the biggest con-job of them all and I had fallen for it. White dress and all. Whatever happened to happy-ever-bleedin'-after? I felt cheated. I had been promised till death do us part and neither one of us was dead, unless you counted brain-dead which Dick definitely was. I had been promised things and entered into a contract on the basis of those promises. I had gone in around the back of the altar of the church and signed a book, a contract. But I had never read the small print. I left anything with small print to Dick. That's how come he had to wear glasses. Too much small print in our lives. Suppose in the moment of sheer exhilaration at landing a man I had signed to say he could feck off to sunny climes whenever he felt like it? You'd think I would have noticed if it had said that, wouldn't you, but I tell you I was so caught up with the moment that I wouldn't have.

Sure, I didn't even notice that one of the bridesmaids had collapsed and was hauled out of the church by the groomsman and two altar boys.

I was so busy looking like a meringue that I didn't even see her passion-killer knickers. Everyone else in the church saw them as she was carted up the aisle with her bright pink chiffon dress up around her neck like a big scarf. In fact, only that the photographer was so quick-thinking and took several shots of the incident, I might never have believed it when the guests recounted the story amid gasps of horror and in some cases delight.

If I did unsuspectingly sign a suspect contract it would mean that the priest was in on the whole scam. My father had given that unholy man a hundred quid to marry me. Not Dick. The priest. You'd imagine after getting the money his conscience would have got the better of him and he would have called me aside and asked if I wanted the 'fecking off to foreign climes' clause deleted.

I knew I could get a legal separation and add Deserted Wife to my list of credentials but could I sue Dick for breach of contract? Love, honour, sickness and health. I don't remember Dick honouring me. Unless of course you count the fact that he had honoured me with his presence and the pleasure of his washing and ironing for the past twenty years. I would take a case, not his briefcase or his suitcase, but a legal case against him. Breach of contract. Fight him in the courts. Hit him where it hurt. I would win the case and pave the way for every other woman whose bollocky husband took off. I would become famous. A household name. I felt much better. I snuggled down under the green candlewick bedspread and tried to identify the smell off it. I think it was clean. The smell of clean and fresh. I hadn't changed my duvet cover since Dick left. That was another thing I would change in my life. The duvet cover. God, but I was getting the hang of this changing my life stuff!

Then again maybe if I sued Dick he would leave me altogether. I would have to bring up the children all on my own. Never more would I be able to use "Ask your father" or "Wait till your father gets home!" – phrases that had slipped into my vocabulary with frightening ease. "Wait till your father calls on Saturday" did not have the same ring about it. It lacked urgency. On the other hand the kids wouldn't be able to play one of us off against the other.

"Dad said I could sleep over in my new boyfriend George's flat tonight."

"Well, I don't like it, Chloe."

"How do you know you don't like it? You've never even seen it."

"I don't like the fact that you're staying in George's flat no matter what it's like but if your father said you can then who am I to argue? I'm only the mother around here."

Later to Dick: "Dick, why did you tell Chloe she could stay with George all night? It's asking for trouble."

"I never said anything of the sort! I just agreed with you. She said you said she could stay and I said if you had said it was all right then it was fine with me."

"Well, in future we'll have to consult each other about everything they ask us. Have a family discussion about every single thing. Get the story right. United we stand, divided we fall, and we seem to be falling all the time lately."

I would have no one to be united with now. I would fall. Flat on my face. I knew it. I had made many mistakes with Chloe and Carl. It didn't seem so bad knowing that Dick had been in on the mistakes. We shared the blame. Well, sometimes. Other times he just laid the blame squarely with me.

"You're the father around here. Put your foot down." Never worked. He either did nothing or lost the rag altogether. No happy medium for Dick.

I would have no one to blame but myself for the mistakes I made with this new baby. Well, this time I would make no mistakes. This time I would do it all right. This time I would go by the book. I would rear this child as if it were a build-it-yourself set of bookshelves, or a DIY kitchen. I would read every instruction and follow them to the letter. I would get all the right tools and bit by bit I would arrive at the perfect child. I would become an expert on Spock, be able to quote him the way I quote Shakespeare. I am a great Shakespeare quoter, 'To thine own self be true' being my particular favourite.

I will be proficient on Penelope Leach and all things babies. I will teach it to love classical music, *William Tell* by Rossini – *The Lone Ranger* to you. I will try harder to understand modern painting or if not understand it then at least not laugh at it. For my other two children I had gone by the code that if they were happy campers then we were all happy campers. I was happy to pack in my job. To swap my life at the cutting edge for sitting on the floor cutting pictures from magazines. Making collages, playing Lego, reading Ladybird books and, best of all, making up stories "out from my head". Oh, happy days!

But it would be different this time. This time I would conform, get in step. Look for the educational factor in everything. Seek out the learning experience. Embrace the new thinking on crèches and the like. This child would be a joy to behold. But hold it I would not. Unless it was to change its nappy, feed it or give it the one hour quality time I would slot in for it. I would not spoil this one. If it appeared to be sick in the morning I would not do my usual rush at breakneck speed to the doctor, only for it to burp and chuckle into the doctor's face. No. If it was writhing with pain at home I would make sure it was writhing in like manner at the surgery. Not that I intended to be cruel or anything but these little bundles of joy have a nasty habit of making liars out of their nearest and dearest. They also have a horrible habit of puking all over your best suit just as you're about to attend the most important interview of your life. And sad as it may seem you have a very slim chance of being offered a job with puke, albeit a baby's puke, down the front of your clothes. This baby would not puke.

Now that I come to think of it the little bundles have an awful lot of ugly habits. They have a particularly nasty one of stealing your heart and your bank balance all at the one time. I was going to watch this one. The first sign of any heart-stealing I would nip in the bud, with a cotton bud – there would be an abundance of those around the house now. And nappies for boy babies and girl babies. At least they were disposable, not the babies, the nappies. I would watch this one like a hawk. By the time this child reached the horrors of teenagehood it would be so conditioned by me that it would never even notice that its freedom was at hand.

I know we are meant to be bringing up our children to make them responsible adults. Independent individuals. But show me one, show me one eighteen-year-old that is adult or responsible. There are none. Come to think of it, I have seen grown men of forty plus sit while their mother sticks a mountain of potatoes and gravy in front of them. The poor woman has been so conditioned that she takes pleasure in the man gulping it all down. Cleaning the plate and announcing: "No one makes it like you, Mammy." That one little line gets her every time. She is only short of giving him a rub on the back to see if he has any wind. Well, not me. Third time lucky. My third child would be a paragon of virtue. I felt it move. Just a flicker. Like a gentle little butterfly spreading and fluttering tiny, little wings. It was beautiful.

"I'll love everything about you. I'll do everything for you. Bring you everywhere with me. You and me will be the best of pals." I rubbed my tummy and whispered to its occupant. "I will play with you and cuddle you, lots. I'll never ever let you cry,

I promise. I'll spoil you rotten. Do you hear me, little baby? You will have a wonderful life even if it kills me."

What the hell, who wants a stuck-up perfect child anyway? How can you have a perfect child if the parent is, like me, far from perfect in the first place?

CHAPTER FOURTEEN

Dr Fingers was in to wake me up at sparrow-fart next morning. If I didn't get out of the hospital soon I would die of exhaustion. I was dying for a good night's sleep. He was bright and breezy and why wouldn't he be? Hadn't he got the job most men would give their eye-teeth for? Peeping and poking at all shapes and sizes of women in all sorts of states of dress and undress and getting paid an arm and a leg for the pleasure. Well, hopefully not a real arm and definitely not my leg. He looked as though he had polished his face. Not a sign of beard on it. He had a wild look about him. Long grey hair held back in a ponytail with a silly hair bobbin. I'm not a great fan of men with long hair. Sort of Wild Bill Hickok look about it. I'm sure he returned the compliment as my moussed hair was holding firm in the Mohican style and the remains of yesterday's war paint was streaked all over my face. I would have been frightened of myself had I the benefit of seeing myself.

I asked him a couple of excellent questions about time scale and estimated date of delivery.

"When's it due? How long?"

He looked impressed. I suppose he thought that a Native American would merely take a walk out behind the tepee and drop the child in the first available field. He prodded and poked and had a good feel of anything of mine that could be felt. All this before eight o'clock.

"Well, about six more months. The good news is that you won't have to stay in here all that time." He tried to make funnies. "You can go home tomorrow and be looked after by your husband. Let him treat you like a lady in waiting."

I wasn't laughing. Little did he know I really was waiting. Waiting for the impregnator to return from holiday. Anyway, I was delighted to hear that everything with me was good, and if a doctor said so then it must be true. He told me my darling baby was perfect. Did I ever doubt it?

Suzie was just as lucky. Her news was broken to her by Clooney. He crooned and purred about her arm and the magnificent manipulation he had performed. We guessed he was good at any form of manipulation. He waxed lyrical on the wonderful healing powers of the young female. Suzie drooled when he told her that, sad and all as he would be to see her leave, she could go home the next day. Suzie had no questions. She was gobsmacked. The physiotherapist was called. Unfortunately she couldn't do anything for Suzie's gob but she did manage to give her a few tips on protecting her arm when having a bath and the like. A lot of fuss and black sacks. Suzie didn't know how she would manage when she got home. I made a rash promise to help out as best I could. She was at a low ebb so we did our 'things could be worse' routine.

"It could be worse. I could have broken my two arms," Suzie said, trying to smile between the tears.

"It could be worse. Chloe could be pregnant."

"Two arms, one leg."

"Chloe pregnant and Carl impregnating Kyrstie."

"Two ankles, one leg, one neck."

"Chloe pregnant, Kyrstie pregnant, some bimbo Dick picked up in Crete pregnant."

"OK, you win," Suzie conceded.

I never wanted to win. I always did. This little game was devised as an antidote to the 'Shit Here' sign. No matter how often we played it I never felt better. I always thought we were tempting fate. Come on, Fate, send us all you've got! Here's a few you haven't even thought of yet! How about these for a couple of great suggestions? Come on, don't be shy. Sock it to me. I'm able. Ready and able. Back for the burden and all that, so give it to me all guns blazing.

Despite all the rumours, hospital food wasn't as bad as I thought it would be. Then again anything I didn't have to peel, wash and boil myself seemed delicious to me. The nurses were nice. They even made my bed for me but every time I nodded off to sleep they woke me up to tell me to have as much rest as possible.

Everything in the ward was blue. Curtains, candlewick bedspreads, walls. Even the other inmate's hair and face. Dyed a peculiar blue shade – not her face, her hair. She wore pale blue nightdresses and a thick blue fleece dressing-gown. We wondered had she been told she would be in the Blue Room. The poor woman did her hair every morning and applied a deep red lipstick. She sat waiting for visitors that never came. If visitors had come she would have missed them because once she dolled herself up in the morning and sat up waiting. Pillows propped at right angles to the bed, she fell asleep again. Leaning over on an incline, at a degree. Mouth open. Snoring for Ireland. Blue eyes closed. Hands clasped together on her lap. Her blue veins like a map of the London underground. She was the oldest person me and Suzie had ever seen. She told us she was a hundred and one. If I lived to be as old as her I reckoned I was in for sixty-one more years of misery.

"Who are you?" she asked me for the umpteenth time.

"I'm Linda!" I shouted at her. Not because she was irritating me. Because she was hard of hearing.

"Do you know my son Liam?" she shouted back. Not because I was hard of hearing but because I was irritating her.

"No. I'm sorry. I don't," I replied for the umpteenth time.

"You must know him! He lives in Dublin. Didn't you say you were from Dublin? You must know Liam. He said he'd come and visit me but he never came. Where is he?"

"I'm sure he'll be up today," I screamed at her. Not because she was deaf but because her son was irritating me. Even though I didn't know him. I was pissed off at him not coming to see his mother in this her hour of need. What harm would a little visit and a few grapes do him? I hoped he'd come. Soon. Before it was too late.

For a long time now Suzie had been having

women's problems. I heard about them regularly. On a monthly basis, in fact. I really didn't want to know too much about it but I tried to be sympathetic. I suggested that now that we were in a hospital and a captive audience that she should get my gyny, Dr Fingers, to have a look at her. So she did.

"Linda, Dr Fingers examined me with the same hands he examined you with. Yuck."

"Now that's disgusting. Weird even. But I suppose we could hardly expect him to borrow a pair of hands or even a set of fingers just for us now, could we? Anyway, what did he say? Is everything all right in the womb department?"

"No."

"Oh, Suzie."

"I know. He says that whole department is a mess and he'll have to do a hysterical."

"Oh Suzie, I'm so sorry! I can't believe it. Me pregnant and you having the full hysterical!"

"I don't know which is worse," Suzie sighed.

I do, I thought.

"You always said you didn't want any more children, Suzie. Maybe this is one of those blessings in disguise." Very well-disguised, I thought.

"Yeah. I was thinking that but it doesn't make it any easier. I'm afraid."

"When will he do it?"

"He has to wait until my arm heals properly. Then it's only a matter of getting me a bed and him whipping it out as he said himself. I don't know how I'm going to tell poor Bill."

"Now is not the time to be worrying about Bill." You've done enough of that. "Worry about yourself for a change."

"I'm sure Bill will be up later tonight to see me. First the broken arm and now the hysterectomy. I suppose a third thing is bound to happen soon."

"Let's hope not."

A while later, after Suzie had dozed off, a nurse arrived in. But not to stick things in us. She was carrying a beautiful basket of flowers. All my favourites, freesias, carnations, irises and appropriately enough Baby's Breath.

"These are for you," she said to me. "Will I leave them here beside your bed?"

"Yes. Thanks. Just leave them on the locker there." I saw a little card sticking out of the side of the basket. I pulled it out.

To Linda. Chloe told me you were in hospital. I'd be prepared to be second-best. Love always, The Dillon Man' – Antonio xxx

Jesus, the gobshite! Imagine if someone had seen it! I hid the note. Tucked it deep down into my bra. I would have to talk to him. Let him know where he stood. As soon as I worked it out myself. The flowers were wonderful. It was a terrific feeling, knowing that someone thought enough of me to send them to me. I was on cloud nine. Full of the feel-good factor. It was a unique experience for me.

I was smelling the flowers and smelling of roses when Chloe sauntered in. She was hidden behind an enormous bunch of pretty much the same type of pretty flowers. All colours. They were lovely. She and Carl had popped in to the hospital very late the previous night but I was asleep and they weren't allowed in. Of course, they didn't know about the pregnancy yet.

Poor Chloe looked worried but lovely in her denim dungarees and pale blue top. She was almost seven foot. Thanks to the white platform runners. There was something different about her but I couldn't put my finger on it. Had she lost weight? Was she tired?

"Halloo, Chloe!" Suzie shouted over.

"Hi, Suzie! How's the arm?"

"Ah, it's all right. I must get you to sign your name on my plaster."

"Yeah. Carl will be up later – he'll sign it too."

I gave Chloe a big hug. What was it that was different?

"Nice flowers. Who sent them?" she asked.

"Todd's Dad. It was very nice of him. No need really. Just because you're going out with Todd doesn't mean he has to send me flowers." I was red in the face. Like a fucking teenager covering up after being caught in a halo of smoke.

"He's like that. Todd probably sent them. Was there a card?"

"I don't know where I put it," I said as the corner of the card dug deep into my tit. "But it was from the Dillons anyway." And Antonio in particular.

"That was nice."

"Jesus!" I spotted what the difference was in Chloe. "Your nose! What have you done? You're mutilated."

"No, I'm not. Stop staring at it."

I couldn't take my eyes off it. It sparkled, blue. Hypnotic.

"Good God, Chloe, what possessed you? Letting someone drill a hole in your nose. I hope to God you were dragged kicking and screaming. Or did you just offer your hooter up, lie down and think of England?"

"Oh, Mam, you're such a fuddy duddy! It's just a little stud. I picked a blue stone because you always tell me to wear blue, brings out the colour of my eyes, you always say. What do you really think?"

"I think it's shite is what I really think." I hated it. But it could have been worse. There I was again looking for worse, calling upon fate to wield his mighty hand and sock it to me.

"Where did you get it done? Did you not think of AIDS?" Jesus, was that all I was good for lately – ranting out warnings on AIDS? I was like a television commercial. Different episodes, same character, same message. "Was the place clean? The needle sterilised?"

"I got it done in a very reliable chemist's and the nose-stud was sealed before he put it in my nose. I checked. I am, after all, my mother's daughter." She wriggled her nose. The stone sparkled. It really could have been worse – she could have had one of the large, bull-like rings in her nose or her tongue. Bringing back the lisp I had spent fortunes to get rid of. She could have a chain hanging out of it looped to the hole in her ear. Dangling across her face. If ever there was a need to chain herself to a railings she would have a ready-made one. Mrs Pankhurst would have been proud.

Of course, she could also have been injecting herself and shoving all sorts of substances up her nose. Having great crack. Boy, I felt better. Tempting fate was worth a risk every now and again. At least I knew she wouldn't be engaging in the latest craze: snorting vodka. No way Chloe would be engaging herself in the latest trend of wasting a good shot of vodka up the nose. She'd hardly take up that endearing little practice and risk squirting someone right in the eye when the drink sprayed out like a fountain from the tiny little perforation in the side her nose. No, the nose-piercing wasn't all that bad. There were some benefits.

All the same she'd never get a job with that thing in her nose.

"I've got great news, Ma."

I could see she was excited. A hole in her nose couldn't be making her this happy. If it was I'd be straight out for a few dozen in mine.

"I've got myself a part-time job."

This was very strange. The guy who pierced her nose must have pierced her brain. Chloe doesn't do work. No, I mean it. Chloe has an allergy to any type of work. We have tried every sort of employment. But it makes her tired and irritable. She even set up her own company once. Minding pets while people were away on holidays. She brought them to our house. Everything was going well until some nice old couple left her their only companion in the

world to be minded. A blue and white budgie.
After staying in our house for one day it died.
Keeled over off its perch. There it was sitting on its
swing reciting 'The Windhover' by Gerard Manley
Hopkins one minute. Then just as it got to the bit
where the poet's 'heart in hiding stirred for a bird'
it dropped down dead. Lay on its back. Little legs
and claws stuck up in the air for fine weather.
Head to one side. Dead. Chloe was very upset. She
wondered would she get paid. I think the bird was
heartbroken. Not that Chloe wouldn't get paid. I
don't think it cared less about that one way or the
other. It was heartbroken because it missed its
owners. Either that or the couple of miserable
hours with us caused it to plunge to its death in an
act of suicide. We tried to replace it. We couldn't.
Well, how many poetic birds do you know? We
had no problem getting another blue and white
budgie. There were flocks of them. It was the
teaching it to recite poetry in ten days that was
causing the problem. Apart from the time factor
there was also the fact that none of us knew the
words. The two students had studied it for their
Leaving Cert. but all they could remember was
something about a 'morning's minion'. Only for
the budgie being dead, I could have asked him to
recite it while I wrote it down. Then I could have

taught it to a new bird. Of course, I wouldn't need to do that if the bloody thing hadn't taken it into its head to keel over in the first place. Anyway, when I enquired in the pet shop, the man said it was very unique for a budgie to talk. He said it required patience and love to teach it. The one that died must have been loved and doted upon by its owners, he added, just to make me feel better. He was right. When I broke the news of the demise they took it very badly. A lot of whingeing and thumping of chests. Apparently they hadn't ever left the budgie with anyone before. It was the first time they had been away for thirty-five years. They showed us photographs. Not of their little holiday. But of the budgie. Sitting on his perch smiling. Sitting on his perch thinking. Sitting on his perch listening to the telly. Hundreds of photographs of the budgie doing all sorts. Each one involved the perch. I wasn't impressed. I thought he looked the same in all the photos. I swear to God within a week we got an invite to the funeral of 'Bard the Budgie'. We didn't go. Chloe wanted to pay her last respects. I said I'd only be in danger of laughing. She said I had no feelings. Maybe she was right. I wish I'd no feelings now.

The trouble with Chloe minding the animals was that she didn't – I did. I got lumbered with every variety of four-legged beast and feathered friend in the universe. I was run ragged, bringing them for walks. I once tied a dog to a pole near the supermarket while I went shopping and went off home without him. I kept thinking I had forgotten something. Bread, milk, tea bags. It wasn't till the next day when I went to feed him that I realised what it was I had forgotten. I never let on to anyone. Even Chloe. When I went back to get the poor animal he greeted me like the crucifixion, paws stretched out wide, standing on his hind legs. I bundled him up into my arms and marched nonchalantly along. Hoping no one saw me. So as I did not want a job shovelling shit and clipping hairs, I told Chloe to call a halt to her company or start paying wages. She packed it in. I never got so much as a redundancy bar of chocolate.

The thrill of receiving a pay packet at the end of the week means nothing to Chloe and goes no way to curing her allergy. For years she has been given a pay packet by me for doing nothing. For years I have been looking for an employer that will do the same for me. I haven't been as lucky as Chloe in my venture. But now I was very proud of her. She had finally got up off her very pretty arse and sought out employment.

"Where?" I asked.

"Pragas restaurant. Todd's dad gave it to me. I'll be waiting on tables. I'll get loads of tips."

Oh shit, I thought. "Tips on how to do dishes and clear tables, I hope," I said smiling. My teeth were stuck together. I hoped my smile looked real enough.

Chloe would be working with Antonio. Of course, she would also be working side by side with the younger Dillon man. Plenty of opportunity for a bit of rubbing and laying on tables, no doubt. Antonio would now get to know my daughter. Befriend her and her mother at the same time. I would get to see him every time I fetched and carried Chloe. Chloe always gets fetched and carried. Her only reason for getting the mobile phone was to ring for a lift. Walking to the phone box was an effort. Something else Chloe is not into: effort.

But there was something else about her sitting there at the side of my bed beaming. She had a sort of a glow. Positively radiant. Jesus, Mary and Joseph. Her hair. It was like a halo around her head. Had she been elevated into sainthood during the night?

"Your hair?" I was getting weak. I managed to point slowly at her crowning glory.

"I thought you'd never notice. Isn't it divine?" Here we go with the divine word again. When had that slipped into my children's vocabulary? If they were going to use such a word why didn't they learn to use it in the appropriate way? Say things like how 'divine' their mother was. That their mother had a divine way of dealing with life. Use it in context. Chloe's hair was anything but divine. Disgusting, desperate, disastrous – any of these D words would have been fine. Divine was out.

"What did you do to it?"

"I used that bottle of colour I bought last week. All my friends think it's great."

"And I suppose they are all rushing out as we speak to do it to themselves?" I couldn't help the sarcastic tone in my voice.

"Ah, no, Ma. Sure they wouldn't copy me. Not blatantly anyway."

I thought as much. Not unless they were all as thick as my flesh and blood. Not many people were going in for the glow-in-the-dark look lately. I hoped it would look better after a few washes. Chloe has to wash her hair every day. So do I. She does. I hadn't for ages now. That was Dick's fault.

"Will it wash out after a while, do you think?" I asked hopefully.

"No, it grows out. Much better value. Sure if it washed out it would be gone in no time. Dipsy, from college, advised me to get the one that grows out."

And my Chloe took advice from a girl named Dipsy. I supposed Dipsy either watched a lot of telly or was a very, very tubby child. Or maybe there was a deeper meaning. If there was, it was lost on me. I didn't ask. There were a lot of things lost on me lately.

"I suppose I'll get used to it," I smiled. Then I worried about wrecking her self-esteem. All the years I had spent boosting it only to wipe it out in one throwaway remark. Lack of self-esteem can be very debilitating. I know. From first-hand experience. "Actually I quite like it. It will grow on me. You should have told me before you got it done. I could have advised you better than any Tellytubby."

Looking on the bright side, and her hair was indeed very, very bright, at least it grew quickly. I made a note to look in the chemist to see if there was anything to speed up the growing process of hair. I could get Dick a bottle while I was at it.

"I promise to consult you on every other piercing, colouring and tattooing I get done."

"Any other? Like nipple and all that? What tattoo?"

"Like I don't know what yet. But I might like more piercings."

My beautiful daughter was going to turn herself into a tea bag. Lots and lots of tiny perforations and now that she was the magical age I could do nothing about it. It could be worse, she could be . . . Even my worst possible scenario was not working. This was the worst.

"If I put up with the nose, will you promise me no more? You'll look like a sieve!" I pleaded.

"Well, I have an appointment for tomorrow for three ear-holes. Well, not big hearing ear-holes, just piercings. I'll just get those done and I promise no more. Now please change the subject. How are you?"

"I'm grand. I'd be even grander if my darling daughter agreed to leaving her body with the few orifices it has instead of adding more to it. They said I can come home first thing tomorrow."

"That's great. We'll get the red carpet ready. I brought you in a nightdress, a nice sexy one. I bought it specially for you. You never know who you might meet in here. I wouldn't want you to look tatty while interviewing young medical students for your daughter."

"Fat chance of that, Chloe. I wouldn't inflict any of them on you. Suzie's doctor is a Clooney though."

"I hope she flings herself at him."

Chloe helped me into the nightie and she was right – it was sexy. Black and lacy. Plunge neckline and shoe-string straps. It pushed my boobs up and out. I had the goods and now they were on display.

"Wow!" Chloe said as she fixed my hair. It was gone way beyond fixing but she tried. "Come on, Ma, tell me the truth. How are you really? What did the doctor say about the fainting?"

"Promise you won't tell your father if he rings. I want to tell the slimebag to his face. And promise you won't tell Carl. I want to tell him myself – I want to see his reaction. Do you promise?"

"God, Ma!" Chloe burst into tears. "Are you dying? Is it that bad?"

"No. The opposite. I'm pregnant."

"Pregnant? Pregnant? Are you sure? Jesus, I thought you were past it! That's great!" Chloe put her arms around me and we had a little weep. She was a grand young one. "I'm going to be a sister. Oh, I already am a sister. Well, a new sister. Mam, are you sure you're not too old for this?"

"Well, it's a bit late to be thinking about that now. The deed is done. I am with child whether I'm too old or not. Obviously my body and God think I am young enough. Anyway, won't I have you to give me a hand? You can come to all the classes with me. Watch the video." If nothing else that might put her off landing herself in any mess. "You can make me endless cups of tea. Look after my general wellbeing and my supply of chocolate. Even though I am an old wrinkly person I think I'll be well able for this."

Chloe flung her arms around me again and I think I heard another little sob. If I did she didn't let on. "It's so exciting. I won't have to sneak sideways looks at the rows of tiny little dresses any more. Now I can really look at all the bonnets and booties properly!"

"Now let's not jump the gun. Let's get used to the idea first, then next week we can splash out." We laughed.

"Ma, I think I'll cancel that piercing for tomorrow. You might need me at home. I'll make do with the nose-stud."

I squeezed her hand.

Chloe glanced over at Suzie who was still snoring peacefully. "What about Suzie? How's her arm?" Obviously changing the subject before the floodgates opened again.

"Better than her womb." I filled her in on the news.

"She must be in bits. Has Bill been up to see her?"

"No, he couldn't get away and all her boys are off on some camping trip or another. I feel so sorry for her. Before you go you might sit with her for a little visit if she's awake, will you?"

"No way," muttered Chloe. "I'm not going anywhere near her. I wouldn't know what to say."

"About her womb?"

"No, about her husband."

"What about her husband?"

"Like she might ask me what I've heard about the Bill news."

"The what?"

"The news about Bill. Oh my God! Don't say you haven't heard?"

"Haven't heard what?"

"Oh my God! Don't tell me Suzie doesn't know!"

"Know *what?*"

"Take it easy! Lie back. Relax. Don't harm my baby, will you? This is going to be a big shock, Mam. I thought you knew."

"Get on with it, Chloe!" I was losing patience with the dramatics of it all and my anxiety levels were building.

"*Shhhh!* Don't wake her!" She looked over in alarm at the sleeping Suzie. "Well, you know Doreen is having an affair?" she muttered.

My heart left the safe position it was in, encased in my ribcage, and headed straight for my throat where it started beating so loud I was sure my blue-rinse roommate would hear and Suzie would wake up.

"Well," said Chloe, "it's only Bill who's throwing his leg over."

"What?"

"Bill is the one –"

"Yes. I heard you. But is it true? It can't be. Not Bill. Where did you hear this? It's nonsense. Bill! I can't believe it. Sure, Doreen wouldn't even look at him. Larry is streets ahead of Bill in the looks department. Poor Suzie! Are you sure?"

"Well, Bill must have something Larry hasn't. Hidden where we can't see it. Anyway, the story has been going round. But it's definite. Morgan told me."

"Morgan?" Nearly all Chloe's friends have weird names.

"Yeah, you know Morgan, lives next door to Suzie. Well, she got a part-time job in some hotel in town. Who does she see only Bill sitting, sipping something with Doreen! It was her first night. Well, not Doreen's first night, Morgan's first night at work. So while Suzie was falling head over heels on a grassy bit, Bill was probably falling head over heels on a brassy bit – Doreen."

"But maybe the hotel thing was a coincidence. They might have bumped into one another. Had a neighbourly drink."

"Well, if they did they ended up holding hands

going into the lift. Bit over-familiar for just bumping into each other, don't you think? Goes way beyond the requirement for the Neighbourhood Watch scheme. More into Love Thy Neighbour territory if you ask me."

"What will I do?"

"Nothing you can do."

"I have to tell Suzie."

"Why?"

"She's my friend."

"Do you want her to remain your friend? She won't if you say her husband is having an affair. Especially when you tell her it's with Doreen."

"When did you get so wise?"

"Long ago. You just never noticed."

"I was too busy noticing how beautiful you are." I winked.

"Well, when you're finished praising your most favourite daughter maybe you'll take her advice and keep your mouth shut. Let someone else tell her. Then you be standing by ready to pick up the pieces."

"I have to be the one to tell her."

"Well, rather you than me."

"Aren't men bastards, Chloe?"

"Not all of them. Todd's brilliant and sometimes I see great hopes for Carl. Anyway, speaking of men,

I have to go. The biggest bastard of them all is giving me a lecture on Social Policy in some godforsaken country or other that's ruled by some even bigger bastard. Carl should be up to see you soon and we'll both be up tomorrow morning to bring you and our sibling home. Carl can drive, God help us. He's making his own of your car. Oh by the way, be prepared. The dreaded Kyrstie might be with Carl. She seems to have invaded his mind. He's obsessed. Every sentence is Kyrstie-connected. He is even gone off his food. I think it's serious, Mam."

"I know. But I sort of like Kyrstie and I don't think Carl means to make her his life-partner or anything. They're just having fun."

"Ma, he eats, sleeps and breathes Kyrstie. He's even turned into this nice person. Offering me lifts and having conversations with me. It's weird. I like her too though – she seems normal enough."

"Well, anyway . . . thanks for calling in to see me, Chloe. I won't say you cheered me up no end. That would be a lie."

"Ah Mam, I love you."

"Ditto."

We hugged.

I lay down and pretended to be asleep. What was I going to do? I could always pack my bags,

sneak off home. To a family that of late felt the
need to tell each other we love each other all the
time. My life was in turmoil and I was going to
have to tell my best friend hers was, if anything,
worse than mine. How could we counsel each other
through this fine mess?

I could always do what Chloe had suggested,
pretend I knew nothing. Let Suzie get on with it. In
her hour of need I could scarper. The bastard Bill.
The slimy two-faced bollocks. I wished I could kill
him. Maybe I could. Maybe I could sneak home,
murder Bill, sneak back into the hospital and never
let on. Then when they found Bill's mutilated body
I would have an alibi. Doreen, on the other hand,
would not. I could arrange that. I could have her
and her expensive suit find the body. I could make
sure that all the evidence pointed to Doreen. Kill
him with a designer knife or beat him to death with
a designer handbag. The name of Calvin Klein
would be imbedded all over his smug little face.
Everyone would suspect Doreen. Was it normal for
a person to be plotting murders every day?

"Linda?" Shit, Suzie was at my bedside. Her face
was right down at me. Face to face. I couldn't open
my eyes. Couldn't look my best friend straight in
the face.

"Linda? Are you asleep?"

"No. I'm just resting my eyes." I had to open them.

"Linda, what's the matter? Is everything all right? Did Chloe have bad news? Are Carl and herself all right?" She was bending right in to me. Ready to comfort me.

"Yes, they're fine, Suz, thanks."

"Is it Dick? Had she bad news about Dick?"

No. She just up and told me your husband was bonking Doreen. So my life is rosy. How's yours?

"No, he's fine. The bastard Dick seems fine. He wonders where I am and I've sworn them not to tell him. He keeps ringing though. Let him wonder. He left me wondering for long enough."

I started to prattle on about Dick, hoping we wouldn't have time to get onto the Bill topic.

"But I thought you wanted him to know you were in here so he'd come home."

"I did but not any more. If he's not coming home for me I don't want him to force himself home out of a misplaced sense of loyalty. I want him to come home because he wants me. I want him to miss me and want me more than anything. I want him to need me and love me. Love being with me. Is that too much to ask?"

"No, Linda, it's not. But you've got to tell him. I am your best friend. Listen to me. Dick loves you.

Let him be with you now. Especially now with the baby and all. Look at me and Bill, how happy we are. Dick and you will be like that again soon." She pulled up a chair and sat down. I was glad. I didn't want her to fall over and break her other arm when I told her what only her best friend could tell her.

"Oh, Suzie!" I started crying. My life was one big cry lately. Would I ever laugh again? Would me and Suzie ever have fun again?

"Don't worry, Linda. I'm here for you. Dick will come home soon. I just know it. Please stop worrying about it, Linda."

"It's not Dick I'm worrying about, Suz."

"What then? Is it the baby? Are you still worried about being old and pregnant? What did Chloe say? I bet she was delighted."

"She was. It's not that. It's not even about anything in my life, Suzie." I held her hand. That confirmed it. I was now officially a touchy-feely sort of person. Anyway, these were extenuating circumstances and a bit of touchy might be called for. "Suzie. I have something I have to tell you. I don't want to tell you but I don't want anyone else to tell you either. If I thought no one would tell you then I would leave well enough alone and never tell you. But I know some supercilious busybody is going to delight in telling you. It might even be Bill himself. Maybe I should wait until after you've seen Bill. Let him tell you. I don't know what to do. I need a friend's advice."

"Linda, you could you try talking English! I lost you right around the supercilious busybodies."

"It's Bill, Suzie." I decided to come straight out with it.

"My Bill?" Her hands shot to her face, covering her cheeks. Just after I glimpsed the colour leaving them. "What's happened to him? Is he hurt? What are you telling me? Where's Bill?"

"Oh, Suzie."

"Linda, for God sake, what is it?"

"Suzie. If you knew Dick was having an affair would you tell me?"

"Of course! Is he? I swear I never knew, Linda. I'm your best friend – of course I would have told you!" She paused. "But what's this got to do with Bill?"

"Well, you know how we were wondering who Doreen is having the affair with?"

"Oh my God! Dick is having an affair with Doreen! Is that why he went away? I don't believe it! I'm so sorry, Linda." She tried to put her arms around me but only managed to hit me on the ear with her plaster cast.

This was much harder than I had thought. So was the cast. Why didn't I listen to Chloe?

"He's not."

"He's not? Well, what then? What are you saying?"

"I'm saying that I know who's having the affair with Doreen. Bill knows too."

"Bill knows? How does Bill know? What's it got to do with him?"

Jesus, would I have to spell it out for the girl? Draw diagrams? Play Pictionary?

"Oh, Suz! Bill . . ."

"Yes, Bill knows. You already said. But who's having the affair with Doreen? Why don't you just tell me! You're making a mountain out of a molehill!"

"Bill, Suz, it's Bill who's having it away with Doreen."

"What?"

"It's Bill."

"Bill?"

"Yes."

"My Bill?"

"Yes."

"I don't believe you! It can't be. Not Bill. Not my Bill."

"I'm sorry, Suz. Really sorry."

"It's not true." She didn't even cry. "Tell me it's not true, Linda." Tears trickled down Suzie's face but she wasn't crying crying. It was more. It was like she was frozen and the tears were the only things alive. Terrible, terrible sadness. I had never seen such sadness before. Except once, a few days ago. In a mirror. How could that bastard have hurt her like this?

"How do you know? It must be a mistake," she finally said.

"I'm sorry, Linda, but it seems it's true all right. He was seen in a hotel with her."

"Who told you?"

"Chloe."

"How does she know?"

"Someone saw them."

"Well, I don't believe it. Some vindictive little sod spreads a rumour and you believe it! I thought you were my friend, Linda."

"But it's true, Suzie. Think about it. He's been missing a lot lately. Spending money. Playing golf with no shoes. He must have been meeting her, not playing golf."

"Don't be so ridiculous! Just because your precious Dick is gone off the rails doesn't mean that everyone else's husband is gone astray too. Bill would never be unfaithful. Dick is the one who's run off, Linda. He's probably having an affair, not Bill."

"Suzie, Dick is not having an affair."

"How the hell do you know? Sitting there so sanctimonious telling me about my life. After all I've done for you! Look at your own life! Nothing to write home about there! Get the mote out of your own eye first, Linda. Don't come to me making accusations about my husband. Find out about your own first!"

"Suzie, I don't know for a fact that Dick is not having an affair but I do know for a fact that Bill is."

"No, you don't. You're just listening to idle gossip. You seem to have become quite an expert on that lately."

"Suzie, being a right bitch to me won't take away the fact that Bill is having it off with Doreen. I'm sorry I was the one to tell you. I'm sorry if I hurt you. Bill is hurting you more. I foolishly made a decision to tell you rather than have you make a laughing-stock of yourself when he lies his head off to you tonight. Cop on, Suzie! Bill is a bastard. He's been whoring around behind your back and you can't shoot the messenger now. Shoot Bill!"

I had said much more than I intended. Gone way past the line between truth and hurt. I had been annoyed at what she said about Dick maybe because I had been thinking it myself. I lashed back the only way I knew how. I kicked her when she was down. Just after her husband had done the same.

CHAPTER FIFTEEN

There are some things that are better off not said. We had said them all. There is an unwritten rule that states how it is all right to listen to someone thrashing off their spouse or child. It is quite another to agree with them or even endorse the rotten things they say. The job of a friend is to listen. I had forgotten that. I had broken the golden rule and spoken my mind. What little of it I had left.

I tried to make up with Suzie. Sat over beside her bed. But things had gone too far. I didn't know if things would ever get back to normal for us. I hoped they would. We needed each other. The only saving grace was that each one of us knew it.

Bollocky Bill came up to visit Suzie and after he left I sat with her again. I said nothing, just sat. She fell asleep. I still sat, waiting. I had learned a lot over the past few days.

"Linda."

"I'm here, Suzie."

"I'm not sure if I can talk. I can't even cry."

"No need. We can talk later. I'm sorry, Suz. I really, really am. I was just trying to help. Guess I made a worse mess, eh? I'm sorry if I hurt you. There are enough people in the queue to hurt us. We don't need to hurt each other."

"I'm sorry too, Linda. You didn't hurt me. Bill managed to do that all on his own. You were right to tell me. I know it must have been hard. Anyway you were right about him and the tart. Bill finally admitted it. Oh at first he kept denying it. Said it was a vicious rumour. That people were jealous of our perfect marriage and how they hated to see how happy we were. I had to keep on and on at him. But he is having an affair with Doreen. It's been going on for a couple of years. I must be a right thick not to have noticed."

"How could you? You trusted him. He was just sneakier than you thought."

"Come on, Linda! All the signs were there. I just ignored them. Hoped they'd go away. Maybe I knew all along but just didn't want to face up to it. We've laughed long enough at poor miserable Larry.

That's what everyone was doing to me too. Me and Larry, the innocent parties. The thicks, more like. I've a good mind to ring Larry and tell him all about it but I can't."

"Let Doreen do her own dirty work."

"The bastard Bill hasn't been working late in the office. He's been working on Doreen. Keeping me sweet with tales of pressure in work and all the other shit I swallowed. Flowers and perfume to keep me happy. I don't know fact from fiction any more. Was everything a lie? When he was with me was he thinking about her? I feel so dirty."

"You have nothing to feel dirty about. It's all down to Bill and Doreen. You hold your head up high, Suz – you have nothing to be ashamed of."

"I loved him, you know. I thought the sun shone out of his backside. The miserable bum let me think that."

"But of course you did. He was your husband. That's the way it's supposed to be."

"What am I going to do, Linda? Doreen must be having a great laugh at me. The whole world must be hysterical."

"Well, do we care? No, of course we don't. Let her have Bill and all your bad luck with him. She won't be laughing when Larry finds out. She'll be in her Dunnes Stores knickers like the rest of us when he refuses to give her a penny!" I had made Suzie smile.

"I told Bill to pack his bags and be gone when I get out of here. Jesus, Linda, it's like a nightmare. I asked him did he love her. He said he thought he did. I asked him did he still love me. He said he didn't know. That he thought a lot of me and didn't mean to hurt me. That hurt me even more. I'm sorry I had a go at you. I just didn't want to believe what you were saying."

"I know."

We sat in silence. I fixed Suzie's hair. The door opened and two very handsome men came in.

"Well, well, Suz! The answer to our prayers! A bit of light relief and of the male variety."

Ken and Carl had chocolates and magazines. It turned out Carl was in the same soccer club as Ken and they had known one another for years.

Ken pecked me on the cheek. Gorgeous. Soft and gentle yet firm. A woman's man. I left Ken to take Suzie's mind off Bill. I took Carl back over to my bed to tell him my bit of news.

"How are you, Mam? You gave us all a fright."

"I'm fine, Carl. You needn't have come up. I'll be home tomorrow."

"Well, I wanted to talk to you on your own before you came home."

"Is there something wrong?" Carl has a knack for picking the worst possible moments to impart the worst possible news.

"No, Ma, it's great. Everything is just great. I have never been happier. Remember you used to tell us that out there somewhere was our soul mate and that we should wait until we find them. Settle for nothing less. Do you remember?"

I did indeed remember. I had used many a ploy to stop my children engaging in sex with every dog and divil and this was one of my better ones, I thought.

"Yes."

"Well, I know Kyrstie is mine."

"I'm glad for you, Carl, but you must consider the fact Kyrstie is a bit older than you. Are you sure?"

"I've never been more certain of anything in my life. We want to get engaged, Ma. Kyrstie won't give me an answer until she hears what you have to say. She says it's not fair if we just spring it on you as a done deed with Dad gone off and you being sick and everything." He was beaming from ear to ear.

Little did he know what the everything was. I wondered if the very big-hearted Kyrstie was setting me up for a major fall. Getting me to give my opinion on the engagement. I was fecked if I did and more fecked if I didn't. Credit where it's due; the girl was clever. I had to give her that. But you have to be up very early in the morning to beat me.

"Well, now, Carl, this is the way it is. I am not the one you're asking to marry you. I can't give you my opinion one way or the other. You have to decide. I can only say that I wish all this wasn't happening so fast and that you weren't so young. Then again maybe that's the best way for you. You have to decide. But if you have to think about it then it's wrong."

After the Suzie debacle I was giving my opinion of nothing to no one. Especially not my own children. I didn't want to lose the closest, most precious, human relationship I had. I wanted to have my son around me for a long time yet. Kid gloves were called for again. I was getting a lot of wear out of them lately.

"I don't have to think about it, Ma. But I have thought about it. I want her more than anything I have ever wanted. She is now part of me. I know all this sounds soppy and I'm not normally soppy but I want you to understand how I feel. Do you?"

"Yes. But what about college, Carl? Will you give up your course?"

"No. We only want to get engaged. Commit to

each other." God but my son was full of shit these days.

He went on with the shit. "Kyrstie and I will finish our course at the same time in two years' time and we will get married then. Please, Ma, what do you think?"

"What about Chrissie? Will you be able to be a good father to her?"

"I love her. She is like a little sister now but soon that will shift and I will become her dad."

"Carl, it's an awful lot for you to take on."

"But, Ma, I love the bones of her, warts and all."

My lovesick son was asking me for approval. I should have been flattered but I was worn out. Fed up with other people bringing problems to my door. Dumping on me. This would be another problem for me to worry about. Roll up, roll up, bring all your problems to Linda. Let her have them all. She has loads and loads, an overabundance, so why not give her a few more?

"Does your father know?"

"No. I spoke to him last night but he never rang today. I never told him about Kyrstie. We talked about you mostly. I think he wants to come home. He keeps asking about you, Ma – he loves you, you know."

"Well, he has a funny way of showing it. Listen, Carl, if you need to find yourself bugger off now and do it before you make any commitments. Do you hear me? Don't wait until you and Kyrstie are married for twenty years to do it."

"Does that mean we have your blessing?"

Had I a choice?

"Did you ever doubt it?"

He flung his arms around me. He was grinning like a toothpaste advert. Maybe it would work.

"Carl . . . I have news of my own."

"Everything OK?" He was barely concentrating. The young in love are a pain in the arse. They want to shout about it to everyone. They want to put their arms around each other and claim possession. In front of everyone. They think they are the only ones allowed to love and be loved. I envy them.

"Everything is fine. But you're going to have a little brother or sister in about six months."

If I had hit him over the head with a bedpan I could not have surprised him more. He just sat staring at me.

"You and Dad?"

Who else? Antonio? Timing.

"Well, your father is the only one I have ever slept with, Carl. Strange and all as it is for you to understand."

"Does he know?"

"I hope not. I told Chloe not to tell him."

Carl was stunned. I had nearly killed him. Tit for tat. I had pulled an ace on him. He did not like it.

"I can't believe it. When were you going to tell us?"

"I only found out yesterday myself."

"It's a bit embarrassing at your age, isn't it?"

Oouch!

"Well, if you and Kyrstie get married in two years will you give up all rights to a family because of her age?" Touché.

"No. I get the point. I am delighted for you. For all of us. I just want to make sure that you aren't taking on anything you can't handle. I don't want you to be in any danger either."

"Will you please stop talking to me as if I'm Methuselah. There are older swingers in town, you know, Carl. I'm not the oldest. I'm young and healthy and everything is going to be fine. Be happy for me."

"I am. I'm happy for all of us. I might get that brother I've always been wanting. Just think! If I marry Kyrstie in two years you will be a granny and the mother of a two-year-old. The sprog will be younger than its niece. Wild, eh? We never were a conventional family, were we?"

"No but I always wanted us to be."

"We're fine. Better than most. I love you." There we go again with this need to tell each other we love each other. Surely we should know that by now.

"You know I love you too."

"I know."

He hugged me. A man's hug. My little boy was gone. I had reared a nice man. I looked over his shoulder and saw his double standing at the door. A good bit older but the image of him.

"Dick."

"Linda."

"When did you get home?"

"As soon as Carl told me you were in hospital, I got a plane home."

I looked at Carl accusingly.

"I'm sorry, Ma."

"Don't blame him." Dick said. "He was upset and I wormed it out of him."

"You always were a worm." I spoke my mind.

"I'll leave you two to it." Carl hugged me goodbye. He gave his father a mock punch in the shoulder. "Behave yourself," he said as he bowed out gracefully without even waiting for Ken. Afraid he would be caught in the crossfire.

"Dick, I don't know if I want to see you." I was

annoyed. This was not how I had imagined our first confrontation. Me in a sexy nightdress in bed. Granted not my own bed, but I felt at a certain disadvantage. Dick was fully clothed. "I really don't know if I want to see you, Dick, you or your tan." He was bronzed all over. It was sickening. The big bastard was looking fantastic.

"How are you?" He pecked me on the lips. I nearly turned away but didn't.

"What happened, Dick? What made you take off like that?"

"I still don't know but I do know why I'm back. Will that do you? And I've done a lot of thinking while I've been gone. I suppose you have too."

"Well, actually no. All I managed to think about was how I was going to cope from minute to minute, hour to hour. That sort of thing. Unfortunately I didn't have the benefit of a sun-lounger or a bottle of suntan lotion to bring on the thoughts. But I can appreciate how nice it was for you lying in the sun thinking. Keeping your mind from getting burnt. What the hell were you thinking about for Jesus sake? My world has fallen apart over the past few days and where were you? Lying on your belly on some godforsaken beach. What do you want me to do, Dick? Welcome you back with open arms? Very pale open arms, I might add. I might have liked a holiday. Why didn't you bring me with you? Sneaking off in the middle of the night. I thought you were dead or something."

"I know it was a bit drastic." He giggled. He actually giggled. Apart from the fact that it was at least five years since I had heard Dick giggle, this was not the time or the place.

"Drastic? It was fucking insane." I was trying to keep my voice low. I wanted to scream and shout. I didn't want everyone to hear me. This would have been much better in the comfort of my own home.

"I still can't believe I had the guts to do it." He giggled again.

"Guts? You think it took guts? It would have been gutsy to stay. Sort it all out here. Only a coward runs, Dick."

"But I sorted everything out for us."

He took my hand and I didn't pull away. Call me a fool, an eejit and a dork. Call me anything you like, I have already called them to myself. Hey, big eejit! Hey, you thicko! You, yes, you holding hands with the slime-bucket that left you. Big brassy bitch. Yes, you! You fool! Stop making it so easy for him.

"Linda. I'm back. We can take up where we left off. It was stupid of me to go without saying anything. I promise I won't do it again."

Had he always kept his promises I might have believed him. His track record on the promise-keeping front was very bad. But I am a sucker.

He pecked me on the mouth again and sat down on the side of the bed.

I found my fists banging against his chest. Blue-rinse must have been enjoying the show, to say nothing of Suzie and Ken. I didn't care.

"Dick, I hate you. Do you hear me? I hate what you've done to me and Chloe and Carl."

"Yes. I know I must have put you through a lot of worry but I'm back now. Full of ideas. Wait until you hear them – you'll be amazed. I had a lot of time to sort things out. I met a few lads on the golf course and we got chatting and one thing led to another and I got to see things clearer."

"So, all and all, you had a bloody good holiday. Is that what you're trying to tell me? Why the fuck did you bother your arse to come back?"

I didn't think I could listen to any more.

"I love you and I love the two kids. The four of us are great together. I missed it, Linda. I missed being one of the four of us." Missed being Lord of the Manor more like.

"How would you feel about being one of the five of us?"

"No, don't tell me. As soon as my back was

turned you bought a dog. I thought we said we didn't want any pets."

"Actually you said that. Anyway it's not that. I'm pregnant."

"How? Whose? Christ, Linda, how did that happen?" He was crestfallen.

"Well, it's like this. There are birds and there are bees and –"

"Very funny. I see we haven't lost our sense of humour. Jesus, Linda, I didn't think it was even a possibility."

"Neither did I. Look, Dick, I know it's a bit of a shock for you. In fact it's a bit of a shock for me too."

"How long have you known? Did you know before I left?" Dick asked.

"I only just found out. Would you have gone if you'd known?"

"I don't know. Probably not. I don't think I would have left you pregnant."

"You would have stayed for a seed inside my womb but not for me or the two outside the womb?"

"You know what I mean."

"No, I don't. And what do you mean 'whose'? What do you think I am? It's yours, of course. You shouldn't even ask."

"I wasn't exactly asking – I was just stunned,

Linda. I thought all that was over. All the nappies and bottles. It's a bit mad at our age. Having a new baby. I had it all planned out. I thought about our life together when I was away. I've thought about nothing else. That was the thing I wanted to tell you about. I want to pack in my job and set up on my own. I thought you'd help me. I could open up a practice in the village. No more working for anyone else. I'd be my own boss. Come and go as I pleased. I'm sick and tired of heading off every day to the grind of working to fill someone else's pocket. I want to fill my own for a change. I didn't tell you this earlier but there is a redundancy package going in work. I want to take it. It's a great chance for us, Linda. A fresh start. I've been doing some figures. The rent on an office wouldn't be too much and I thought we could live on your salary until I got started. Carl and Chloe are all grown up. I finally see that. They'll be moving out soon. We could make a go of it on our own. But now, with this baby? Well, I'm not so sure. Will you be able to keep on at work? It would be great if you could. You'll have maternity leave. Between that and annual holidays it might work out. What do you think?"

I think you're a bastard. "Well, you seem to have it all sorted out nicely. I don't know if we'll be able to manage on my salary alone though . . . it's tough going as it is, on the two salaries. But I suppose we could give it a try."

He looked at me and nodded. "I think we can manage. Don't forget I'll get quite a good package from the job. We can manage on that until I get things going. Carl and Chloe won't be around for much longer either."

"Well, if that's what you want I won't stand in your way. I'll agree to it on one condition. You never mention to Carl or Chloe what you just said to me. Never put pressure on them to move out."

"OK. So will we do it?" he asked. I nodded. Dick smiled. He was delighted for himself.

There was little point in standing in Dick's way. Whoever was foolish enough to do that would be mowed down. Dick took no prisoners. How in the name of Jesus would we manage with two eternal students and a new baby on my meagre salary? Maybe I could grovel for a rise. Pick up some overtime or bring some work home from time to time.

Dick was overjoyed. Everything was going his way. His newfound self was thrilled with all his ideas and the fact that they were being so well received.

"Will you talk to Carl and Chloe tonight, Dick?

Tell them how sorry you are that you buggered off without saying goodbye to them."

"I suppose. I'd better. I'll never hear the end of it if I don't, will I?"

We hugged and Dick went home. He had let us all down. I didn't need to tell him. He knew. I was sure he was sorry. He just found it hard to show it. I was glad he was back and staying. I don't know why.

Ken went home and Suzie and I swapped notes. Ken was going to bring Suzie home. Well, not home to his house but he was going to collect her from the hospital and bring her home to her own house. I suspected Ken would be doing a lot for Suzie. In more ways than one. We were both smiling, which given our recent history was a good sign. I suspected both our smiles were a little less than genuine. Forced even.

It was blatantly obvious that Suzie and me would never get to Crete. Crete had just been one of our pipe dreams and we knew it. It wasn't such a major disappointment that we wouldn't be going. Our lives were so unsettled at the moment. Anyway we couldn't afford it. What with Suzie kicking Bill out and Dick giving up his job. Also there was the problem of my fitting into the thong with my being pregnant and all. Ridiculous and all as it was before, now it would be hideous. We were very matter-of-fact about it. Promising to go another time. We both knew that another little dream was ruined, another bubble burst. But when you're at the bottom like we were there was only one way to go. Up. We were definitely on our way.

CHAPTER SIXTEEN

Big posters with big bright red lettering saying 'WELCOME HOME, MA AND SPROG!' were hanging in the hall and all over the place. It looked great. This was obviously a red-letter day. Dick, Carl and Chloe had gone to a lot of trouble for me. I'd love to be able to say that they had gone to the same trouble with the house and got stuck into cleaning it. But that would be a lie. And you should know, by now, how I hate lies.

I'd love to be able to tell you that the smell of home cooking wafted from the kitchen blending with the smell of fresh polish. But no. The place was as I had left it. A kip. I was just grateful that the doctor hadn't said he'd make a house call. I would have had to get the kids to put me in the car for the examination. The car was the only habitable room in the house. Carl and Chloe would have had to stand around the car holding their coats open wide. Wide enough to cover the windows. Dr Fingers would have to be told I lived in a mobile home. It wouldn't be my first internal in the back seat of a car.

I would also love to be able to tell you that I came home from hospital looking glamorous and wearing shoes. That too would be a lie. I came home shoeless. In a blue suit that had seen much better days. A short jacket and much shorter skirt. It wouldn't have been so bad if they had brought in a blouse or top to go with it but no. I had to button the jacket to hide my once perky bosoms. No tights. No underwear. I had given them the distinctly unglamorous outfit I had come into hospital in and asked for a change of clothes. I would have been better travelling home in my nightdress and dressing-gown. I nearly wasn't let out of the hospital because I had no shoes. Then Carl came up with a bright idea. Well, everyone else thought it was a bright idea so I thought it must be. He had a sports bag in the boot of the car. Housed in this sportsbag were the biggest pair of runners you have ever seen. The sort you could fill with compost and plant a young forest in. Now I know I said I have big feet

but not that big. The runners weren't even j.
plain white. No, these had all sorts of stripes in al.
sorts of colours. The type that said 'look at me'.
Everyone did. I found it difficult to walk at first.
The shoes didn't want to leave the ground. At last
Dick and Carl got on either side of me and linked
me. I plodded along in the too small suit and the
too large shoes. Turned quite a few heads.

The first thing that greeted me when I came
home, after the beautiful posters, was Dick's sports
bag. Lying in the hall vomiting out dirty clothes
that he had been kind enough to bring back from
Crete for me to wash. Obviously his newfound
self, like the old one, didn't know how to wash his
own clothes. I made up my mind to put an ad up in
the local supermarket for a woman or maybe even
a man to clean the house for me. I was sure we
could find a suitable person. Blind with no sense of
smell.

The kids were glad I was home. They asked
what was for dinner and could I collect them from
the various outings they had planned, none of
which included me. Dick took up his position in
front of the telly and for a moment I wondered had
he ever left. Was this it then? Life with Linda goes
on as before.

I escaped. Called over to see how Suzie was

managing. I wondered if she was aware that the whole neighbourhood was talking about her. I, for one, wouldn't be telling her. Once bitten, twice shy. News of Doreen and Bill's carryings-on was the topic on everyone's lips. It had taken over from me and Dick. I was relieved. But poor Suzie. I'd have to do my best for her. She was where I had been a few days ago. Now it was her turn. Her 'Shit Here' sign shining bright as a star. I supposed she'd give me a key. She had said something about going to take up where I left off on the couch.

But when I arrived she was all dressed up. She looked fantastic.

Her house looked fantastic. Clean.

"Come on in. You can make us a cup of tea while you're here."

I followed her into the kitchen. It was as clean as mine was dirty. Not a bacterium in sight.

Suzie's kitchen is all wood. Wooden floor, dresser and presses. Dried flowers hung everywhere. Rows and rows of spices lined the walls.

"How's Dick?" she asked, trying to unscrew the tea caddy with one hand. I took it from her.

"Here, you sit down. I'll do it. Dick's fine."

"God, Linda, I envy you. It must be great to have him home. All lovey-dovey, I suppose."

"Well, not quite, but I suppose it will take time.

I'm still a bit pissed off with him. Anyway, how are you? Any news of Bollocky Bill?"

"I'm better than I thought I'd be. Not a whisper out of Bill. He took all his things. Some of mine too. The bastard cleared everything out while I was in the hospital. Can you believe it? Doreen is probably sifting through the lot as we speak. She won't keep much. Nothing has labels. He even took some pictures off the walls. Can you believe it? You know the one Greg did for us last Christmas? Well, he took that. I loved it. He didn't. He only took it to hurt me. As if he hadn't hurt me enough. Well, I'm not going to let him best me. He did me a favour. I'm not going down under all this, Linda. I'm determined not to take to the couch."

"Well, good for you! Don't worry about the painting – I'm sure Greg will do you another one. Have you been talking to him? Does he know about his dad and Doreen yet?"

"No. He rang earlier. The three of them are coming home as soon as they can to see me. They feel awful that they couldn't get here earlier. But they've arranged the quickest flights they could get. I don't know what I'm going to tell them."

"The truth," I advised.

"It'll be great to see them. Ken said he'd like to meet them too. He's a nice man, Linda. He seems genuinely concerned. He promised to call in to see me later." I reckoned he'd call in often. Maybe he'd even be given a key. I had a funny feeling he would do his best to help Suzie get over Bill. I was hoping she'd enjoy his best.

"I'm sure he is. I'm sure he thinks you're a nice lady too. A very nice lady."

"Do you think so? Wonder what would give him that impression?"

"Maybe the fact that you are."

"God, but you're full of it these days, Linda!" Finally my friend laughed. Not a long, loud laugh but enough for me to see the old spark. We sipped our tea and made plans. Not exotic plans. On my way back across the road I met Larry. He was walking up my driveway.

"Larry. How are you?" You poor bastard.

"Hi, Linda. I was wondering if Dick was in?"

"Come on in, Larry. He's just watching a bit of telly." I didn't know what to say. How to sympathise with him. 'Sorry to hear Doreen is bonking Bill' seemed a bit blunt. So I ignored it. Ostrich-like.

I opened the door and Dick jumped up when he saw Larry was with me. He was very anxious to get rid of Larry before Larry even came into the room. At least that's the impression he was giving when he physically pushed him back out. Gently, but still. He was nodding and winking at Larry in a most peculiar way. Larry didn't know what was going on. I think he was a bit afraid actually.

"Will you stay for a cup of tea, Larry?" I shouted over Dick's shoulder as Larry disappeared backwards out the door.

"Thanks, that would be nice." Larry looked relieved. Like I had saved him from a good hiding.

I went into the kitchen. I could hear the two of them talking in the hall.

"For God's sake, don't mention the war! Don't mention the war! Do you hear me, Larry?" Dick was saying. Well, I think it was war. It sounded like it anyway.

"What?" Larry was saying, "I don't understand you, Dick. What the hell are you going on about?"

I rooted through the empty margarine cartons and milk bottles, to put on the kettle. I got out the cups and made room for them on the table. There were no tea bags so I put a spoonful of coffee in each cup. Something caught me eye. A present. It was nobody's birthday. But right there in the middle of the table, all wrapped up in white-patterned paper, was a gift. There were little Greek drawings and symbols all over it. Hydro-somethings or other, I think they were. Dick had told me he had bought me a present. This was it. Perfume? Lingerie? I opened it, excited, expecting the best. After all he had a lot to make up for. Fair play to him all the same. He had probably spent a fortune on me. Well, I was worth it. I tore open the wrapper, decapitating one of the little Greek men. Not jewellery, not a handbag or a little ornament. No symbol of his undying love for me. What was it only an ashtray. A fucking ashtray. A terra-fucking-cotta ashtray. Just in case I didn't know where it was from, A PRESENT FROM PISKOPIANO was printed in bright blue letters all over it. In English.

Larry was just leaving when I barged into the TV room. I could hear him making his escape.

"That's grand then, Dick. Good luck now. I hope you look after it as well as I have. It should give you no trouble. I'll drop it off to you in the morning. If you could just make out two cheques. One to me and one to Doreen, we'd be delighted."

"I'll arrange that. Bye now, Larry, and thanks."

I followed them out into the hall.

"What this?" I stood there and waved the offending pottery in the air. Right under Dick's nose.

"I thought you'd like it." Dick was chuffed with himself "To add to your collection. You know the way you collect ashtrays from all over the world. Now you've got one from Crete."

"I'll give you a bloody ashtray! Right between the eyes!" I raised the ashtray.

"I think I'll be off then. See you." Larry beat a hasty retreat.

"Oh, have you already got one from Crete? I'm sorry. I didn't know."

My blood was boiling. It is a great credit to me and a measure of my unending patience which had been tested many, many times over the years, that I didn't shove the ashtray down Dick's neck there and then. Shove it down so far it came out the other end. He went back in, to assume the position in front of the telly.

"Since when do I collect ashtrays, tell me? Go on, tell me! Go on then! I'm dying to hear." Waving the offending ashtray at him.

He stood up and walked into the dining-room. Opened a door of the cabinet. Ashtrays from every flea-ridden armpit of every corner of the world were piled high. Hidden. Dick swept his hand in a flourish toward them. He was delighted. I left the room. I got a plastic bag from under the sink and threw the ashtray into it. I took out all the others from their hiding place in the press and unceremoniously dumped them one by one into the bag on top of each other. Crashing and smashing them. It was magic. The relief!

"Jesus, Linda, what are you doing? Do you not like it or something?"

He seemed genuinely shocked as he watched me smashing. I looked at him. I thought of all the crap I had put up with for all the years I could remember. I tried to forget.

"What did Larry want you for?" I said as I bashed away. I was making a great effort at normal conversation.

"He asked me last night did I want to buy his BMW. He's given me first refusal on it. Doreen wants her half so he has to sell it. He just called to see was I still interested."

"What did you say?" My blood was way beyond boiling point. Exploding point.

"I jumped at it. I said we'd give him two cheques. One for him and one for Doreen. She needs the money to buy a little place for her and Bill."

"Well, fuck you, Dick! Just like that you go and buy a car! Who am I? Am I anybody? Jesus, if I was your housekeeper you'd consult me more. You'd even clean up before I came over to clean. A holiday isn't enough for you, you selfish bastard. Now you want a car. Not any old car for our Dick! No, a bloody great BMW! You're going to pack in your job. Let me work to keep us. Well, you've hit

390

the jackpot this time, haven't you? Won the holiday *and* the car. Well, you can go jump, Dick! I thought marriage was about sharing and the only thing I seem to get a share in around here is the shit. Besides, you can't buy Larry's car. You can't give Doreen the money for her and my best friend's husband to set up a little love-nest. Have you no morals? Have you gone stark raving mad?"

"Well, Larry seemed all right about it. Said she was a financial noose around his neck. Seems he'll be glad to get rid of her."

"Doreen or the car?"

"I don't know, probably both."

"Typical. What about my best friend Suzie then? What about her? How do you think it will go down when I tell her we financed the hot-spot for her husband and his lover?"

"Well, if we don't buy the car someone else will. I don't see what's wrong with us getting it. You're just overreacting as usual."

"Overreacting? No harm? Just like there's no harm in buying your wife a fucking ashtray! Dick, I really missed you when you were away. I hoped every day that that would be the day you'd come home. But I didn't really miss you. It wasn't you yourself I missed. It was only the thought of what you could be if you tried that I missed."

"What? Linda, what are you saying?"

"I'm saying that I don't want to do this any more. I'm tired of doing it."

"Do what?"

"This."

"What?"

"What I've been doing all my life. Pleasing."

"What?"

"Pleasing you. Doing whatever you say. I'm sick of it. It's hard work and I'm tired. I want to please myself for a change."

"But you can please yourself. No one is stopping you. You're a bit emotional now, Linda, being pregnant. I'll get Chloe to make us a cup of tea and then you'll be all right."

"No, I won't. I don't think I can be true to myself if I'm trying to please you. I don't like what you do. Or the way you do it. I think it would be best for us all if you took your dirty little sports bag from the hall and buggered off back to Crete."

Dick started pacing. Up and down. Up and down. I wished he'd sit down. I wished I'd said nothing. I had gone too far. I knew it.

"Dick?"

"Don't you open your mouth. Do you hear me? You've said enough."

"But, Dick!"

"Shut up. Do you hear me? Just shut up."

"But –"

"I said shut up!" He came over close to me. I could feel his breath on my face. He shoved me along ahead of him. Pushed me up against the wall. Took a grip of the collar of my jumper. Pushed it up under my chin.

"Will you just shut up, Linda! This is my house! No one is going to ask me to leave. Do you hear me? I will come and go as I please and I won't ask you for permission. Neither will I ask your permission to spend my own money. You're such a smart bitch! Well, I'm buying Larry's car whether you like it or not. And I'm giving up my job whether you like it or not. And I'll tell you something else for nothing, no one is going to push me around or tell me what to do! Do you hear me?"

I was terrified. I could see he was trying his best not to hit me. Or was I just hoping he was? I decided to keep as quiet as I could. Then he might let me go. Jesus, he was possessed. His new self was worse than the old self.

"Dad, what the hell are you doing?" Poor Chloe was at the door. She was biting her lower lip. She always does that when she is really frightened.

"It's nothing, Chloe! Just go to your room! I'm grand. I'll be up to you in a minute," I shouted to

393

her. Jesus, go away, I pleaded at her with my eyes.
She stood there staring. Pools in her eyes. She was
rooted to the spot. Shaking. I wanted to run to her.
Hold her. Tell her everything was all right. I was
afraid to move.

"Go away, Chloe! This has nothing to do with
you. Your mother and I are sorting things out. Leave
us alone. Get out, Chloe!" He turned as he shouted
and let go a little of his grip on me. I pulled free and
I ran over to Chloe. I stood in front of her and
blocked her. Dick was furious. I could see it in his
eyes.

Chloe pushed me aside – gently – not the way
Dick had done.

"Dad!" Chloe spoke softly. Dick was wild now.
Chloe didn't know. She couldn't read his eyes. I could.
I was terrified. "You can't just do what you like to
Ma. She's been in bits since you just took off and left.
You're such a big man. Shoving and pushing her
around. Taking off when you feel like it. I suppose
you'll start on me now. Push and shove me around.
Well, you won't, because the first time you do I'll ring
the police. Don't think I won't. I'm not going to put
up with the shit she's put up with all her life. Trying
to keep the bright side out for me and Carl. We have
you sussed now. You frighten me, Dad. You really
frighten me. But I love Ma more than you can ever

frighten me. So do what you want to me but I'm not going to my room and leaving her with you. Mam deserves better than you. So do Carl and me. You turned your back on us. We welcomed you back with open arms and now look at you! You're pathetic." Small little tears forced their way down the side of her nose. She was trying to be brave. Holding it all in. She was shaking.

I heard a key in the door.

"What the hell is going on in here?" Carl shouted.

"I came in and caught Dad shoving Ma around." Chloe finally fell apart.

I couldn't speak. I was watching. Seeing everything I had spent my life building come crashing down around me as I knew it would one day.

"You bastard!" Carl started shouting. "I stood up for you. I told Chloe she was wrong about you! But she knew. Chloe saw what you were. A bloody coward."

"And you wonder why I left? Look at you. All running to her defence." Dick was pointing at me. "Neither of you taking my side. You always were a mammy's boy. You didn't even ask what she has done." He was pacing again.

"We don't have to ask, Dad. Nothing she did should make you treat her like this."

Dick collapsed into the chair. He was beaten and he knew it. I was relieved. He looked like I'm sure I looked when I read his grotty little note. Revenge is not sweet. I felt sorry for him. But not sorry enough that I wanted to take him back. He had breezed back into our lives without a by-your-leave. Not a bit of grovelling to be seen. Who the hell did he think he was? Calling the shots again. Taking up where he had left off. I had coped for nearly two whole weeks without him. I could cope a hell of a lot longer, especially if I got the blind housekeeper in to give me a hand.

Dick had done me a favour when he left. His pedestal slipped, came crashing down and now there was no going back. He could never regain his lofty position. Carl, Chloe and me had made a good fist of things with no fists to worry about. We were happy. We could still be happy.

I finally found my voice. "I think it would be best if you left, Dick."

"So do I," Chloe added. "I'm sorry, Dad. I just don't know what else to do."

"Me too," Carl said. "You've gone too far."

"So you're all against me? Is that it?"

"No, Dad, we're not. In fact we all love you. You're just against yourself." Chloe is a very wise woman.

Dick went upstairs and packed a few things in a holdall. He left without saying goodbye. He was used to that.

Chloe finally gave way to the tears that had been dammed. I held her as she sobbed her young little heart out. I hated Dick for doing this to her.

Carl said nothing. I could see his jaw flex. He was biting down hard on his teeth. There was no doubting his manhood now.

The bell rang. I rushed out. I thought it was Dick back. It was Antonio. I fell into his arms.

Todd was with him. Looking for Chloe.

"I was just dropping Todd off and wondered how you were. I never expected a welcome like this!" He held me tight. Stroking my hair gently. I looked over at Chloe. I hoped she would survive all this.

Todd was holding her, close, stroking her hair. She was crying like a baby in his arms.

"Come on," he said. "I'm going to take you out somewhere nice." I hoped he would take her out of herself. I was tempted to ask if I could tag along.

"I love you, Ma." Chloe hugged me as she left.

"Me too. I love the bones of you." God, I was a right eejit, crying again. I looked over at Todd. "Will you make sure to look after her for me? She's precious." Such drivel! Under ordinary circumstances I would have made myself puke. I was very emotional. The bladder near the eye and all that.

"You know I will."

It dawned on me that there was only so much I could do to protect my children and I had done it all my life. Done the best I could for everyone. Except me. It had been hard going keeping us all together for so long. It was stupid. I was the ringmaster keeping this circus going, only Dick was the one cracking the whip. I had lost all control of my life yonks ago. It was come-back time.

Funny thing is, I felt sorry for Dick. Weird, eh? There is no accounting for feelings. I felt guilty. Like it was my fault. I was a failure. I blamed myself. If I had said this he wouldn't have done that. If I hadn't exploded he wouldn't have either. Then again I always blamed myself. If I had just kept on treading on eggshells, taking the shit, then everything might have been all right.

"It's not your fault." Antonio read my thoughts. We watched as our two children, young adults, walked off hand in hand into the sunset – well, not the sunset exactly but it was love's young dream anyway. "When Todd's mother died I felt guilty. Guilty that I hadn't done enough. That if I had done something sooner, made her go to the doctor earlier, she would never have died. But she did die. It took a while for me to realise there was nothing

I could do. It was all out of my hands. This is out of your hands too, Linda. You deserve better. Maybe now you'll get it. I could make it better for you. If you'll let me. I love you."

I turned into him and he held me, tight.

"You look tired," he whispered, concerned.

I was sure I looked shit. I didn't care. Well, I did really but there was very little I could do about it. It would take an awful lot of plastic surgery to make me look half-human again and at this hour of the night I didn't know anyone who would perform such a difficult operation. I was gone well beyond anything Elizabeth Arden could do for me and Max Factor didn't factor on my sorry state when he developed his panstick. Sheer Genius he may have been but magician he was not.

I was knackered. If I could only make it up the stairs to bed that would be such an achievement. A bloody miracle. I could do with one of those. A miracle would be very nice just about now. Antonio took my hand. He rubbed his thumb against my skin. Like you do when someone you care about is hurting. So he cared about me. I could feel it. Sweet Heart of Jesus, what was I going to do? I wanted him. Ached for it. But I was wearing my five-pairs-for-five-pounds knickers and my second-best bra. And I was tired. So tired.

"Come on. Let's get you tucked up in your bed. You just might get some sleep." See. I was right – he did care about me. Ugly ol' me. He led me by the hand up the stairs. I let him lead me. I wanted someone to lead. Antonio was good at it. I'd say he was good at a lot of things.

I stood beside the bed watching him turn down the duvet. I was tired.

"Want me to leave while you get undressed?" he asked, walking to the door.

"No. Don't go," I whispered. I stayed standing where I was. My heart started thumping very, very loudly. I was sure he could hear it when he put his arms around me. I felt his hand softly on my neck. I looked at him. He was beautiful. The tiny little laughter lines around his eyes were beautiful. Soft. I reached up and touched them. Like a blind woman I felt his face. I could look at him all my life. He bent and brushed his lips against mine. I could smell the cocktail of Armani and him. I loved him. I wondered if he knew. I smiled and kissed him. Deep, devouring kisses. Our tongues warm against each other. I wished I'd had a bath. Worn my best lace knickers like they do in all the films. My legs were wobbly. He held me up. I felt such a wanting. My body was crying out to be touched. He knew. Slowly, softly he felt every inch of me. Down my

neck, across my boobs, down to my waist. His two
hand gliding across my belly-button, sneaking up
under my blouse to my bare flesh. Devouring me
all the time. It was like teenage love again, without
all the fumbling. His hands expertly circled over
my belly then deeper until the tips of his fingers
made my groin ache. I wished I'd had my bikini
line done. The perfect equilateral triangle. Then
again maybe he wasn't interested in perfect, maybe
he was only interested in me. I pushed my body
tightly up against him. I could feel him. I ground
my hips into his. He was kissing my neck. Biting it
softly. Tiny bites. He opened my blouse and I
slipped it off. Unhooked my bra and freed my
boobs. They looked swollen. He kissed my nipples
then sucked them. I pulled at his shirt, heard a
button tear, felt his hot muscular body. I wanted
this man, big-time. I opened his trousers in a frenzy
and felt his flesh. Wanted to feel it rub against mine.
He peeled off my skirt and knickers. I couldn't wait
for him. He was all over me and still we were
standing, now both naked, pressed hard against
each other, hands exploring everywhere. All my
erogenous zones were going ape, and at the same
time. I was one large E-Zone. We lay on the bed.
All cellulite and stretch-marks. I never felt as
beautiful. Antonio caressed and held me. I had never

been loved before. Oh, I had had sex but this was the first time I had been made love to. I never knew there was a difference until now. All dicks are not the same. Thank God. I would have died, there and then, if I thought Dick's dick had come back, attached to Antonio, to haunt me. Sweat sparkled from Antonio's body. His bronzed chest on top of mine, breathing with me. Hearts beating together. He pulled himself up on his elbows and looked at me. Deep into my very soul.

"I love you," he whispered to me. "I have always loved you. I am going to love you forever."

"I know," I said. Then we devoured each other, writhing, pushing. Deeper and deeper. The room went black. I floated. It was orgasmic. He held me for a long time, then touched my face and told me he loved me again. And after a while I cried. My fucking husband had just left me and I was crying. I was so happy. I felt different. Something other than Dick was missing. For the first time in years I wasn't afraid. It was terrific.

Antonio touched my face. "You are the most beautiful woman I have ever seen."

I wanted him again. I never wanted it to end. I stepped out of bed, naked, and took his hands. It was a long time since I had stood in front of anyone naked and not felt ashamed of all my lumps and bumps. As I led him to the shower I glanced in the mirror. I saw what was missing. No sign of the sign. The 'Shit Here' sign. It was gone. If I'd known how easy it was to get rid of it, I'd have done it years ago. Never, never let yourself go down under the shit, I thought as we stood in the shower. The hot spray beating against our bodies. Antonio rubbed scented oils all over me. I moved towards him. Wanting him.

"Stand still. Don't move an inch. I'll have you crying out for me before I'm finished."

I was crying out for him anyway, even before he doused my body in oil until it seeped deep into every pore. Crying out for him to hold me. I stood still and he came to me again.

I was crying out for love.

CHAPTER 17

It was a fantastic day. The sun was shining and there was a great buzz about the house. It was six months to the day since Dick had left. Five months, three weeks and six days since Antonio had moved in. I didn't regret any of it. Antonio had healed all wounds. He loved me warts and all.

My outfit was all laid out. Ready. This was the big day. Antonio had been up very, very early making sure everything was the way I wanted it. He had taken to reading my mind and minding me. I loved it.

"Come on, Ma. Today's the big day. Up and at 'em." Chloe was all excited. She had never been bridesmaid before.

She guided me and my bump out of the bed and

into the shower. I was huge. Beached whale time. This pregnancy had followed the same pattern as the other two. I had ballooned. My skin was so stretched that it was almost transparent. Royal blood pumped through me. Honest. I could see the blue beneath the thin layer of skin.

"Linda, where are you?" I could hear Suzie come into the bedroom.

"I'm in here!" I shouted from the cubicle. I hoped I wouldn't get stuck.

"Well, come on then! The groom says you're to get a move on. Come on, Linda. Me and Chloe are all set to beautify you. You can't keep the groom waiting."

They cleaned, exfoliated and toned my face. Chloe put on my make-up and though I say it myself I did look fantastic when they had finished.

"You look brilliant." Chloe was beaming. Proud of her ma.

"Are you decent?" Carl shouted into the bedroom at us.

"Is she ever?" Chloe shouted back.

"Don't mind her, Carl. Of course I'm decent. Come on in."

"Give me a few minutes alone with Ma, Suzie, will you?" Carl asked.

"Right," Suzie said. "I know where I'm not

wanted. Anyway, I don't think I want to stay. I have a feeling there's going to be a lot of soppy stuff about. I'll see you all downstairs. I hope Ken remembered the camera."

Chloe turned to leave.

"Wait, Chloe." Carl put his arms around her. "You're the best sister a brother ever had. You know I'll always be there for you, don't you?" He handed her a little box. She opened it. It was a locket. A picture of him and her on one side and a picture of me on the other.

"Thanks, big brother." They hugged. Chloe was crying.

"Now I thought we said no tears today," I said. "This is supposed to be a happy day for all of us. Come on now. Go and fix yourself up, Chloe." I knew it wouldn't take much to make me cry.

"Ma." Carl sat down beside me on the bed and put his two arms around me. "I love you. Love the bones of you. Thanks for everything."

"Carl, today is going to be a great day. A new beginning for us all. From now on things are going to go according to plan, I feel it in my waters. And aren't my waters always right? I am so proud of you, Carl."

He handed me a little box and stood up and left to get ready. There was nothing more to be said. I opened the box slowly. Relishing the sentiment of the giving. There lying in the box was a bracelet. Gold. A little heart hung from the chain. *To thine own self be true* was printed on one side. *Love, Carl* was on the other. I held it in my hand. Then close to my heart. I put it on. I knew I would never take it off.

I put on my dress. Then my feathery hat. They were yellow. The likeness to Big Bird was uncanny. Jesus, what had possessed me? I would have looked great at a fancy-dress ball.

"Wow!" Antonio said as I walked down the stairs.

"You look great." Chloe was beaming.

"Fucking fantastic."

"Carl, please, no bad language. Just for today. Just for me," I pleaded. I doubted that I looked great or fucking fantastic. As for the wow factor, I was sure that was missing. But because the three people I loved most in all the world said it, I felt it.

Suzie was elegant. She wore a black knee-length dress and a cropped white jacket. Her black and white hat looked ready for Ascot. Ken held her hand all the way through the ceremony.

Kyrstie wore a long, flowing, ivory lace dress. She was followed up the aisle by Chloe and Chrissy.

Two big beige meringues. Carl stood waiting for her at the altar. He was so handsome.

I was nervous making the father of the groom speech. Especially as I was his mother. Antonio sat beside me giving me all the moral support he could muster. I was rattling.

"Firstly I would like to say thank you to you all for coming and making today such a wonderful day. I knew a lot of people would turn up to see Carl all polished up in his tux." I felt a little twinge. Not in my heart where I had expected to feel it, but in my waters. "It is a very proud day for me. When Carl first mentioned to me that he would like to get married I rang the doctor. He assured me that there was nothing physically wrong with Carl. I then rang a psychiatrist. He assured me that Carl's complaint was very common. But that there was very little he could do for him. 'Love,' he said, 'is an incurable illness.' 'But is it contagious?' I asked him, worried that we all might catch it. He assured me it wasn't but I am beginning to doubt him." I looked at Antonio, then at Chloe, who was radiant.

Another twinge. Jesus.

"I know Carl and Kyrstie are very, very happy. Since Carl met Kyrstie, Chloe and I have had to listen to him waxing lyrical about her. He has had a

permanent grin on his face since they first met. Look!"
I said pointing directly at Carl. Carl was obliging
by grinning from ear to ear.

Now a pain. A definite pain.

"We have had to suffer that cat-who-got-the-
cream look for months now. To be honest we're
sick of it and just as pleased Kyrstie agreed to
marry him. And," I looked directly at my son, "I
hope he will never lose that look."

Another pain. Sharper. I grabbed the table.
Antonio grabbed my elbow.

"Thank you all for coming. A toast to the bride
and groom."

I cut my speech short. Left out all the funny bits.
Like when Carl took his first girlfriend to his Debs
and asked the florist for a cortège of orchids. Or the
time he took one girl to a concert, lost her and came
home with a completely different one. Swearing a
hole in an iron bucket it was the same girl.

Jesus, the pain again.

"What's wrong?" Antonio asked. He was my
best pal now. I never told Suzie that. She was still
my best female pal – well, after Chloe.

"I don't know what's wrong but I have a feeling
the baby wants to make an appearance at its brother's
wedding." Holy shit. I felt something warm down
my legs. My waters. The bloody waters had broken.

More like the floodgates. It was everywhere. All over the plush carpet.

"Sit down! Sit down, Linda!" Antonio looked all worried.

Chloe rushed over. Todd was with her.

"Is it time, Ma? God, what rotten timing! I'll tell Carl." She ran off. Well, scuttled to be more precise. Running and the big puffy dress didn't quite go together.

A great crowd gathered around me.

"Get the car and bring it around the front!" Antonio shouted to Carl.

I was in bits now. My hat was sideways on my head but I couldn't get it off. Suzie had stuck pins into it and my head to keep it on. Well, not my head exactly, more my hair. Whatever she had done, one thing was sure: she had done a bloody good job of it. The hat wasn't coming off. No way. The feathers were tickling my nose. I started sneezing. Then the pain got worse.

"Linda are you all right?" Suzie was holding my hand.

Antonio lifted me up. He staggered backwards then found his footing and ran with me to the door of the hotel. Chloe followed in the quickest pursuit she could manage in the dress. Carl was in the driver's seat of the car.

"Linda, will you marry me, please?" Antonio asked as he bundled me into the car.

"For God's sake, Antonio, you know I love you. What more do you want?"

"I want you to say it to everyone."

"I love Antonio!" I shouted to the top of my voice. "Happy now?" Oh. Oh. Christ, another stabbing pain.

It was nothing new. Not the pain – that was new and pain seemed a rather feeble word to describe it – vice-grip around the belly seemed more appropriate. Antonio wanting to marry me was nothing new. He asked me nearly every day. I think it's too soon AD. After Dick. But Antonio keeps asking. I hope he never stops. One day I might even say yes.

Empty cans, old boots and a sign saying *Just Married* were hanging from the back of the car. We drove at breakneck speed through the village to the hospital. Antonio carried me in. I don't think he will ever recover.

"Well, well," the midwife said, looking at us sternly. "Looks like you just made it. Priorities in the right order and all that. But I don't think it's a hospital threshold you're meant to be carrying her over." She laughed at her own joke. No one else did. "I presume you're the groom?" She was pointing at Antonio.

"No, he is." Antonio pointed at Carl.

Suzie, Ken and Todd arrived.

"Well, you two come with me then." She pointed at me and Carl. "Only the mother and father are allowed in now. The rest of you can come in later."

"Wh! Wh! Wh!" I was breathing out. Doing what all the books said to do. "Wh! Wh! He's not the father." I managed to point at Carl.

"But I thought you said he was the groom? Who were you marrying?" She looked at me, puzzled.

"I – Wh! Wh! – wasn't getting – Wh! Wh! – married. He was but not – Wh! Wh! – to me. I'm his – Wh! Wh! – mother."

Just then Kyrstie arrived with Chrissy. The veil gave the game away.

"Ah, here's the bride!" The midwife said. "What a lovely dress! Did you have it made? It's the nicest dress I've seen in a long time. Walk up there and let me have a look at it. Give us a twirl. Betty!" she called a nurse – great, she would look after me. "Betty, come here and look at this wedding dress. Betty is getting married at the end of the year. She might like a dress like that." Betty arrived and more ooohing and aaahing and pulling up skirts and examining veils went on. I kept panting for all I was worth. Chloe looked faint.

413

Antonio spoke up. Thank God. "Sorry to interrupt but I think the mother-to-be is in need of some attention."

"Are you the father?" the mid-wife asked.

"Wh! Wh! Wh! Wh!" I said.

"No," Antonio said.

"You then?" She pointed at Ken.

"No." Ken backed away.

"Not you?" she said to Todd.

"No."

"Thank God for that. I thought you looked a bit young."

Todd seemed to take this as an insult.

"Being a father would not be an impossible task for me," he said as if he had been trying very hard to prove it. I felt weak.

The midwife raised her voice. "Who is the father of the child?"

"Dick!" we all chorused.

"And which one of you is Dick?"

"He's not here," Antonio said.

"Right. So the only one missing is the father. Is that right?" the midwife said.

"Yes," I said.

"Can – Wh! – my boyfriend – Wh! Wh! – come in with me?" I asked.

"And which one of this fine selection of handsome

men here would that be?" There was an edge to
the midwife's voice I didn't quite like.

"Me." Brave Antonio spoke up.

"Can I come too?" Chloe asked.

"And who might you be?"

"The bridesmaid. Her daughter. I did all the
classes with her."

"Sure why don't you all come?"

I think she said it as a joke. But she should never
have said it. We all barrelled into the room.

The doctor looked aghast at the crowd. I started
screaming. The thoughts of all this entourage standing
waiting, watching between my legs, was too much.

"Get the hell out, the lot of you!" I panted and
puffed, the contractions coming fast.

"Can't I stay?" Antonio asked. Chloe rushed over
to me and hugged me. "Let him stay, Ma! You need
him. Carl and me will be outside, waiting. Good
luck!"

I was so proud of her.

"All right, Antonio can stay. The rest of you
wait outside."

The pain was sharp and fast. It was too late for
an epidural. The nurse whipped off my very expensive
tights and knickers. She kept talking about centimetres
but nothing about painkillers. My two feet were
put into stirrups with not a horse in sight. Dr

Fingers did his bit. I couldn't see what he was doing. I had my eyes closed in excruciating pain. All I knew was he was sitting on a stool talking to a part of my body that had hardly ever seen the light of day, let alone had a whole conversation conducted to it, while I lay, legs apart on the bed.

"I can see the head," Dr. Fingers said from my nether regions.

Antonio ran to the double doors.

"He can see the head!" he announced. The crowd cheered.

"I may have to do an episiotomy," Fingers added.

Antonio stepped back.

"Do what you eeeehhh –" I had to push, "bloody well like, just get it out of there. Christ, it must have the biggest head in the universe!"

Antonio dabbed my forehead with a damp cloth. I wished he'd stop. I didn't know which end to concentrate on.

"Hold my hand." He did and I squeezed the life out of it. Wasn't that what I was supposed to do? Isn't that what everyone does in childbirth?

"Would you like to watch the birth?" Dr. Fingers asked me, stupidly. "We can prop you up and you can watch if you like."

"Are you stark raving mad? Eeeehhhh! Feeling it is more than enough for – eeeeehhhhhh – one person. If you were lying up here – oooooooohhhhhhh – where I am, you would not want to be looking at what – eeeeeeehhhhhhhh – was coming out of your innards, causing you this unimaginable pain! Unless you're a masochist. Ooooooooohhhhhhhh! You're not, are you?" I didn't want any old masochist delivering my baby.

"Right now! Push!" Fingers went back to rooting in my nether regions. All I could see was a head sticking out from between my legs. For a moment I thought I had given birth to a fifty-year-old man with a pony-tail.

"It's a girl!" He grinned as he pulled out a sticky wet morsel that looked like a clove-drop, all red and white and gooey. She was beautiful.

Antonio kissed me and ran for the doors.

"A girl!" he announced.

The crowd cheered.

The tiny morsel was put up on my chest. She was beautiful. I started crying with the sheer joy of seeing her. That and the fact that the pain was gone. When I looked around I could see Antonio was on the verge of tears too.

"I'm going to call her ahhhhhhhh!" Jesus, another pain!

"That's a lovely name. But you might have to come up with another one. There's another baby."

"No. No. I'm only having the one," I said. Knowing what I was able for was always one of my virtues.

"Well, it's a bit late now," Dr. Fingers said.

I had this horrible urge to push. So I did.

"It's another girl!" Fingers was delighted.

"Are there any more?" I asked. Afraid there might be hundreds. Afraid I would go into the Guinness Book of Records for the oldest woman in the world to have a hundred babies.

"No, that's the lot! Identical twins. Well done, you!" The two little peas in a pod were propped up on my chest. Antonio kissed me again and made a dash for the doors.

"It's twins!"

The crowd cheered louder.

"Is Ma all right?" Carl and Chloe asked.

"Your mother is perfect, just perfect. You two can come in now. Then the rest of you will have to wait a little longer."

Antonio handed each of my children a new sister. Chloe was crying.

"Are you still calling one Faith?"

"Well, we had decided on Faith so I think the oldest one should be called that. But now I don't know what to call the second one." I was deliriously happy.

"Well, let's hope you don't have any more, Ma. I don't think I'd be able for it." Carl looked a bit green around the gills.

"Hope's got nothing to do with it," Chloe laughed. "Haven't you learnt that yet, Carl? I hope you're not relying on hope as a contraceptive! Hey, isn't that a great name?" Chloe said. "Hope! Why not call the second baby Hope?"

"Faith and Hope. I like the sound of that. We could do with a bit of that around here," I smiled.

The two babies were taken over to be cleaned up. They screamed. Whether it was because each missed its womb-mate or a sign of the relationship they would always have, only time would tell. Maybe they were screaming at the crowd that by now had filled the room and were enjoying the first public appearance. These babies would be spoiled and loved by everyone.

Carl rang Dick and told him. He and his latest love, Fleur, were pleased and hoped I was happy. Happy? I was charmed with myself.

Just then Antonio fell to his knees. I knew it had all been a bit too much for him. He was going to pass out. He spread he arms out and looked up at me.

"Linda, I love you. Please marry me?"

Last week he had chosen a romantic trip on a

canal barge to pop the question. I had said no then. Now we were in the labour ward of the Rotunda Hospital. And one of my best features was sporting a row of bright blue stitches. Not a bit of romance in sight. What the hell made him think I would say yes?

He looked at me and smiled. And then he did it. He winked at me. Winked that wonderful way he does when he's letting me know how wonderful everything is going to be.

So maybe it was the wink or the hormones, or maybe it was the two little clove-drops, or the camaraderie and *joie de vivre* of Carl, Chloe, Todd, Kyrstie, Suzie and Ken. Maybe I was drugged on the happiness of it all. Whatever it was I took his hand, kissed it and said, "Yes."

He held me and kissed me.

The crowd cheered.

Then again maybe it was just love.

THE END